Curtis Adler, originally from Wisconsin, USA, now lives in Dublin. He is married with two children.

January Colours

Curtis Adler

POCKET BOOKS

TOWNHOUSE

First published in Great Britain and Ireland by
Pocket/TownHouse, 2003
An imprint of Simon & Schuster UK Ltd, and TownHouse and
CountryHouse Ltd, Dublin

Simon & Schuster UK is a Viacom Company

1 3 5 7 9 10 8 6 4 2

Simon & Schuster UK Ltd
Africa House
64–78 Kingsway
London WC2B 6AH

Simon & Schuster Australia
Sydney

www.simonsays.co.uk

TownHouse and CountryHouse Ltd
Trinity House
Charleston Road
Ranelagh
Dublin 6
Ireland

A CIP catalogue record for this book is available
from the British Library

ISBN 1 903650 31 3

Typeset by Palimpsest Book Production Limited
Polmont, Stirlingshire
Printed and bound in Great Britain by
Cox & Wyman Ltd, Reading, Berkshire

I wish to thank Anne Thurston for her insight and honesty in assessing an early draft of this book. I would also like to thank Hugh, Ella and Gráinne for indulging this and many other whims.

To Gráinne

CHAPTER 1

In which Mamie McDevitt returns home.

'Surely you must be lonely, living in that big house all on your own,' said Joan, leaning forward with a look of concern.

Mamie McDevitt maintained her polite smile. Around them, the hum of voices, the steady rustle and flow of shoppers in the post-Christmas sales.

'It's been ten years now since John's death,' Mamie replied. 'I'm well used to keeping my own company.'

Mamie had grown to expect these expressions of concern from her old friend. Dear Joan, she thought. Joan Kennedy, who had always been the pretty one, the one to keep the conversation light and meaningless, the one who could be counted upon to laugh brightly, or listen submissively to her bore of a husband, or chime in with a truism to fill any hint of silence.

Of course Joan had married well, as they say, and her children had married well, while Mamie had married John, just John, who was brilliant in his way, but not in the way the world would ever recognise. And Mamie and John did have a child, but they had lost him at the age of four to some ghostly disease that they never could identify. Their subsequent childless state had for these many years rendered

Joan concerned, and perhaps, in her own polite way, quietly triumphant.

Or was Mamie being uncharitable?

'Of course Martin is very worried about you, living there all on your own,' Joan continued. 'Ever since your last lodger moved out.'

'Martin is very good to think of me,' Mamie replied, 'but I'm not in any hurry to have a new tenant. Especially if they're anything like that last fellow . . .'

Mamie probably would have lost touch with Joan years ago, were it not for the rather hasty marriage of Joan's daughter Deirdre to Mamie's nephew Martin Walsh.

'You know Martin's business is absolutely flying,' Joan said. 'He's never at home before seven in the evening. I don't think he has time to attend to his *own* house, and I'm afraid that he'll *never* get round to that redecorating he's promised you.'

'Not to worry,' Mamie said, pouring Joan another cup of tea. 'Sure the house could fall down and I'd hardly notice. I never go upstairs. In fact, I'm living very nicely in the two front rooms downstairs. And I don't relish the thought of an army of builders and decorators invading the place.'

Since her husband died, Mamie had quietly withdrawn from those rooms upstairs, where they used to sleep, and where their son had spent his brief life. Now, between feeling her age and, perhaps, growing into a new – what was it? wisdom? – she felt less and less desire to control the space around her.

Her nephew Martin had indeed been helpful as her interest in the house declined. In the summer he'd often come round at the weekends to whip the gardens into shape, or to attend to minor repairs. And he did help her to renovate the upstairs as a self-contained flat, and he saw to everything with regard to tenants, assuring her of the necessity to have someone about, just in case . . .

But over the years the house had steadily fallen into disrepair. Nothing had been painted since John's death – apart from Mamie's tiny kitchen and the flat upstairs – and lately Mamie had noticed a creeping odour of dampness emanating from the carpet in the hall.

'Of course, you *know* you're sitting on a goldmine,' Joan continued. 'Martin tells me that your house, even in the state it's in now, would be worth, what was it he said? Four hundred thousand pounds at today's prices. Isn't it unbelievable, Mamie!'

'Yes, I'm sure Martin knows the value of these things,' Mamie replied. She smiled and sighed a widow's sigh.

'And are vee finished today, laydeez?'

A waitress with a heavy foreign accent began to clear away the tea things.

'Yes, thank you,' Mamie replied, reaching for her bags beneath the table. 'I'd really better dash. You know how I like to be home before the dark sets in.'

'Yes,' Joan replied, that look of concern returning. 'So difficult for you now, when the days are so short . . .'

Years ago, Mamie thought, didn't everyone take the bus into town?

She stood on South Great George's Street, bundled in her woollen coat against the icy wind.

Now only those very badly off would ever be *seen* on a Dublin bus, she thought.

A mixture of pity and regret came upon her as she noted the people in the queue: the rough-looking men, the tired women, the children with sweet-stained lips.

Oh, how she hated being reminded of the old days!

A moment later a small yellow bus pulled in and she struggled aboard, taking the last seat available at the back. The bus trundled slowly forward, stopping abruptly every few yards in the heavy afternoon traffic.

It had been weeks since she had ventured into town, and she seemed to see everything afresh.

A glass-fronted restaurant with a spiral staircase to an upper floor. Whitefriar Street Church, grey and imposing as always. An Arabic food store, a group of Muslim women busily chatting outside. The old art-deco theatre, for so long a cinema, now what? An amusement hall.

Dreadful, she thought.

The bus came to the bridge over the canal and stopped at the lights. She turned to look out over the sombre scene: the tall bare trees and the grey sky reflected in that still, black water. The grassy banks looked sodden, flattened by wet leaves and chilled through by the heavy, cold rain of a wet January.

Eventually the bus lurched its way through Ranelagh and came to Mamie's stop on Sandford Road.

'Are you all right there, missus?' the bus driver asked.

'Yes, quite all right – thank you!' she called, as she took the long step down to the pavement.

She waited for the bus to pull out, then waited again for the traffic to ease. A cold mist had begun to fall and she shivered as she waited. Eventually she crossed the road, walked the few steps to her house, and opened her creaking iron gate. She stepped inside, closed the gate behind her, rooted in her bag for her keys.

It was then, when she had found her keys and looked up at the familiar white house, the heavy black door, that she had her vision.

Or was vision too strong a word? But so powerful it was!

Suddenly summer and bright. Her cotton dress with the tiny floral pattern, and her hat – so long since she'd thought of that white summer hat. And John – he must have been waiting at the front window with young Sean, waiting for her return, from where? A valise – the country – a funeral – something . . . And she had been standing just there, in that very spot, on that lovely summer's afternoon, when they had opened the door and stood before her, little Sean in John's arms, her two boys in short sleeves and with big, beaming smiles.

'There she is! There's our Mummy!'

And Mamie stood, transfixed now, as the mist turned to rain, and felt that vision, so happy, so long ago.

So, so warm.

CHAPTER 2

In which Paul Boyle leaves his home.

On Friday morning, Paul Boyle reached over to the window ledge, picked up the alarm clock, and held it up to catch the light from the streetlamp outside.

6:58. Same time every morning.

He pushed in the button on the top of the clock and set it back down on the window ledge. Then he rolled over to embrace his wife.

But she wasn't there. Strange, he thought. She's never up before me.

Paul sat up, threw back the duvet and stepped out of bed. He fumbled for his slippers beneath the chest of drawers, and took his dressing gown from the hook on the bedroom door. Then he walked down the dark stairway.

'Margaret?'

No reply. She must have gone out to the shop.

He entered the bathroom and proceeded to carry out his morning ritual. A few minutes later he emerged, shaved, showered and awake.

'Mags?' he called once again. No reply. Very strange.

He had hardly seen her during the past week. She was working much too hard, he thought. Her PhD thesis was keeping her late in the library more and more often. Her teaching load at the university had increased this term because Robert was out sick and she had offered to cover his tutorials for him. The extra teaching was good financially, but it meant she had less time to work during the day, hence the long hours late into these winter nights.

She was talking about it less, he noticed. Wasn't sharing her ideas the way she used to. Even though Paul knew nothing about her subject, she used to have him read her work, to try to understand. Because, she thought, if he understood her arguments, even if he disagreed, then they must at least have been expressed clearly.

But lately, nothing. He hadn't read anything she'd written since September, and he was afraid to enquire whether she was making progress, or what her supervisor thought, or whether she had had any feedback from the literary journals. Instead she seemed to want to keep it inside, as if her life out there, outside their home, was too dark to discuss, too bleak, like this endless stretch of short, dull winter days.

And when she returned home after a long day at the university, she was often too keyed up to be able to relax. Always prone to insomnia, she was staying up then dozing off before late-night television with increasing regularity. Twice last week Paul came downstairs to look for her in the middle of the night to find her curled up uncomfortably on the couch in the cold sitting room, wrapped in a well-worn blanket, an electronic hush emitting from the blanked-out screen.

She was anxious, Paul felt. And down, too.

Paul walked back up the narrow stairs to their bedroom. He dressed in a white shirt and his grey suit.

Where was she? Must have gone to work already. She must be in a bad way, he thought, to have left the house this early. She was late again last night. She'd hardly slept.

He returned downstairs. He recalled that there was a meeting at the office this morning – a new client, a great opportunity, a *marvellous* opportunity, as Jack had insisted yesterday in his Kerry accent. He wanted the whole management team there, bright and early, input from everyone, got to have a plan, *it's make or break time, lads!*

Paul walked into the silent kitchen, flicked on the kettle, took a cup and saucer from the press, set them beside the kettle, reached below for the instant coffee. Then he dug a spoon out of the drawer, spooned coffee into the cup, and switched off the kettle, which had just begun to boil.

And then he glanced at the kitchen table, and saw the note.

Paul,

I don't know if you've noticed how bad it's getting. But it is – really bad.

And it doesn't help when I overhear messages on your mobile phone, like the one on Wednesday from 'Elaine', whoever she is. Not that I blame you, the way I've been. But your little Elaine didn't help.

I've always hated this cliché, Paul, but I need some space for a while. I can't go to Mum – I want to keep her out of this. I'm sorry, Paul – but I want you to leave. I can't focus right now – please take some clothes and things with you. Take the car.

But don't come back tonight.

Maybe we'll talk at the weekend. I'm sorry. Please don't come home tonight. Have Elaine if you have to, but don't tell me about her, and don't come home tonight.

Margaret.

Right, he thought. Okay.

He sat down at the table.

So. She wants me out. Right. I suppose I'd better go, then. I mean pack, and then go. Right.

He glanced at his watch.

Meeting. Damn. Okay. Better get packed then.

He emptied the cup in the sink, set it on the counter, walked away, returned, rinsed the cup out and placed it on the rack to dry.

He walked upstairs. Back in the bedroom he reached under the bed and pulled out a small suitcase.

Damn, he thought. She's done this before. Four years ago, back in Illinois. When she was wrapped up in her Master's. At least in Illinois I could go to my mother's house. Where am I supposed to go now?

He pulled a few clothes from his wardrobe, from the chest of drawers, from the back of the chair.

This is great, he thought. I'm going to be late. This is really great.

He dragged the case down the stairs, and fished in his pockets for his keys.

Fuck this anyway, he thought as went out of the front door, into the black, foggy morning. Fuck this totally.

Fucking Elaine.

CHAPTER 3

In which Felicity recalls happier times.

Early on a dark, wet Friday. Sandyford Industrial Estate, County Dublin.

Felicity Grant, thirty-nine, bent her head against the cold wind as she dashed across the car park. Reaching the angular office block she unlocked the door, entered the building, then pushed the door shut behind her, turning the latch to lock it once again.

She walked down the dimly lit corridor and up the stairs, running her hand through her long hair, blown and tangled by the wind.

She came to the offices of Spyral Multimedia and used her keys to gain entrance. She tapped a code into the security box to deactivate the alarm.

It used to be so much better, she thought, as she switched on the lights. In the old building, our old offices. Cramped, yes. And draughty. And the stairs – I hated running up and down those stairs. But back there, in town, so close to everything. Somehow, it seemed so much better then. I used to *look forward* to coming in each morning.

She crossed the open-plan area, which was used for software development, and entered her small office. She flicked on the lights and set her bag on her desk. She took off her coat and hung it on her coatstand to dry.

She remembered so vividly, three years ago, when Spyral was still a new company. She remembered coming in for her interview, wearing her mauve suit with the pin on the jacket – a silver swallow – and her cream blouse.

When she joined Spyral, she'd already known Jack for several years. She'd worked with him when he was still a salesman. She recalled the day of the Spyral interview, sitting across the table from him. He was all puffed up with his new role as MD of his own company. He tried to impress her, went on about all the 'marvellous opportunities' that lay ahead, and the hard work that would be required by everyone to get the company on its feet. But she saw straight through his attempts to impress, to intimidate. He wanted her for the job, needed her to help him get organised – it was obvious from the start that the job was hers.

The interview itself was almost comical: his chubby face, his Kerry accent!

Then she remembered meeting Ruth, the serious one – so thin, so earnest in her grey sweater, her straight hair clipped back so tight. Such long questions, such persistence, such drivel: 'Now Felicity, I want you understand the *material contribution* we're expecting from the *financial function* that you will represent . . .'

And would she ever forget Dee's sorry excuse for an interview? He was the Principal Graphic Designer. He sat across from her, curled up like a gnome, with his earring and his ponytail. He told her he knew nothing about accountancy, wondered if she really *liked* figures, then asked her if she'd ever been to Kathmandu.

She'd never experienced such a collection of misfits. She took the job immediately.

And then they won that first big contract, the one for the Department of Agriculture. All through Jack's contacts, of course: his father had been in the government at one time. They took on Paul, the American fellow, to advise them on the scientific aspects of the project – he had a background in botany. And how Paul organised that office! Called regular project meetings, kept everyone tight to schedule. He watched the budget like a hawk. So that by the end of the project, they didn't know how they could survive without him, and he joined Spyral on a permanent basis.

Felicity still remembered those early days so fondly: going for lunch on Fridays to the canteen in the Development Centre on Pearse Street, those lovely long Friday afternoon lunches, with Dee slagging Ruth's feminism, and Paul trying so hard to fit in, to be Irish. Jack even joined them on occasion, when things were going well. The laughs they had!

And Felicity herself, feeling, for the first time in so long, that she had found something to belong to.

She sighed as she sat down, smoothed her skirt, put her bag in the bottom drawer of her desk. She turned in her chair, reached over and felt the stiff, dry leaves of her azalea on the window ledge.

Dead, she thought. It's the air. Too warm in this office. Atmosphere too artificial.

She overturned the pot into the bin beside her desk.

And during those first years, she remembered, Spyral made money. Contracts kept rolling in, the staff got larger. And they did superb work – all music and colour and creative graphics and animations – Dee driving the design, Ruth writing the scripts, Paul managing the whole thing. And remember when they had that television actor in the office to do the voiceovers, and the old women on the street outside waiting for autographs?

Those days Jack was in brilliant form, doing his one-minute-manager bit, telling everyone how marvellous they all were. Every morning at 10:45 she used to dash out to the bakery across the road and buy him a Danish pastry for his coffee break. And he used to wink at her – so silly, now that she remembered it. And he seemed so jolly, so flushed with the success of his crew, as he got fatter and fatter!

But now, Felicity thought, it's all changed. Ever since they moved office, the mood had changed. Jack had met his skinny blonde dolly bird, and they seemed to have dreadful rows all the time, and he seemed miserable. And then the little floozy dumped him, which made it worse. And the pace had picked up: Dee, Ruth and Paul had been working so hard, and the stress was showing, on all of them. There was nowhere nice nearby for lunch, and they were all too busy anyway. The team spirit had suffered.

And worst of all, despite all the activity, the business was none too healthy.

They'd done a big project for the Orbit Group, but Orbit was in trouble. Rumour on the street was that Orbit was going under, and their creditors would never get paid. If that happened, Spyral would be out of pocket big-time – over two hundred grand.

Jack knew all about this, and Felicity was adamant that the staff should know. But Jack was equally adamant that the whole thing be kept quiet.

'Keep it to yourself,' he said. 'There's still a legal battle going on, and I don't want to worry anyone. If the junior staff get a whiff that we're in trouble, they'll be gone like shite from a goose. And then where would we be?'

So Felicity had kept the real situation a secret from her colleagues. But as time passed, the debts were mounting, and if the cashflow didn't improve soon, Felicity knew Spyral would be in deep trouble.

Too old, Felicity thought. I'm too old for this. In fact, we're *all* too old for this.

And it was true. Ruth and Paul were in their late thirties, and Dee was over forty – far older than the young turks out there in the market. Everyone was hiring young and cheap, experience didn't count for anything any more.

As for Felicity herself, she could pick up another job easily enough, her accountancy skills would transfer anywhere. But the sheer *effort* of it all: the job-hunting, the interviews, the new offices, the first-day-at-the-new-job, the looks she'd get as an old maid in a young industry ... she didn't think she could face it all again.

Couldn't anything stay the same? she thought. Couldn't she depend on anything, or anyone, just for a little while?

An hour later, Felicity, Dee and Ruth were assembled around

the table in the conference room. A cafetière sat steaming in the middle of the table, waiting to be plunged, surrounded by five mugs.

'Where the divil is Paul?' Jack asked from his position at the top of the table.

'I haven't seen him yet this morning,' said Felicity, 'and I've been here since seven-thirty.'

Jack looked down at his watch. He stood up, paced nervously, his chubby fingers fiddling with a gold pen.

'Not like our American friend to be late,' he said impatiently. 'But I don't like to start without him . . .'

Just then the boardroom door opened and Paul entered, his face flushed from running up the stairs. He avoided eye contact as he sat down, apologising under his breath.

'Right then,' Jack began, 'now that we're all here, let's get down to business.

'First, I want to commend you all on the marvellous work you've been doing for the Accounting Standards Board. I had lunch with Dan O'Sullivan yesterday, and he's absolutely delighted with the way the project is shaping up.

'Now, I've come across an opportunity for which I believe we are uniquely suited, and we need to respond quickly. The company is called MountAgro. They're a global player in the agricultural products market.'

Dee looked up from his notepad. 'MountAgro,' he said. 'They're that big farming crowd. They do cloning and that carry-on.'

'Yes, I've read about them,' Ruth said. 'What do they want from us?'

'Two of everything,' replied Dee.

Jack's heavy eyebrows met in disapproval.

'They're opening offices in Ireland,' he continued gravely, 'and they want to discuss the possibility of us doing an educational package. For schoolchildren. Something about genetics. This is your area, isn't it, Paul?'

'Yes,' Paul said, with hesitation in his voice. 'Sort of. Sounds very interesting.'

'I've told them all about you,' Jack continued, 'and they are very excited about our team. They want something big, something good, something that will help calm fears about their products. Everything is fair game, from soy beans to Dolly the sheep. They'll leave the details to us, as long as we stress the *positive* aspects of genetics. Parents, children, how genetics can help us avoid diseases, how genetics can feed the world's poor. That sort of thing.'

Felicity noted Jack's smile, looking just a bit like the old days.

'But look, lads, we've got to get past the first hurdle. They're flying in here to meet me on Monday, and I need to be ready for them. So I want you all to drop whatever you're doing and get together for some serious brainstorming. *Today*. I want some ideas on an approach that will really impress these fellas. Are you clear on what's needed?'

'Yes, Jack,' in unison.

'Well done. Paul, can you touch base with me later this morning with a progress report?'

Paul nodded his assent.

'Right, thank you all. I know you'll give this your best shot!'

Jack snapped his notebook shut and carried his heavy frame gracefully out of the room.

A general pause. Then Dee stood, reached forward, plunged the coffee, and proceeded to fill the mugs on the table.

'Bloody hell,' he said resuming his seat with a sigh. 'First thing in the morning, no fucking coffee, and a crowd of mutant cabbage-growers on our doorstep. Enough to do your head in.'

Ruth sipped her coffee, then set her mug gently on the table.

'MountAgro is getting a lot of coverage in the press these days,' she said, thoughtfully. 'And it's not a great story. They're putting small farmers out of work. Especially in developing countries. And they've funded all that research into genetically modified foods – I mean, *all* the research – so of course they say GM foods are safe.'

'It's propaganda,' Dee said. 'They want us to write their bloody propaganda.'

'But they've probably got money,' Felicity said. 'And if we don't do it, there are others that will . . .'

'What do you think, Paul?' asked Ruth. 'You know this stuff. And you'll have to pull this together. Are we siding with the enemy here?'

Paul flicked through the pages of his notebook.

'I don't know,' he said, distracted. 'I think we'd better find out a bit more before we take a stand.'

'Right,' Dee said. 'You're the boss. Should we meet back here in half an hour and throw some ideas around?'

Nods of assent.

'And by the way, Paul,' Dee said as he stood. 'You look shite. Are you feeling all right?'

'Yeah, sure,' Paul replied, forcing a smile. 'I'm fine, thanks. Just fine.'

A few minutes later Paul returned to his desk. He sat down, opened his diary, tried to focus on the day ahead.

He had tried to keep Margaret out of his mind during the meeting, but the reality of his situation rushed in upon him now. He noticed that he was perspiring.

The skies out of the window looked heavy and dark with cloud. He liked this job. He liked the people. They had welcomed him when he first arrived in Ireland; now he felt part of the team. And they were good, Paul thought. Good at their jobs. Good people.

But this morning, his surroundings seemed to take on a new and unwelcoming aspect. His modern curved desk, his black diary, his oversized computer monitor – all so new, so mechanistic, so impersonal. He looked at the office around him, watched his colleagues working, typing, concentrating. They suddenly appeared cold, functional, like the office space itself – its aqua-flecked carpet, its plastic-wheeled chairs, the strange maze of its cubicles.

He could be anywhere, he thought. Any industrial block, in any country, anywhere in the world.

Paul stared into his diary, unable to focus.

Margaret might really mean it this time. He didn't know what she wanted, how long she wanted him to stay away. He had nowhere to stay that night.

Paul's mouth was dry. He picked up his diary, rose from his chair and walked out of the office. He wandered down the corridor to the canteen.

The canteen was shared by four other companies. Only one table was occupied – a few secretaries smoking in the far corner. Paul took a mineral water from the fridge and approached the cash desk.

'There's a nasty morning for you, Paul,' said the attendant.

'It is, indeed, Noreen – thank you,' he said as he paid her.

'Sure, at least it's Friday,' she sighed, staring blankly across the room.

He picked up the bottle, walked towards the notice board and pretended to read.

He removed the cap from the bottle and drank quickly. The cold water calmed him, seemed to anchor him in the room. He drank more, again feeling the perspiration on his forehead.

He found himself reading a notice in the middle of the board.

Small flat available to let. Variable lease. Some caretaking duties required. Very reasonable rent.

Paul recognised the contact name. He worked in the same building. Owned a furniture company on the second floor.

Then he read the notice again. And feeling nothing, as though driven by something quite outside himself, he ripped a corner from the notice, wrote down the telephone number.

Small flat. Caretaking.

Nowhere else to go.

Right.

CHAPTER 4

In which Margaret walks tall but takes a tumble.

On that same damp Friday morning, shortly past seven o'clock, Margaret Boyle closed the door gently behind her. She stood on the front step for a moment, inhaled sharply, and then walked away from the house beneath the streetlamps' yellow glow.

She walked quickly, her heels making a determined clickety-click as she put greater and greater distance between herself and the house, that house where Paul was now waking, descending the stairs, and calling her name.

In a few minutes she reached the end of Eglinton Road and rounded the corner. The inbound traffic was already beginning to build and the glare of the headlights hurt her eyes. She stopped to button the top of her coat against the misty air.

She tried to block her thoughts. She slipped into clichés of liberation and self-determination. She told herself repeatedly that this was what she needed. She had a right to her own space. To think things through. To focus on what mattered to her, and to her alone.

For a while.

Maybe for ever.

Oh Christ, what am I doing . . .

She walked across the bridge, peering down into the black moiling water of the Dodder. She continued walking up the hill, entering the university complex at the Architecture building. Then she walked down the long path that wound between the playing fields, still in darkness at this early hour. The white sports complex loomed out of the hazy blackness like a ship run aground.

A few minutes later she walked up the steps to the Arts Block. Reaching the door, she stopped, suddenly overcome, as if drained of energy. She paused to get her breath under control, and then she pulled open the door and greeted the security guard, as she did every morning.

'You're first in again, Mrs Boyle!' he said.

'Always was an early riser, John,' she called back, with false enthusiasm.

She passed him and walked into the grey, poorly lit corridors.

Margaret had a reputation for being a dedicated teacher. Since taking up her three-year contract at the university last year, she had received special recognition on the basis of feedback from a student poll. She was cited for her 'empathy with student concerns' and her 'lively, challenging classroom style'.

When she had received the letter from the Dean of Arts, she threw it in the bin. She had never mentioned it to Paul.

It had seemed such a step down for her, this award for Teaching Excellence. So far, so, so far removed from what she had set out to achieve. Because back in Illinois, where her real academic studies began and where she had met and married Paul, her future had looked so bright, so clear: almost limitless.

· When she entered the Master's Program at Champagne-Urbana, she was something of a phenomenon.

From the very first lecture in Illinois she had experienced a heady sense of growth and stimulation. She loved the informality of the place, the accessibility of her lecturers. She challenged them constantly, forcing the faculty to move beyond their usual fixed touchstones of culture and belief and canon. Her interests expanded, diverged, blossomed. She broke boundaries, became 'interdepartmental'. Her requirements exceeded the capabilities of the English Department, burst into History and Medieval Studies and even Biology. She gathered a string of supervisors, each engaged in a separate sphere of her wide-ranging research.

Her Master's thesis was still being talked about amongst the faculty. Never before had the members of that august panel, the Master's Review Board, been led to discuss female masturbation, menstruation, suicide, jealousy and murder, Sappho and Hildegard of Bingen and Julian of Norwich, eighteenth-century pornography, Queen Victoria, Masters and Johnson, needlework, k.d. lang and Larry Flynt – all during the course of a one-hour oral examination.

And they adored her there, adored her unashamedly: an Irish girl, in this sheltered Midwestern university town, with her accent, and her turn of phrase, and her friendly manner, and her cool, pale, unpainted face. And by God, they agreed, she was a first-rate student: diligent, insightful, clear and determined.

In short, she flourished. In two short years she published two articles (and a silly, romantic, but lucrative short story). She gave three conference papers in three corners of the US. She had lunch with the head of the Modern Language Association. She became smooth and confident in the face of those surprisingly awkward propositions from departmental chairs:

'Gee, Margaret, I loved your paper so much, I wonder if we might have a talk about your future. Maybe over a drink or two?'

Despite her success, she never fully warmed to America. Relationships within the Department tended to be competitive, especially as the job market tightened. After six months she had despaired of forming any intimate friendships. Then she met Fay Fischer, from Boston, who was consumed with a thesis on body art. For a brief span the two women formed a close friendship, as well as gaining notoriety on campus: dangly earrings, black clothes, dense feminist conversation. But then Fay died, tragically, during that first summer, a clot cutting off her breath in a cool archival basement.

And Margaret became bitter. Her feminism sharpened, her feelings of anger and loneliness fuelling a mistrust of the political status quo.

And much as she hated to admit it, she longed for home.

Paul had been there during this time, this low period during Margaret's second year in America. She knew him first as an acquaintance of an acquaintance, but then, as her alienation deepened, Paul became a badly needed support. Quiet, solid

Paul with his sandy-red hair – Paul who made sense of her anger, and helped her work through her fears, and even showed her how to enjoy her time, the short time left to her in that dream-bright land. And as her stay in America drew to a close, she drew Paul to her, asked him to stay beside her, and married him, as if to recapture the sense of wonder she once had, to hold on to the sense of excitement that Fay's death, and her overwork, and her bitter knowledge of the world had clouded over.

They decided to return to Ireland, even though Paul had never been there before. Margaret had well-formed plans to return to this university where she had spent her time as an undergraduate, to extend her studies into matters Irish and matters British, to explore her vision of women and colonisation, and develop her work into the PhD she had craved since she was sixteen years old.

And so, last year, she was awarded a three-year teaching contract. They gave her this office on the third floor, which now, at 7:45 a.m., looked out over blackness to a river of headlights on the dual carriageway beyond. This office where she had worked so hard, written so well, but, up to now at least, achieved so little.

It was here, in this office, that she had opened those letters – three so far – those polite rejections of her articles, articles into which she had poured her heart and mind and body for so many weeks, late into the night, checking, polishing, refining. And so far her efforts had produced nothing except this growing collection of brief, curt, standardised notes: 'This fine work simply won't meet our requirements for the next few issues, but thanking you for your interest . . .'

Three letters. The third, just yesterday. Things just not working out.

Why? she thought. How? What could Paul possibly see in me, in such a failure?

She had tried, yes, she had tried to work this through without involving him. She had phoned her mother only last week, met her at the Westbury Hotel for tea (Mum's choice, of course). Tried desperately to connect, to find a way out of her feelings of depression, her disappointment in Ireland, and in herself.

'But Margaret, dear, you're doing so well,' her mother said, cradling her teacup in her hands as she leant across the table. 'Teaching in a university! And married to Paul, such a lovely fellow, and living in that lovely house . . .'

'I know, Mum . . .'

'You're both working, and you're saving to buy a house of your own, and you know Daddy and I would be glad to help when the time comes . . .'

'Yes, Mum, I know all that, but . . .'

'And of course with Paul doing so well you could always take time off to have children . . .'

'But Mum, I'm not achieving anything here!'

'Ah, Margaret, dear, can't you stop striving for a while and simply enjoy what you have?'

Margaret went silent, then, and Mum hailed a friend of hers across the room, and Margaret slipped away, deeply distressed, claiming some fictitious appointment.

Now steam rose from black coffee in a Styrofoam cup on her wooden desk beneath the cold fluorescent lights. She stared blankly at her notebook, trying, unsuccessfully, to focus on preparations for her nine o'clock tutorial. She felt weak once again, noticed perspiration on her forehead, shivered. Glancing at her notes on Virginia Woolf she heard, despite herself, a voice. That voice. The voice she overheard inadvertently on Paul's mobile telephone yesterday, on his answering service:

You have a new message.

Hi Paul, this is Elaine.

Northern Ireland accent.

I'm just dying to talk to you.

Dying.

Elaine.

Margaret leaned towards the fourteen first-year students of English Literature who attended her tutorial each week.

'Breastless,' she said, watching the reactions on their young faces. 'Virginia Woolf says here that Clarissa Dalloway feels *breastless*. Why?'

Silence.

'Come on, then,' Margaret prodded. 'What's happening here?'

A tall blonde girl broke in. 'She's feeling rejected, like. Because Lady Bruton didn't invite her to her party.'

'Okay,' Margaret responded, 'she's not invited to a party. And so, naturally enough, she feels as though her boobs have fallen off. Am I missing something here?'

Giggles, little squirms of discomfort.

'Tom,' Margaret challenged a red-faced boy at the back. 'What does Clarissa feel?'

Tom shifted in his seat.

'She feels, well, flattened.'

Laughter.

'What do you mean, flattened?' Margaret asked.

'You know. Not round. Like her body is a stick.'

'I see. How about you, Susan?' Margaret challenged a girl with an especially young face. 'What does this have to do with Lady Bruton?'

'It's sex, like,' Susan stammered, red-faced. 'She feels that Lady Bruton is sexier than she is.'

'And is she?' Margaret asked. 'Is this Lady Bruton sexy? Heavy make-up? Short skirts?'

'No, miss,' said earnest Mary. 'She's older – she's a Lady. High up in society.'

'So what's the threat, then? Why does Clarissa feel so threatened by this older woman?'

Silence. Margaret looked around the room. All eyes were on her, these innocent eyes focused on her, waiting for her to feed them the key to this passage, this novel, this life. She scanned the room: the brown hair, red hair, the shiny hair, the not-so-clean hair – such innocents, such lovely young Irish innocents!

Then one face seemed to emerge from the group. Not a round-faced youth, but an older fellow, with definite features. Very short black hair, brushed straight back, two earrings in his left ear. A bit more mature, a bit of backbone, a bit tougher than the rest. He was not one of her regulars, and he had never before spoken in class.

'You, you're Tony aren't you?'

'Yeah, that's me,' he replied, looking directly into her eyes.

'Tell me, Tony, what's going on here? Why does this Lady Bruton make Clarissa feel sexually inadequate?'

He paused for a moment before he spoke. There was silence in the room.

'I'm no expert on high-class Englishwomen,' he began, speaking with a heavy Dublin accent. 'But it seems to me that sex is more than being young. It's all about confidence.'

The class turned in their seats to assess this new voice.

'Confidence?' Margaret asked.

'Yeah,' Tony continued. 'Clarissa's younger, so she's probably, like, more attractive than Lady Bruton. But sex is about power. Lady Bruton is intimidating because she's got position in society. She's got confidence. Clarissa's got nothing.'

'Yes,' Margaret replied. 'That's a very good theory.'

But then she stopped, feeling the shivering, the weakness come on her again.

'Very good theory indeed, Tony. But is this *your* theory, or, excuse me,' she paused, her breath coming short. 'Oh God, I'm sorry. You'll, you'll have to excuse me . . .'

And then the room began to spin, she would remember later, slowly, as if caught in a whirlpool of slow time. Her face flushed as she slipped, so slowly, forward, forward. And as she fell it all seemed to go fuzzy, and empty, and she would later recall the room sliding into circular motion as she fell forward, and then sideways, and then down, down onto the floor.

And then the blankness thereafter, as the class, so stunned, watched her fall into nothing, and close the tutorial, and close the book, and close her eyes.

CHAPTER 5

In which Paul finds a new home and a new profession.

Later, on that same Friday afternoon, Paul spoke briefly with Martin Walsh on the telephone.

'Hello, Martin? This is Paul Boyle, from Spyral Multimedia. Upstairs from your office.'

'Yes, Paul – can you hold there for just a moment?'

'Sure . . .'

Paul detected a country accent and a hint of impatience. As he held the line, he heard Martin continue to speak.

'Connie, can you fax that over to Johnson Brothers for me . . . Yes, all right, when you've got a moment . . . Sorry, Paul, now, what can I do you for?'

'I saw your notice in the canteen, about accommodation. I was wondering whether the flat was still available.'

'It is, indeed, Paul, yes it is. It's what in New York they would call a "studio apartment" – you know, small, but self-contained, and very easy to keep. It's at the top of the house. My auntie, you see, she's living in the house, on the ground floor. And I'll tell you, Paul, I just don't like the idea of her being there on her own. I'm looking for someone who'd be there, you know, at night and on weekends. Not to look after her – she's well able to look after herself, I can tell you! – but just to be around the place, just in case, you know, something should go wrong.'

'I don't have a problem with that, Martin. The thing is, I'm actually a bit stuck for somewhere to live in the short term, and . . .'

'Now, I'll tell you right upfront, Paul, the place isn't any palace. I've been meaning to do it up for some time, but you know how difficult it is to get people in these days, what with our Celtic Tiger and all.'

'I'm sure it will suit me very well, Martin. I'm really just looking for a small place for a short time to . . .'

'I tell you what, Paul, I'm in the middle of something here. Why don't we meet at the flat after work this evening, and you can have a look for yourself? Say six-thirty – 29 Sandford Road in Ranelagh – do you know the area?'

'Yes, Martin, I know the area very well.'

Paul left the office at 5:30. The sky was black, a light rain was falling, and the evening traffic was performing its dismal crawl from the industrial estate into town.

As he drove, Paul tried to keep his emotions from his mind. He flicked around the radio stations. The dull vibrations of the Angelus. The Peace Process, stalled again. Another brutal punishment beating. An ad for pensions. An ad for a car.

He tried the BBC. Local councillors vying for funding. New performance indicators for the NHS.

Back to Ireland. Hurling. Another ad for pensions.

He pulled in off Sandford Road some distance from the house. He took a deep breath, got out of the car, walked briskly up to number 29. It was a large, black-and-white, mock-Tudor house, in the middle of a row of similar houses.

Martin Walsh was sitting in a Range Rover parked directly outside. When Paul approached, Martin climbed out of the car. Paul noted that Martin was a large, heavy man with a crumpled navy suit, a navy shirt, and a yellow tie. He was finishing a conversation on his mobile telephone.

'Yeah, grand, yeah, okay, get whatever you can out of him, right? And look, I'm in the Burlo any time after about eight – give me a ring – righty-o, mate, talk to you – ah, hello, you must be Paul,' he said in a hurried manner, extending his large right hand.

'Hello, Martin,' Paul replied. 'I appreciate your taking the time to meet me here . . .'

'No bother. This is the place, anyway,' Martin replied, inserting a key into the black wooden door.

As they entered the house Martin switched on the light, a bare bulb hanging over a small, dark hallway. The carpet was a brown floral pattern, badly worn and damaged with damp. Two doors led off to the right; to the left, a telephone on the wall and a narrow staircase.

'Auntie Mamie lives in the front rooms,' Martin said as he began to climb the stairs. 'I'll introduce you on our way down. You're up at the top. I used to let the middle floor, but as I was saying, I need to get the place done up.'

Up two flights, past three doors, and up two flights again. At the top, three more doors. Martin digging a heavy ring of keys out of his pocket, opening one door after the next.

'Here's the sitting room,' he said, entering. 'I told you the place was no palace, but you get a nice view of the schoolyard out the back. The fireplace works grand – had the chimney swept just over Christmas.'

A metal bed. Two sagging comfy chairs. Bookshelves. A paper shade on the light hanging from the ceiling. Martin's bulk dominated the space as they walked from room to room.

'Your kitchen's on the small side, but then you probably wouldn't be cooking much, would you? The loo's through there.'

The kitchen had a small table and two wooden chairs. All the ceilings sloped down, garret-style, and each room had a skylight window.

'Okay,' Paul said when they had finished the tour. 'The flat is fine. I'm eager to find a place. I don't know how long I'll need it – it will probably only be for a short time, a month maybe, I don't know what you had in mind for a lease . . .'

'Right, Paul, here's the story,' Martin cut in, brusquely. 'My Auntie Mamie needs someone around, right? As I was saying to you, I'm keen to get someone in here so she has someone to call if anything goes wrong. I've put a bell here, you see, and she has a button below. I'm sure she won't bother you, now, she's as hale and hearty as they come. But you know I just hate the thought of her stuck down there if she can't make it to the phone in the hall.'

'Yes, fine, I understand,' Paul said, 'but you see, I can't commit to a long lease . . .'

'As I was saying to you, mate, the place needs to be done up, and I just want something coming in until I can get the decorating under way, you know what I'm saying? I'd be looking for six hundred a month from you, and we won't have to bother about a lease.'

'Six hundred a month?'

'That's right. First month in advance plus a security deposit, comes to twelve hundred pounds, and I'll need that upfront, in cash. Now I know what you're thinking, mate,' Martin continued. 'But it's an absolute jungle out there. When this place is fixed up I could get eight hundred easy in today's market.'

Paul thought for a moment. The rent was very high and the flat was in bad shape. At the same time it was cheaper and more spacious than a hotel room, and it was available immediately.

And then something struck him: those summer jobs, those paintbrushes and drop cloths, all those years ago.

'This decorating,' Paul said. 'What have you got planned?'

'The whole lot,' Martin replied. 'Starting with the big room downstairs – the back one, beside Auntie Mamie's place. Rip up the carpets, fix the skirting boards, strip off the wallpaper, replaster the walls, get a new fireplace – the works.'

'And when do you plan to start?'

'ASAP. But like I was telling you, I can't seem to get anyone. All the reliable decorators are booked up with new housing estates, and I don't want any cowboys hanging around the place. Why do you ask? You know anyone who could do the job?'

'Martin, what are painters charging these days? Sixty, eighty pounds a day?'

'Yeah, it'd be around that I'd say. If you find a good fellow. But come on, man, out with it. Have you got someone in mind?'

Paul looked directly into Martin's eyes.

'I might have a little time on my hands . . .' he said.

And so, without further thought, Paul entered into a deal. He agreed to look at the large room on the ground floor, buy whatever was needed, give Martin the receipts, and redecorate the room over the next few weeks. In return, Martin knocked the rent down to two hundred pounds a month, 'just to cover the upkeep on the place.'

Martin gave Paul the keys and hastily descended the stairs for his Friday night appointment.

Before he left, though, he called in to his aunt's flat from the base of the stairs.

'Mamie? Auntie Mamie? It's me, Martin,' he said, banging on the door in the hallway. 'I've got someone here, Auntie, an American fellow. A gentleman. He's moving in upstairs.'

As Paul reached the bottom of the stairs, he could hear stirrings from within the ground-floor flat. Eventually the door opened, very slightly, and a small, elderly woman put out her head.

'Ah Martin, hello,' Auntie Mamie greeted him, squinting up into the light from the bare bulb. 'I heard someone upstairs, and I hoped it was you!'

'Right, Auntie Mamie, this is Paul. He's an American. He works with me, you know, in Sandyford. He'll be taking the flat upstairs.'

'That's lovely now,' she smiled up at Paul. 'I'd come out

but I'm in my dressing gown. Isn't it an exciting life I lead, in my dressing gown at seven o'clock of a Friday evening!'

Paul was about to extend his hand but Martin cut him short.

'Paul's moving in tonight, so you two will have plenty of time to get to know one another. He's going to be doing up your old sitting room, Auntie Mamie. He's a dab hand at the old decorating, you know. I'm sure you two will become great pals. Now listen, Auntie Mamie, get inside with you, you'll catch your death standing in this hallway. I'll drop in tomorrow to leave in the new kettle. Go back inside now, there's a good girl, good night, now, good night.'

Auntie Mamie dutifully withdrew, smiling an embarrassed but welcoming smile.

'So there you are, mate,' Martin said as she closed the door. 'She won't be any trouble to you. You've got your keys, right? I'm off. Talk to me on Monday about what you need to do up that room. Good luck, now, and all the best!'

And Martin was gone, that is, with three hundred pounds, comprising rent and deposit, stuffed into the pocket of his trousers.

Paul stood in the dark hallway for a few moments, fingering the keys to his new, albeit temporary, home. He listened at Mamie's door, from which issued the murmur of a radio talk show.

After a moment's hesitation he left the house. A few minutes later he returned, carrying his suitcase through the door and up the stairs. Then he came downstairs and left the house once again, walking through the rainy night towards Ranelagh village.

For the next two hours, he sat at the bar in an especially dismal local pub. Ordinarily a moderate drinker, this night Paul drank, steadily. He lost count of those smooth, black, heavy pints: that slow, centuries-old source of comfort.

In the eventful weeks that lay ahead, his memory of that whole, strange day would grow dim. He would ultimately recall, however, sitting at the bar, and removing his mobile telephone from his breast pocket, and phoning the familiar number of his, that is, of Margaret's house. He knew he listened for a long time to that hollow, insistent double ring, double ring, double ring. Perhaps, after ringing off, he searched his coat pockets for that other number, the number he had never used before, that Northern Ireland number he had vowed he would never try. But though he wasn't sure, he seemed to recall that he never found the number, and never phoned her, and never left a message for her on her answering machine.

And the more drunk he became, the less strange became the time and place in which he found himself. The day he had had, this pub, the city, which during the day had become so alienating, was now comfortable once again. He felt as if he were sending roots downward into this wet soil, feeling connections form, recede, and then form again with each slow, cold swallow.

CHAPTER 6

*In which Paul experiences a rude – or rather,
a polite – awakening.*

The sky began to brighten shortly after 8:00 on Saturday morning. By 8:30, bright sunlight flooded through the dormer window in Paul's new bedroom.

Paul, however, was not well. He opened his eyes to the harsh light, slowly remembering where he was, and then, why he was there, and then, how he had spent the previous night. And then he experienced that painful sensation, those drill bits, driving into the base of his skull.

Margaret. Oh Margaret.

He rolled over to face the green wall and tried to return to sleep. Ten minutes passed. He had just lost consciousness of the pain and of the morning, when a tentative *knock knock knock* woke him once again.

He heard someone call his name from outside the door.

'Paul? Good morning, Paul!'

Opening his eyes, he croaked, 'Hullo, who is it?'

'It's me, Mamie. From downstairs.'

'Oh God,' he groaned. Then, trying to lighten his rasping voice, he responded, 'Yes, Mamie, just a moment – I'll be right there.'

He was still dressed from the night before. He stood up, unsteady, as if the room were in motion. He couldn't seem to straighten his head to an upright position. After a moment's hesitation, he stepped across the room and opened the door.

Mamie stood before him like a smiling garden gnome. Her small body was covered in a shapeless housecoat, supported by chubby legs and clean, pink cotton slippers.

'Good morning, Paul,' Mamie began energetically. 'Now I know I'm a desperate interfering old woman, but I heard you come in last night and I had a feeling that you'd been going through a tough old time of it, and I couldn't help thinking that the best thing for you would be a proper hot breakfast, particularly for a nice American chap like you who's not used to the way we drink Guinness here – which is our national pride but indeed is also our national downfall! – and so I've taken the liberty of preparing a little something for you, and I would hope you could indulge a meddlesome old woman just this once – and I assure you, I won't be troubling you again! – but if you'd just come down and have a little something, then, sure, your day will get off to a proper start and you can get down to, you know, working out where you are and what it is that you're going to do next.'

She was still out of breath from her climb up the stairs, and she had to pause to inhale, all the while smiling up at him as though she had known him all his life.

'Now you take just a minute to pull yourself together, and then please come downstairs and we'll have our breakfast and a little chat, is that all right?'

Paul attempted to stammer his thanks but she had already turned to descend the stairs.

Ten minutes later he was seated at a small table in Mamie's sitting room, his face still reddened from vigorous scrubbing. He looked out of the front window of the house, through the lace curtains, across the untidy front garden and onto busy Sandford Road. It was a dismal scene: the brilliant sun had already been tempered with cloud, and rain, whipped by gusts, now dappled the dirty windowpanes.

Paul shivered slightly. Mamie emerged from her small kitchen and brought him a glass of water in which bobbed two tablets, spewing effervescence.

'There you are now, Paul. Drink this up and you'll feel much better. I'll have a nice mug of coffee here for you in two shakes.'

Paul's head was throbbing. From the moment he sat down he began to question the wisdom of agreeing to eat with this strange little woman, but he was in no condition to argue. He lifted the glass and drank deeply of the bitter, fizzing water.

He set the glass back on the table. Almost immediately his head cleared. He could focus again on his surroundings. It was a minor miracle. He shook his head with disbelief.

'That should chase away whatever ails you,' Mamie said, smiling, as she took the glass from the table.

A moment later she returned with two steaming plates. Paul inhaled deeply the rich aroma: sausages, grilled tomatoes, grease-flecked discs of black and white pudding, and bright yellow fried eggs. A plate of brown soda bread appeared in the middle of the table.

'You take your coffee black, isn't that right?'

'Yes, thank you, yes I do,' Paul said, feeling better, but still helpless.

'This is lovely now,' Mamie said as she sat down. 'I never cook a full Irish breakfast like this for myself, living here alone. When my husband and I visited New York, I used to adore the breakfasts there – eggs Benedict, that's the one, isn't it? Those thin muffins covered with ham and eggs, and that sauce – hollandaise sauce, isn't that it? Some of the happiest mornings of my life, I swear to God, were spent eating eggs Benedict and reading the *New York Times* – lovely!'

She smiled across at him with clear, shining eyes.

The breakfast was delicious, homely and hot, and Paul soon felt fully revived. Mamie continued to talk as they ate, about her husband, his work in the civil service, their travels, and his untimely death.

'Ah God, it's all behind me now,' she concluded, patting her mouth with a paper kitchen towel. 'But here I am, rabbiting on about nothing, and I've learned nothing about you. Tell me – what is it brings a nice young American chap like you here to these damp shores?'

Paul managed a weak smile. 'I almost feel that you know the whole story already,' he said.

'Oh? Why's that?'

'Well, you knew that I was out last night. You know I don't drink much. You know I'm stuck in a bad patch. You even knew I drink black coffee. How did you figure all this out?'

'Ah now, it's not difficult for a wise old Irishwoman to know these things. First of all, Martin told me you're a Yank, and that you work in the same building as he does. Now these days, Americans coming over here to work in these high-tech companies, like the ones out where Martin works – these Americans aren't short a shilling, as they say. And yet you're going to rent the upstairs of this house, which is, as I'm sure you'd agree, hardly a fit place for a penniless student, let alone a well-paid computer whizzkid like you. Then there's the wedding ring you're wearing – with no sign of a Mrs Paul anywhere. So there would seem to be some trouble somewhere, isn't that right?'

Paul nodded, his mouth hanging slightly ajar.

'And the rest is easy. I saw your face in the hall last night, and you've not got the face of a drinking man, and I've been a light sleeper since you were in nappies, so I heard you come in about twenty minutes after the pubs were due to close. So it seemed to me, and I believe I've been proven right, that you'd be ever so slightly in a bad way this morning. And the coffee was easy,' she added. 'All Americans drink their coffee black, regardless of the state of their health.'

Paul smiled, and nodded once again.

'And finally, Martin said something about you doing some decorating in the sitting room. Now before Martin puts on his usual airs, I must remind him, and you as well, that although Martin provides the services of a caretaker and does me infinite favours for which I will forever show my sincerest gratitude, *this is my house*, and not Martin's. I've lived here for forty years, and I'm not about to leave it just yet. And if you're going to be restoring it to its former glory, I want to get onto your good side right from the start, so I'll have a say in the colours you'll be picking!'

Again, her smile, a smile that expressed her direct and clear intentions.

'Now for the moment you don't have to tell me a thing about yourself, though the suspense is dreadful! But I would like to show you the room next door, which is in a frightful state, I assure you, and we can have a wee chat about what's to be done. I know you'll want to get started straight away: nothing better than a good project to keep your mind off things! Would that be all right?'

'Yes, yes indeed,' Paul replied, utterly disarmed. 'Yes, that sounds like the perfect plan . . .'

As soon as breakfast was cleared away, Mamie and Paul stepped out of her flat and into the hallway. Before entering the next room, Mamie paused.

'We used this room as our sitting room when we were first married. Then, after John died, I rented it out for many years to an unpleasant little man from Sligo who sold second-hand cars in Harold's Cross. I don't think he ever said more than a begrudging "hello" to me in all the years he lived here.'

She sighed, then fumbled in the pocket of her housecoat for her keys, eventually opening the door.

It was a large, empty, L-shaped room, with two long windows across the far end looking out on an expanse of overgrown back garden. It had a peculiar, not unpleasant smell, with the sweetness of rotted fibres.

Patterned, mud-coloured carpet covered the floor, punctuated with round black spots from the bottoms of hot saucepans and amoeba-like stains from spilt liquid. A high skirting board ran round the room, chipped and flaked and gapped in spots where a stove or shelves or some other units had once been installed.

The walls themselves showed the weight of successive wallpapers, heavy and padded, like an old story elaborated at every telling. The outermost layer showed climbing ivies in brown and green. Corners both above and below were peeling to reveal other, brighter and flamboyant patterns from times past.

A chimney breast on the wall facing the door, now covered over, had once housed a fireplace.

Up above, the nine-foot ceiling was surrounded by an elaborate plaster moulding. The moulding did not appear to be original, but rather like something that had been stuck on with impatience, with obvious breaks in the middle of each wall. At one end of the room the moulding threatened to fall from the wall entirely.

Two tired bulbs hung down at either end of the ceiling, covered by cheap paper shades.

Despite the sorry state of the decor, Paul felt drawn to the room. It was a room worn down by loss, frustration, deterioration, and obvious neglect. He felt as though it reflected his situation, as if the room were an embodiment of age, and emptiness, and lack of fulfilment.

As a decorator Paul immediately recognised the room's attractions. It was spacious, displaying the high-ceilinged generosity of another era. It was built of materials solid but unfamiliar to Paul, far from the wood-and-plasterboard American interiors of his youth. The room was not old in Irish terms – perhaps one hundred years – and yet it was clearly not new, displaying the values of a time long past, untouched by the polished prosperity of contemporary Dublin.

And he thought of his situation: the uncertainty, the new time on his hands, his desire to remain busy, to keep his mind occupied until his life with Margaret was set right again.

He walked into the room, ran his hands along the walls, as if feeling in the thick wallpaper the texture of the past. He said nothing, intrigued by the space, imagining its past while assessing its potential for renovation, standing as if caught between two eras, one past, one about to be born.

Mamie too was silent for a moment, surveying the empty, decaying space.

'Holy Mother of God,' she said, softly. 'When I think back ... The times we used to spend here. And how it used to look ... What a *desperate* state it has fallen into!'

CHAPTER 7

In which Margaret receives a visit from a decent bloke.

Tony Dunne was, essentially, a decent bloke.

He was raised in a Corporation flat in Dolphin's Barn on Dublin's southside. Despite its playful name, Dolphin's Barn is known well by the local police: angered by poverty, soaked in alcohol, and fraught with domestic violence. And in that environment, either you grow up a fighter, or you don't grow up at all.

The heroin first came to Dolphin's Barn around the time Tony Dunne was born. One of his earliest memories was of a hot summer's day when he wandered into the grey concrete flat to see his mother on the floor in the kitchen, writhing and cursing, and his father shouting at him to 'get outside, you little shite, can't you see she wants you out of here!' Tony remembered the sense of terror he felt as he ran from the building. That night he fell asleep in the grass by the canal. He could recall looking up at the window of the flat from below, and sitting somewhere on a kerbside, and being fed sweets by the neighbours, and returning home two days later.

He still recalled those days when his mother was unwell, standing in her room, watching her sweating in bed, transfixed by fear and frustration and, ultimately, rage.

From an early age, then, Tony recognised that drugs caused trouble. After some nasty experiences in his youth he swore off them, especially heroin. When he was a teenager he stole some money from school and used it to buy some gear, and then he began to deal – grass, heroin, crack, whatever happened to be on the circuit. The business was lucrative enough, but it caused him occasional pangs of conscience. Especially when he thought about the suffering that his customers went through to pay for the stuff. Especially the young girls, trying to support their fellas' habits. When Tony was feeling flush he'd try to supply them for free, to save them from the whoring, the humiliations and the beatings. And if he received the occasional payment in kind, he knew he was a much safer bet than the bastards they'd meet on the street.

Tony prided himself on only dealing from known sources and delivering top-quality goods. He wasn't especially into money, and he wasn't into the turf wars that went on between the junkies in town. He never had ambitions to turn into a big supplier like the guys who brought in the gear from Holland or Liverpool. For Tony it was just a part-time thing to keep some extra cash coming in and, sometimes, just to keep the other junkies out of his area and away from his brothers and sisters.

Once or twice he'd been told that he could have done very well for himself. Because as time wore on, he began to earn the respect of the big dealers. It was mostly because of a freak accident, a rare loss of temper. Tony was only doing what he had to do on that day when Jacko Nathan tried to unload some bad gear in the East flats, *Tony's* East flats.

Tony never went out of his way for a fight, but he wasn't in the mood that day to fucking negotiate, because these were his people and nobody else was going to supply them with bad gear, enda story. Tony ended up kicking the shite out of Jacko and throwing his bleeding body out into the road. The cars had to drive around him for almost an hour before an ambulance came to cart him away.

Tony stayed out late that night, shagged some new girl he didn't know, and felt pretty wrecked the next day.

After that particular incident they told him that the General knew all about him – you know, before the General got cut down by that fellow on the motorbike – and the General would be happy to talk to him any time, but Tony didn't really want anything to do with the General, he just wanted his own turf and his cash in the hand.

Lately, though, it was getting tougher out there. The guns, they seemed to be coming out of nowhere. Everyone was saying it. You couldn't get into a proper row on the street any more without some bastard showing up an hour later with a shotgun. Which meant his turf was being threatened more every week, and he figured he'd either have to join the death squads himself or pack it in altogether.

But the problem was that Tony Dunne wasn't into drugs, or gangs, or any of that shite. He was a tough enough bastard when he needed to be, but he really just wanted a bit of a quiet life. He was a bit of a bookworm. He actually finished school. He loved reading. He preferred a good book to any kind of dealing or hustling or fighting. He was into Nietzsche and Kafka and Kundera. He new that it was a very strange habit for someone in his position, but he justified it to himself, saying that there was fuck-all else to do in Dolphin's Barn when it was pissing rain outside and you were sick of the carry-on at the pub and it was too bleeding cold to sit at a match.

And all that reading paid off, not because he learned anything of particular relevance to dealing drugs in Dolphin's Barn, but because it developed Tony's powers of concentration. When he was a kid he could read through anything, even the constant stream of new babies wailing in the flat. If anyone threw anything at him when he was reading – a toy, a sock, a knife – he'd catch it without missing a sentence. Which was why he was such a good dealer. You see, when Tony looked at you, nothing could distract him. He'd scare you the way he'd look at you. You knew he wouldn't mess you around because he was so tuned into what you wanted, and he could read people like books, and understand where they were coming from, and he could sense a lie, or fear, or if you didn't have the dosh, nothing got past him, not past Tony Dunne, not a chance.

The girls said the same thing about him – that he was solid as a rock (giggle) – but no, really, he'd like look at you so hard when he was like talking to you, even when he was like pulling your knickers off (giggle) and he'd just keep staring into your eyes like he knew everything about you, and then he'd just like keep going and if you were going to come Jesus he'd let you come and never miss a beat you know (no giggle), because like he was one serious shag, except that you never really knew what he was thinking, because like even if you thought you did, but then the next day it'd be like he never knew you, and you'd realise you didn't know anything about him in the first place, just that you wanted to be close to him, again, and again.

So Tony had had a think about what to do next. He had a day job at a warehouse, to help out a mate of his, but he was tired of it. He'd had a couple of bad days in a row and he was getting a bit worried because his little shite of a boss was getting narky with him about leaving early, even though Tony had explained that he had business to do. Then the third day came along and Tony could feel that sensation in him that he was getting close to snapping, and he figured he'd better not let loose on his boss because the implications of doing his boss in would be a bit more serious than the implications of kicking the shite out of little Jacko Nathan. So Tony decided to pack it in and do what he had been dreaming about for a long time.

So he got himself enrolled as a mature student at UCD to study English Literature.

Yes, fucking English Literature.

And when College started and the lads in the pub asked Tony if he was doing any dealing at UCD, he told them not to be fucking stupid, that the West Brits at Belfield didn't do drugs and you'd be mad to even bring drugs near the place, because if you came from Dolphin's Barn and you started dealing drugs at UCD you'd stick out like a massive fucking sore thumb.

That's what Tony told them all right. But he knew shortly after he arrived at UCD that he had made the right decision. He was onto a seriously good thing. Because when you walk through UCD looking like Tony looked – the earrings and the black leather and the hair and the scar on his cheek – people noticed you. Half of them were scared of him, and they were nervous when he sat down beside them at first, and even if they did start to talk to him, he noticed that they tended to be just that bit too polite, and maybe smile a bit too much. The fact is, he learned eventually, they were thinking two things. First, they wouldn't want him at their parties, because he (or his mates) would nick everything, and Mummy and Daddy would be furious.

Second, however, they were thinking that Tony should be able to get his hands on some decent gear if they needed it.

And so they'd talk to him quietly, in the toilets in the college bar, or over by the lake, or at the side of the concrete footpath behind the bushes on the way to the restaurant, and the conversation would start out about the lecture or the tutor or the weather or some irrelevant bullshit, but eventually they would come to the point and Tony would take the order in his usual professional manner, looking them straight in the eye to let them know he heard them and he'd do the biz for them and if they tried to mess him around their body wouldn't surface any time soon.

All of which means that Tony was clearing a comfortable couple-hundred-a-week out of our clean, well-mannered college boys and girls, enough to upgrade his mobile telephone, have his hair done very professionally, trade up to a two-litre Golf – though with all these extra-curricular activities, it left very little time for his actual studies.

On that foggy, Friday morning in January, when Margaret Boyle, despite having prepared thoroughly for her nine o'clock tutorial on Virginia Woolf, fainted in front of the class, Tony Dunne rushed to Margaret's aid.

Actually, Tony had had plenty of experience of people passing out. So when Margaret turned that bloodless shade of white and began to tip forward in her chair, Tony immediately recognised the signs and rushed to catch her, cushioning her head before it could strike the floor, easing her downwards to a safe position. His fellow classmates were shocked to see him loosen her top button – recall how they mistrusted him! – but by the time they understood what had happened, Tony had his telephone out, had dialled the emergency services, and had directed an ambulance to the place, that is, to the very room where they were still seated, amazed, as though watching a scene from an avant-garde film.

Yes, Tony had witnessed far worse situations many times before: grisly scenes with needles, and blood, and bottles, and reeking vomit. But he had never expected to see Margaret Boyle in such a vulnerable state.

Margaret was the first tutor that Tony had spoken to at UCD, back in October. During that first week he was trying to get started on the right foot, to be punctual, to be exactly where he was expected to be at the time required, to bring order to these first few days in what appeared to be an endless labyrinth of long corridors and short conversations. On this particular day, he had been wandering around the Arts Block for half an hour, armed with computer print-out providing an indecipherable schedule of lectures and tutorials. His attempts to seek direction had been brushed off by cold administrators, a sarcastic librarian, and the rude secretary of the English

Department, and by the time he finally arrived in Margaret Boyle's room he felt frustrated and was perspiring freely.

He was the first to enter. Margaret stood at the front of the room writing on the blackboard. She was very small, very young-looking to Tony's eyes – he had expected academics to be far older – and when he entered the room she stopped writing, turned to him, and said 'Good morning' with a tired half-smile.

'I don't know if I'm in the right place,' he said.

'I don't know either. Let me see your sheet.'

And she walked over to him, sat down at the desk beside him, looked at his schedule, and pointed to the line with her name.

'This is the place, Tony,' she said, with an ironical little smile. 'You can relax now.'

And then she returned to the board.

It was that unexpected decency, then, that had remained with Tony Dunne. A small thing, he knew. But he registered it at the time, for here was a woman, he was sure, who would help him out if things got tough.

And so, when she fell forward from her chair on that dismal Friday morning, he immediately sensed an opportunity to help her out in some small way, to get into her good books, and so to get his studies back on track, save his academic career, and preserve his livelihood.

Which is why, at 10:00 the next morning, Saturday morning, Tony Dunne was walking down a hospital corridor and turning into a long room to see Margaret Boyle sitting up in her bed, looking a bit tired, a bit washed out, but rather better than she had looked yesterday, when he had last seen her, passed out on the floor of the UCD English Department.

Earlier that morning Margaret had awakened in a public ward in St Vincent's Hospital which she shared with five other female patients.

She was propped up with a pillow behind her head. She wore a cotton nightgown with tiny pink and orange flowers, issued to her yesterday shortly after she walked unsteadily from the ambulance into the hospital.

A tube ran from her left arm to a bag of clear liquid suspended at the side of the bed. A tray containing a bowl of cereal, a carton of milk, a plastic container of orange juice and a small metal teapot was before her on a narrow shelf that had been swung over her knees. The tray looked as though it had been sitting there for some time. The other women in the ward had obviously finished eating, and their trays were being cleared away.

She felt weak, drained of her usual energy, as if her muscles lacked the strength required to lift a spoon to feed herself. Little shivers ran through her legs and then upwards through her torso.

She glanced down at her figure in the bed. She had lost weight recently, too much weight. Her body made only a slight bump in the bedclothes. The hospital nightgown, despite its cheery colours, made her feel shapeless, as if she had inherited the body of a young boy.

An experienced nurse approached.

'Now now, Margaret, you haven't touched your breakfast.

You've a bad dose all right, and I'm sure you're feeling poorly, but it's just a nasty old virus. You must try to eat or you'll never regain your strength.'

The nurse withdrew a thermometer from her breast pocket and inserted it into Margaret's mouth.

'Young girls these days just don't look after themselves the way they should. Seems to be all the rage to starve yourself. You turn yourself into a skinny little rake and then you're weak and vulnerable to every passing bug. You young girls don't seem to realise that there's nothing beautiful about being starved and sickly. Sure *health* is beauty. You show me a healthy young girl, *any* healthy young girl . . .'

The nurse paused, lifted her glasses to her eyes, and examined Margaret's chart.

'Hmmm, I see . . . seems we're not so young as all that . . .'

She removed the thermometer from Margaret's mouth, held it up to the light, and made some peremptory scribbles on the chart.

'Now Mrs Boyle, will Mr Boyle be coming in to see you by any chance?'

'I don't know. He's away. He doesn't know.'

'Ah, that explains things. We've tried phoning him at your home number, but there's been no reply. Have you got a number where we might reach him?'

Margaret shook her head.

'Right. Now, Mrs Boyle, I'll have this tray removed, but I'll be back with a cup of tea and a biscuit in an hour or so and we'll see if we can't get you eating again.'

Then the nurse made a brisk exit.

Margaret sank back into her pillow and closed her eyes. She took a deep breath, which caused a pain to run through her chest. She hoped she could restrain her urge to cry.

An hour later Margaret awoke to find a young man standing at the foot of her bed. He had piercing blue eyes, very short black hair brushed straight back, and two silver earrings in his left ear. He wore a black leather jacket and he carried a large bouquet of yellow tulips.

Margaret did not immediately recognise him. She reached up with her left hand to brush her hair from her eyes, but her tubes became fouled in the railings at the side of the bed.

'Sorry,' he said, smiling. 'I didn't realise you were tied up . . .'

'Tony?'

'That's me. Nice gaff,' he said, looking around the room. 'Can I, ah, put these down somewhere?'

'They're beautiful,' Margaret said weakly, extending her right hand to take the flowers.

'Ah look, why don't I just set them here. I'm sure one of these friendly sisters will find a vase somewhere. So, how are you feeling?'

Margaret smiled weakly.

'I must say, Ms Boyle, that was one very dramatic exit you pulled off yesterday. Scared the shite out of us. Of course I thought it was *my* fault. There I was, blathering on about sex and Virginia Woolf, and down you go onto the floor, and I'm thinking to myself I really need to watch what I'm saying. Nice classroom, nice students and all. Don't want to shock anyone, you know what I mean?'

'You're very good to come in,' Margaret said.

'Not at all. We were all worried about you. And I have to say, it was worth the visit just to check in downstairs. I've never been made to feel so welcome in my life. They think I'm your husband. I've your reputation ruined. Thanks be to Christ I remembered to bring the flowers – otherwise they'd think you were married to a right wally.'

Margaret managed another weak smile. 'He's away. On business.'

'I figured as much. Well look, now, Ms Boyle, I'd better be on my way and let you get some rest. Here's my card, in case you need anything, what with hubby away and all. Give me a bell if I can do anything at all for you. I'm very good with cats, by the way, though dogs don't usually take very kindly to me . . .'

'You're very kind.'

'Right, I'll be off then. You're looking great, by the way, under the circumstances. I hope you're feeling better soon.'

'Thanks, Tony.'

Then he waved, turned, and walked confidently out of the ward. Margaret could feel the stares of the other women settle on her as Tony departed.

'Lovely flowers,' one of them cried out.

'And a lovely delivery boy as well!' said another.

Laughter all round.

Margaret glanced down at the card that Tony had handed her. Tony Dunne, First Arts Student. Dolphin's Barn address.

Very kind of him, Margaret thought. Such lovely flowers.

Very kind indeed.

CHAPTER 8

In which Paul prepares to renovate.

By early Saturday afternoon Paul had gathered the supplies
he needed to begin his assault on Mamie's sitting room. The
activities of the morning had focused his energies, given a
purpose to this empty day.

He placed the bags from the hardware shop in the centre
of the room and began to lay out his new tools.

A shining, black-headed claw hammer. Two saws – one
thick, squared German saw with short teeth for mitring, and
one long English saw for finishing. Three boxes of strong
masonry nails, from one to three inches. Three screwdrivers
with yellow and black handles. A stubby chisel for removing
plaster. An array of blades for applying fresh plaster: an icing
knife, a putty knife, and a broad, shiny trowel. A razor-sharp
utility knife.

Three grades of sandpaper, made in the Czech Republic.
Two towels and two large drop cloths, six feet square. A large
box of filling plaster. A five kilo bag of gypsum plaster from
Wicklow. Three containers of paint stripper for stripping the
skirting boards.

He laid the new tools like a surgeon with his instruments,
or like a priest preparing for Mass.

It had been years since he had undertaken such a project. His mind was drawn back to his summers in Illinois, working with farmers to rebuild wind-damaged buildings, or painting the interiors of refurbished downtown warehouses transformed into chic retail outlets. He recalled the quiet pleasure of new tools, new brushes, new drop cloths, new tins of paint as a job was about to begin. And he remembered the heavy, humid air, the long Midwestern afternoons, his hands toughened with scrapes and scars, and the snap of that first cold beer at The Tapper at the end of a long day.

He stood up from his tools and walked to the end of the room, looked out of the window into the back garden, now heavy with January rain. The garden walls were hardly visible through the overgrown foliage, but a well-worn path bisected the grass. He recalled Mamie's remarks about Martin tending the garden, but clearly nothing had been done there for several months. The pictures were coming back to him now – pictures from *The Irish Garden* – a gift from his mother-in-law, too big for their bookshelves. A massive round hydrangea. The huge, floppy, elephant-eared leaves of the *Gunnera manicata*. A bed of decayed wild flowers, difficult to identify now, possibly foxglove. A large yew at the end, tired-looking and heavy with rain.

He turned to face the room.

He had tried that morning to buy the boards to replace the badly patched skirting that ran round the base of the walls. Before leaving the house he had prised a piece from the wall to enable him to match the pattern – rugged, hundred-year-old pine, seven inches tall, simple bevelling. Thick paint from years of interior decorating. Paul peeled back six coats: whites, creams, one strange green and, in the middle, an unusually depressing brown.

Ancient cobwebs and dust clung to the back of the board.

Paul brought the sample with him to the hardware shop. A polite, elderly attendant took him through the modern equivalents: low, five-inch boards with curls and grooves, nothing quite right. Paul said he didn't want to replace all the skirting, only the parts where the original had been cut away. The attendant directed Paul to try a joinery in Harold's Cross.

Paul eventually found the joinery, a workshop in a desolate collection of warehouses, hidden well off the main road, behind the gardens of a row of run-down houses.

The rasping sound of circular ripsaws. Paul handed the sample board to a dirty little man with tough, tobacco-stained hands. He examined the piece carefully.

'What length?' he shouted.

'About thirty feet. I need one fourteen-foot board and then some shorter pieces. I'll cut the shorter ones.'

The man squinted grimly again at the sample, looked back over his shoulder into the workshop.

'I can have it for you Tuesday,' he shouted.

'Fine. Do you deliver?'

'No problem.'

'How much?'

The man looked at Paul for the first time.

'A hundred and twenty quid,' he shouted.

'For thirty feet of pine?'

The noise from the workshop increased.

'Your fourteen-foot board is longer than standard,' the man shouted. 'Have to order that. Then there's the set-up. Can't buy this bevelling off the shelf.'

Paul hesitated. The man held the sample board out for Paul to take away.

'Okay. All right,' Paul said, handing back the sample. 'Tuesday.'

The room was chill and silent as Paul began to work. Mamie opened the door behind him.

'Mind if I look on for a moment?' she asked, standing in the doorway. 'It's been so long since anything has been done to this room.'

Paul smiled at her. He carried a large screwdriver to the corner of the room and bent down.

'I think we'll start at the bottom and work our way up,' he said.

He pushed the screwdriver between the carpet and the skirting board and levered up a corner of the carpet. Then he grasped the loosened carpet with both hands, and began to pull.

The carpet, fastened to the floor with carpet tacks, came away with a jerky motion: rip, rip, rip. Paul followed the edge of the room, pulling the heavy carpet up to reveal the colourless boards below. He worked his way slowly all around the edge of the room until the carpet was freed from the floor. He moved his tools off the carpet, and then began awkwardly to roll it across the room. Dust filled the air as the heavy roll grew in weight and circumference.

Halfway across the room Paul stopped, pulled out the utility knife, knelt down and proceeded to cut the carpet across the middle.

'Two pieces,' he explained. 'Easier than trying to move it all at once.'

In a few moments he had completed the two rolls of carpet. Mamie made way as he dragged the rolls out of the room and into the hallway.

Then they stood together looking into the room, which now resounded with a new hollowness. The floor was grey with age, its wide boards so long hidden under dust and mould, now exposed to the air for the first time in decades.

'You need tea,' Mamie announced.

'No, I'm fine thanks,' Paul replied.

'No,' she objected, 'I mean to clean the floor. Wait here.'

Mamie scurried off into her flat, and Paul could hear noise coming from her kitchen. She returned in a few moments with a large pan of brownish water and a broom.

'I can still remember the shine we used to get from our wooden floors when I was a girl,' she said, walking into the centre of the room. And with that, she began to scatter wet tea leaves everywhere, leaving a pattern of dark wet spots on the dusty grey floor.

'Now, Paul, I'll leave you to sweep up this mess . . .'

Paul began to sweep, and the wet leaves gathered all the dust from the floor. As he swept, the varnished surface came up to a rich, deep golden hue.

When he had finished, the floor showed the wear of fifty years earlier, the wide boards scuffed and almost softened by marks from heels, from wooden furniture, from dropped crockery, from decades of walking and running and dancing.

Dust hung in the air like incense, and the golden colour reflected from the floor filled the room with new, warm light.

'Now, that's a good start for the day,' Mamie said, reappearing at his shoulder and folding her arms over her chest. 'But my dear man, you certainly have your work cut out for you.'

CHAPTER 9

*In which we witness a Dublin property deal
in the making.*

On Sunday night at 7:30, Martin Walsh threw his half-smoked
cigarette onto the tarmac in the car park of the Kingston
Arms Hotel. He checked his watch nervously as he entered
the foyer. Scanning the room for acquaintances, he breathed
in deeply and strode with false confidence across the foyer
into the lounge.

The hotel strove to present an image of heavy opulence.
Thick curtains in lush pinks and burgundies hung down
over tall dark windows. Gilt-framed reproductions of medieval war scenes decorated the walls. Ornate high-backed
chairs surrounded dark wood tables. Even the carpet seemed
excessive for a busy hotel: rich dark reds interwoven with
golden crests.

It was a place of well-heeled, old-world masculinity: servile
staff, expensive beef dinners, and deep-voiced conversation
over brandy and cigars.

Martin could be found here regularly on Sunday nights.
This was where they met, the foursome of school chums
from St Mary's, to have their last pint of the weekend, to
discuss the match, to schedule their golf and to assess the

state of the world. Only lately, Martin felt that something had changed. He didn't look forward to these gatherings the way he once did. Lately he had even considered giving it a miss. He found himself mulling over excuses, thinking through the implications of quitting the scene altogether and just letting the three of them get on with it.

Because, lately, there had arisen differences between these four – or, more accurately, between Martin and the other three. They were professionals, while Martin owned his own business. Richard had lost so many teeth playing rugby at school that he went into dental surgery and had become one of Dublin's leading practitioners. Johnnie and Peter had both studied law – Johnnie was now a full partner in a large firm of solicitors, and Peter was an established barrister.

In the early years, mind you, Martin's business had set him way ahead of his colleagues in financial terms. But lately, and especially since Martin had lost his furniture case against that computer firm (despite Peter's dedicated assistance), their fortunes had reversed. And so, perhaps, had their interests, their attitudes – even the jokes weren't the same as they once were. The others didn't complain about their wives any more – if they ever had – in fact, there was a disturbing note of 'new-man-ism' in their views.

In his better moods, Martin told himself he was imagining things. Old school mates don't just fall out. He had been through a bad patch lately, and of course he felt things – and friends – were against him.

But it was with him all the same tonight, that feeling of hesitation, that eagerness to get a few pints inside him (on top of the Bordeaux he'd had that afternoon) to make this work once again, like the old days, like the good old days.

Tonight the lounge was populated by British businessmen, elderly American tourists, and a contingent of hangers-on who had watched the rugby match on the wide-screen television earlier that afternoon.

At the far end of the bar Martin spotted the three men. Johnnie and Richard were seated on tall bar stools, and Peter – tall, thin and commanding – stood between them. Johnnie and Richard wore corduroy trousers and brightly coloured golf sweaters; Peter, as usual, wore a jacket of soft tweed and an open-necked shirt.

'Gentlemen,' Martin greeted, with handshakes all round, 'how are we doing on this appalling evening? Dear God, how a bit of rain brings this city to its knees.' He signalled the bartender. 'The same again for these fine gentlemen, and a pint of Budweiser for myself.'

'My dear Martin, we were starting to get worried about you,' said Richard, reaching for his pint on the bar. 'We thought you'd done yourself in over France's performance today.'

'Have you ever seen the like?' Martin replied. 'It was like watching Castleknock in seventy-five all over again.' He pulled up another tall stool and sat down.

'So, Martin, you obviously placed your bet?' Richard asked.

'I did indeed,' Martin replied, leaning back. 'And I'm down fifty pounds for my troubles.'

'Dreadful habit, gambling,' Peter said gravely.

'Get up outa that,' Martin retorted. 'You used to be the worst of all of us for betting.'

'I suppose I was. Bit of a mug's game, really,' Peter said.

'I'd choose the stock market any day,' Johnnie said. 'Same thrill when they're up, still hope when they're down.'

'Yes, your Iona's certainly doing well . . .' Richard said.

'What's this?' Martin asked.

'Don't tell me you've missed this story,' Peter said. 'Dear Johnnie here has a mole planted in one of our leading Irish companies, and he's making an absolute killing.'

'Iona, is it?' Martin asked. 'Who are they when they're at home?'

'Software,' Johnnie replied. 'Complicated business. Relatively high-risk, if you don't know the game. And besides, the stock has topped out. I've just sold the whole lot. Pick it up again in about two months when it drops back.'

'Right,' Martin said. 'Thanks for the tip.'

He drained his pint, and called the bartender for another.

'Now, gentlemen,' Peter began, 'speaking of opportunities: I was having a quiet one in the Clarence Hotel on Thursday last, when who comes into the bar only our old acquaintance Dermot Reilly.'

'Dermot Reilly. I didn't think he was in Dublin much this weather,' Martin said.

'He tells me he's just passing through,' Peter replied. 'It's that Kildare Foods dispute in the papers. He's recently been appointed to the board. They need some land re-zoned to extend one of their processing plants. The environmentalists were claiming it was some sort of breeding ground for songbirds. Now Dermot's in with the DPP, and he got some inside information. He prepared Kildare's case so well that the birdwatchers got thrown out on a technicality. It was in the *Irish Times* on Friday.'

Knowing nods all round.

'How-and-ever,' Peter continued, 'more to the point. Dermot tells me he's got three little properties that he's had for donkey's years up in Stoneybatter. He'd nearly forgotten that he owned them, but it appears the mortgage will be completely paid off in June, at which time Dermot comes into full possession of the aforementioned. A terrace of large, four-bed Victorian houses in need of some repair, situated, need I remind you, in a neighbourhood that is gaining value very rapidly. The long and the short of it, gentlemen, is that Dermot wants to sell, very privately, and is willing to offer the opportunity to a select few bidders.'

The three men nodded sagely.

'I of course told our esteemed friend,' Peter said, straightening to his full height, 'that a consortium of trusted acquaintances would willingly aid and abet his endeavour to release himself of these properties. And my offer of assistance was accepted with good grace.'

'Jesus, Peter, this is sounding very good,' Richard said in a low voice, 'but I'd say he's looking for big money.'

'Indeed not. He assures me that he'll part with the whole lot for a publicly quoted price of six hundred thousand Irish punts for the three properties, inclusive.'

'Six hundred grand!' Martin broke in. 'The man is mad. He'd fetch two-fifty, maybe three hundred *each* in today's market.'

'Ah, yes, but if he charges full rate for the buildings, the taxman taketh the balance. He's planning to get an inspection done, generate a report that says they're falling down, and sell the whole lot for next to nothing. That's why he's doing it on the QT.'

'So what's the catch?' asked Johnnie.

'I believe the term used today is "hello money",' Peter said, leaning in towards the other men. 'Essentially he's looking for two hundred K cash upfront, non-refundable, for the privilege of bidding for these properties. Upon receipt of same, he enters into negotiations for the buildings and closes the sale for four hundred K. All on the quiet. He'll report four hundred K to the taxman and put two hundred K in his pocket. The purchasers end up with seven hundred and fifty K's worth of bricks and mortar. Dermot will even finance the sale – but not, of course, the introductory fees.'

The three men considered the proposition. Martin drank deeply of his fresh pint, set his glass on the bar, and raised his finger for silence as he swallowed.

'You're saying,' Martin began, 'that if we hand over fifty K each in a sealed brown envelope, our man Dermo will hand us over the deeds to his houses, charge us a small monthly fee, and we're in possession of seven hundred and fifty K's worth of property?'

'Seven hundred and fifty thousand indeed, and growing at fifteen per cent per annum.'

'How long will he give us to come up with the dosh?' Johnnie asked.

'I asked him to give us a few days to consider,' Peter replied.

'If we're going ahead, he'll give us one month to deliver the initial payment.'

Peter set his pint on the bar.

'Gentlemen, what's our verdict? Are we in?'

'Sounds very enticing,' Richard said.

'Sounds too good to let go,' Johnnie agreed.

Martin paused before replying. 'Fifty grand upfront, in one month . . .'

'Jesus, Martin,' Johnnie said. 'It's a no-brainer! We can give them a lick of paint and sell them next autumn for seven-fifty, maybe eight hundred grand. We'll clear forty, fifty, maybe sixty K each. Sell your fucking Range Rover if you have to, but don't let this one get away!'

Martin looked into the three faces, arrayed in challenge.

'Right, boys, let's go for it.'

And glasses were raised in lieu of signatures to the deal.

One hour later Martin dashed from the hotel through the car park in the heavy rain. He fumbled for his keys in the pockets of his wax jacket, found them, and climbed into his Range Rover.

He sat behind the wheel, looking out at the shafts of rain illuminated by the streetlights outside. He lit a cigarette.

'Fifty grand upfront, in one month,' he said to himself.

He turned the key to start the engine. He felt tired, unclear of what he had agreed.

'Fifty grand,' he muttered.

The Range Rover lurched forward through the car park, and then stopped before pulling onto Lansdowne Road.

'Bloody hell,' he muttered to himself. 'Where in the name of Jesus am I going to dig up fifty grand?'

CHAPTER 10

In which Felicity fears the worst.

1:30, Monday afternoon. Felicity stood before the door of Spyral Multimedia, took a deep breath, exhaled slowly. Attempting to compose herself, she smoothed the front of her navy woollen coat, ran her hand through her hair. Then she walked through the door and across the open-plan area towards her office.

As she had expected, Jack's Kerry accent boomed from his office as she passed.

'Felicity! Would you ever come in here for a moment?'

'Yes, Jack,' she called. She turned calmly and entered Jack's sanctuary.

She knew that it was the wrong morning to mitch from work. She knew that the representative from MountAgro Agricultural had been into the office to make his presentation. And she was, as she had explained to Jack, deeply apologetic that, due to her mother's sudden illness, and her father's continuing poor health, she was not able to attend this morning's important event.

But at the back of her mind she was relieved, relieved to have had a real and plausible excuse. She'd had a sense of foreboding about this MountAgro thing, since last week, since she first heard about the contract. It had been with her all weekend. Something about it didn't fit, something about this deal filled her with misgivings. It was as though her recent discontent with the office, with Spyral, with work – even with her entire life – seemed to be wrapped up inextricably with this MountAgro opportunity.

The office: so new, so bland, so tasteless, so artificial.

Genetically modified food. Perfect, but unnatural. Sickness masquerading as health.

This was not the first time she had felt like this. She'd been through this before, she knew the signs within herself: the lack of motivation. The listlessness. The bad nights, the anxiety for no obvious reason.

And so this morning, despite all that was happening at Spyral, she was inwardly glad that she'd been out of the office. When her mother phoned her at 7:30, whingeing as always about her back, her chest, her running eyes, and everything else that was habitually paining her, Felicity breathed a sigh of relief, welcomed the opportunity to miss work for a morning, even managed to retain an interest as her mother recited her ailments and maladies on the way to, and in the waiting room of, and on the way home from, the doctor's uncomfortable surgery.

Jack Donnelly, well groomed and sitting in his new office at Spyral Multimedia, was in very good form. He sat back, rubbed his hands together briskly, satisfaction oozing from his rotund body like that of a man about to tuck into a feast.

He examined his clean, closely trimmed fingernails, looked

up at the photographs of himself on the walls, massaged the heavy gold ring adorning the little finger on his right hand.

Yes, he told himself, he was the right man in the right place today.

To begin with, he'd had a marvellous weekend. Had he fallen in love? No, not really. But he was certainly smitten. Besotted. Seduced, really. God, those bright young eyes. Those dainty little shoulders. That smooth, flat tummy, peeping out from her short top . . . ah, yes, for just a moment he allowed himself to drift back to Saturday night: such a marvellous night, such a marvellous, marvellous girl!

And now, MountAgro Agricultural coming into the office, *his* office, asking him and his team for a quotation for the largest project they'd ever undertaken. And the thing was wide open, MountAgro wasn't talking to anyone else, it was his, Jack's, for the taking.

Right man in the right place, our Jack! He smiled openly to himself.

He looked out into the development area, saw Felicity approach, looking even more dour than usual.

'Felicity! Would you ever come in here for a moment?'

Jack waited as Felicity took off her coat. Don't know what it is with her lately, he thought. Always was a bit of an old maid. But lately she seems so down, so negative. And just as the company was about to take off!

'You got my message?' Felicity said, sitting down. 'I'm sorry I wasn't in.'

'I know, I know,' Jack replied. 'These things can't be

helped. But we did our best to forge ahead without our Chief Financial Adviser.'

'So how did it go? The meeting – with MountAgro?'

'It was absolutely marvellous,' Jack said, grinning as he leaned back in his swivel chair. 'Everything went exactly according to plan. He's a smooth customer, I can tell you – a slick American operator. Peter Murphy is his name – tells us his grandfather's from Cork. His company's got big plans for Ireland. Opening up an R&D facility in Kildare, and new administrative offices in Donnybrook. Ireland is going to become the centre of MountAgro's European operations. He's secured a significant sum in Irish Government grants.'

'Gosh. But what about the project?' Felicity asked. 'Can we do it?'

'Of course we can do it!' Jack retorted. 'Sure, it's right up our alley. Educational software, multimedia, for the schools. All about genetics. He wants it developed for Ireland first, then we'll localise it for the rest of Europe. His goal is quite simple: to teach European kids that genetics holds the key to all our futures!'

'And the others, Paul and Ruth?' Felicity asked. 'What about Dee? How did they react?'

'Sure, how *would* they react?' Jack asked. 'This is a major opportunity! I told them they're to get started on a prototype straight away. Paul is setting to work on a full proposal. We could have a purchase order for this project within a few weeks. This is just what we need, Felicity. We'll be in the clear in no time.'

She looked at him across his desk, his hands folded behind

his head, his boyish certainty so charming, but so unnerving. She knew the state of the company's financial affairs. She knew exactly how much was in the bank, how much was going out each month.

'I'm really, really pleased,' Felicity said, standing. 'I'd better, you know, log on and get caught up . . .'

'Felicity,' Jack said, leaning forward. 'This is the big one. This project will sort everything out for us. And then everything will be back to normal. It's going to be grand. All right?'

'Yes,' she replied. 'I . . . I'd really better get to work . . .'

Jack watched her leave the room. Poor old Felicity, he thought. Always was a worrier. Even when things are going so well.

MountAgro, he thought. And that girl. That lovely, lovely girl!

Felicity left the office and walked down the corridor to the canteen. Ruth and Dee were at a table across the room. They hailed her as she filled her mug with coffee.

'So where were you?' Dee asked as Felicity sat down at their table. 'You missed the great Monkey Man.'

'Monkey Man?' Felicity asked.

'Dee is convinced this guy is the missing link,' Ruth said. 'Dee figures he's a gorilla who joined MountAgro to move up the evolutionary chain.'

'Yeah,' Dee said. 'Only he didn't quite make it to the top.'

'Go on with you,' Felicity said. 'What was he like?'

'He was corporate,' Ruth said. 'Very slick. He gave us a presentation on the company. Lots of ski-slope growth curves. World domination stuff.'

'So what does he want from us?' Felicity asked.

'Bloody propaganda,' Dee said. 'It's like I was saying last week. He wants something to brainwash the kids with. Never mind Nature's imperfections, never mind variety, or the wonder of new life springing from old seeds. This guy is into perfection. Full stop. I'm telling you, eugenics is one step away.'

'Come on, Dee,' Ruth said. 'He wants an educational package, that's all. He knows it has to present a balanced view or it won't be let into the schools.'

'I don't trust the guy,' Dee said. 'And I don't like this project.'

'Fine,' Ruth said. 'So we decide, now, that we won't do it. It's up to us at the end of the day. Jack can't force us to take this thing on. What do you think, Felicity?'

Felicity looked down, swirled the dregs of coffee left in her mug.

'I . . . I don't know,' she said. 'I should have seen the presentation. What does Paul think?'

'Hard to say,' Ruth replied. 'He's keeping to himself these days. Very odd.'

'I'll tell you what he thinks,' Dee said. 'I'd say Paul's all for it. Haven't you seen him lapping up this proposal? He's American, after all. Imperialism is in their blood.'

'Ah now,' Ruth countered. 'That's a bit harsh, don't you think?'

'Right,' Felicity said, nervously. 'I'd better be off – lots of catching up to do . . .'

She left them at the table.

Something there, she thought. Something in their tone. Not nice.

Dee meant it. And so did Ruth.

Something not right here at all.

As Felicity re-entered the office, she saw Paul at his desk. He was a fast typist, and today he seemed to be hammering the keys with special anger. She approached, almost afraid to interrupt. Then she sat on his desk and waited for him to notice.

No response.

'So,' she said, finally. 'What did you think of Monkey Man?'

'Just a sec,' he said brusquely. 'Just finishing this sentence . . .'

Paul continued to type.

Felicity gazed around the room: two short-haired young men hunched over keyboards, a girl on the phone, another fellow with a ponytail digging through a file box on the floor.

'Sorry about that,' Paul said, looking up. 'You missed the show this morning.'

'I know. Mother. Sick again. Nothing serious.'

'I saw you in with Jack,' Paul said. 'You got the story?'

'Yeah. Jack's convinced this MountAgro deal is won already.'

'I'm not so sure,' Paul said. 'We've never done anything this big. If MountAgro checks out our references, they may come to the conclusion that this project is beyond us.'

'Dee is against us taking it on,' Felicity said. 'He doesn't want to be writing propaganda for evil multinationals.'

'It's hardly propaganda,' Paul said. 'I studied this stuff in college. This is going to be an educational package, or I won't allow the material to pass. Nothing's going to go into this thing that isn't scientific, factual, demonstrable. We could turn this project into something very valuable, Felicity. This is exactly what Spyral should be doing.'

'You might have a battle on your hands, Paul. Dee is going to need some convincing.'

'He'll come around,' Paul said. 'At least, he'd better. We're going to need him and everybody working on this prototype full-time if we're going to win this contract.'

'It might not be that easy . . .'

'Okay, I've been warned,' Paul said. 'But that will have to wait until tomorrow. Right now I've got to get this project plan issued for Jack's approval.'

And Paul returned to his typing.

'Hey,' Felicity said. 'Paul. I know you're busy. But are you okay?'

Paul looked up from his keyboard, paused for a moment. He seemed about to say something. But then he just smiled sadly.

'I'm fine, Felicity. But thanks.'

And a moment later he was once again engrossed in his task.

Oh dear, she thought as she walked away from his desk.

We've got problems here. And the trouble is only starting.

Paul was indeed engrossed in his work. All weekend it was the redecorating. Now the proposal. Anything, he thought, anything to keep him from thinking about Margaret, about his situation.

He was nearing the end of the first draft of his project plan when his mobile phone rang.

'Hello, Paul here.'

'Paul – I've finally found you.'

'Declan, long time no hear. How are you?'

'Jesus, Paul, I've been trying to contact you at home since Friday. I couldn't find your bloody mobile number – is your home phone disconnected or what?'

'Ah, it could be,' Paul paused. 'You weren't talking to Margaret?'

'No, I wasn't talking to anyone. The goddamn phone just rings and rings. Listen, there's an absolutely brilliant gig on this Friday and I want you and your good lady wife to drop whatever boring plans you've made and come along.'

'Friday night? Gosh, I don't know . . .'

'Look, mate, whatever you've got, cancel it. I'm telling you, this is a *major* gig.'

'I'd love to, Declan, but—'

'Jesus, Paul, I'm talking about Fred Hersch and Tom Rainey, together, at Whelan's! These guys are the biz, Paul. You're not going to hear better jazz this year. They're keeping it totally quiet, no hype, no publicity, just word of mouth. The tickets are gold dust, but I know the bloke who's fixed it. So what do you say, old man?'

'I'm sorry, Decko – but I'm not sure. You see, it's Margaret.'

'What's wrong with her? Invite her to come along. A few pints of the black stuff, Paul, and some sweet contrapuntal syncopation – that'll set her straight. Or is jazz anti-feminist?'

'No, Declan, I'm afraid it's a bit more serious. You see,' Paul said, lowering his voice, 'I've sort of moved out.'

'Moved out?'

'Yeah. Well, like, she asked me to leave.'

'Oh shit,' Declan said quietly. 'Jesus, I'm sorry, mate. Look, let's talk about it. Can you come over tonight? I'll check with Sally but I'm sure we've nothing on. Come over. We'll feed you. Maybe we can have a wee chat after the kiddies disappear, right?'

'Yeah, Declan, thanks, I'd like that. Yeah, okay, tonight . . .'

'Good. Right. Sorry about this, old man.'

'Yeah. Thanks, Decko.'

Paul rang off and set down the phone.

He'd told no one about Margaret. It was as though he was hearing it for the first time.

He stared into his monitor.

Right. Margaret has kicked me out. Sally and Declan know about it. I have to go to dinner to explain this thing. Need to make sense of it myself first.

Tonight. Oh Christ.

Right.

CHAPTER 11

In which we have dinner with the ideal family.

Paul met Declan Sheehan eight years ago in a lab session at the University of Illinois at Champagne-Urbana.

Over the years, in both Illinois and Dublin, Paul and Declan had come to know one another quite well. Their wives, Margaret and Sally, also had a good relationship, though to a lesser extent than their husbands.

Since Paul had left his home in Illinois and moved to Ireland, Declan continued to feel an avuncular sense of protectiveness for his friend. Because Declan's friendship with Paul pre-dated his marriage to Sally, even now, when Paul visited Declan in the Sheehan home in Sandymount, Sally always felt like the newcomer, as if a foreigner in her own land.

Sally and Margaret often spoke of the close bond between their husbands, a bond marked by boyish passions for pointless, external things:

Business. Chemistry. Jazz. Guy stuff.

Declan was forty, thus a few years Paul's senior. During the late 1980s Declan had left Ireland when unemployment figures were rising like an ascending stairway. Declan chose to pursue his postgraduate studies in Illinois, in chemistry, largely because a number of his mates from University College Dublin had ventured there. Teaching fellowships were readily available and it seemed a reasonable way to fund oneself through one's twenties, until something better turned up.

Upon his arrival at the Champagne-Urbana campus, Declan's first contacts were naturally enough with the Irish community. He met Margaret at a student pub during his first week and got to know her as the weeks wore on, but never warmed to her views. During that same semester he and Paul had been randomly assigned as laboratory partners. Their friendship grew amidst sulphurous smells. Male bonding occurred in an almost literal sense, as both men had an interest in natural adhesives – Declan, from his boyhood days making model aircraft, and Paul, from his background in botany.

Declan was responsible for introducing Paul to Margaret, in a brief and embarrassed encounter, at lunchtime, standing in a crowded canteen, when all three were carrying trays with sandwiches on yellow Styrofoam plates, and none could locate a place to sit down for five rather long minutes.

Within a year, Paul and Margaret had married in a small ceremony, and Declan had returned to Dublin. Living at home, with no job on the horizon, Declan amused himself with a series of experiments in his parents' Dublin garage, experiments that he had begun in his spare time in the university lab. Experiments with materials, with adhesives, and ultimately with paper. Beginning in the warm summer months, extending into the cool autumn, then even during the coldest, darkest months of the winter, Declan made paper – sheet after sheet of handcrafted, wholesomely organic Irish paper.

His techniques were his own. His ingredients spanned the globe – from Irish linen to Indian cinnamon, from French garden mushrooms to sawdust from California redwoods. He developed his own hardware for straining the messy concoctions, a tool which he would ultimately patent as 'Decko's Deckle'. He bought an oven and experimented with temperatures. He bought inks and experimented with colours, saturations and hues. He made translucent paper, shiny paper, scented paper, paper textured with tea and oats, and one kind of paper which was tested by the gardaí: light, disposable, and well-nigh bulletproof.

As spring approached, Declan began to take his papers out of their dark abode and into the open air, giving his offspring their first exposure to society. First to relatives, then friends, then friends of friends. Then, as summer approached, streetsellers, craft dealers, small artsy shopkeepers. Then organisers of craft shows, and then catalogue retailers.

And then wholesalers, and senior buyers from foreign retail chains.

Within a year Grey Dove Papers, manufacturers of fine Irish handcrafted specialist papers, was launched. Soon thereafter Dublin's finest gift shops were handing items to wealthy tourists in Grey Dove bags; Italian watercolourists were applying tints to the Grey Dove 'Creative' range; and Japanese executives were signing strategic alliances, unaware of the significance of the Grey Dove watermark floating behind their signatures.

And Declan himself prospered. First five, then eight, then fifteen faces surrounded the table at the annual Christmas lunch, warmed by the glow of success, inspired by the emerging good cheer of an economy in full bloom.

Sally had been the first receptionist to answer the telephone with her chirpy refrain, 'Grey Dove Papers, how can I help?' She then became the first to resign from the new company, three weeks before the wedding. The birth announcements of the twins the following year were hand-printed on the Grey Dove 'Soft Touch' range, lightly scented with the fragrance of Connemara wild flowers.

Soon Paul and Margaret returned to Ireland, and Declan introduced them to his wife and infant twins. By now Sally and the twins, Harry and Hanna, knew Margaret's generosity, as well as her moods. They knew Paul's accent, his quiet voice, his occasional reticence. And while Declan and Sally knew that Paul and Margaret loved one another, they also knew enough not to be overly surprised that Paul was coming to dinner, tonight, on his own, very much alone.

At 7:00 Paul approached the red-brick house and rang the bell.

The door opened instantly and a boy and a girl, each five years old, each with bright red hair, began to half-sing, half-shout, 'Hi Pauly, hi Pauly! Where's Magsie? Where's Magsie!'

'Hi Harry, hi Hanna,' Paul responded, with an attempt to match their enthusiasm.

'Come in, give us your coat, where's Muggy! Where is she?' they persisted.

'I'm afraid she wasn't able to come tonight . . .'

'Harry! You said they were *both* coming!'

'Hanna, I *thought* she was coming! How was *I* supposed to know?'

'This isn't fair!' Hanna shouted angrily, running back into the protection of the house, with Harry chasing close behind.

Paul closed the door behind himself and followed them sheepishly down the hall. He entered the high-ceilinged sitting room.

'Ah Paul, how are you?' Declan said, straightening up before a large fireplace.

The children were volubly explaining that Margaret wasn't there.

'Harry said she was coming but she's not here!' Hanna shouted.

'I *thought* she was coming, Mummy didn't tell me she wasn't coming!'

'Now, children, I'm sure you could offer to take Paul's coat for him . . .'

'We *did*, but he didn't give it to us yet!'

Within a few minutes Paul had been relieved of his coat and had calmed the natives by distributing the traditional chocolate peace offerings. Declan excused himself for a moment. Paul sat down before the fire, looked round the room, noticing for the first time the plaster mouldings, the high picture rail surrounding the walls, the flawless wainscoting.

Soon Sally entered. She was blonde, pretty and petite, almost insignificant in her smallness, looking much younger than her thirty-four years.

'Hi, Paul,' Sally said, softly, as if entering a sickroom. 'I don't know what's happened, but I'm so sorry.'

Paul stood and she reached up to kiss his cheek.

She stood before him for a moment, looking into the fire, wiping her hands nervously on a brightly coloured apron.

'As soon as Declan told me, I tried phoning Margaret,' she said, as if confessing. 'I've been trying all afternoon. I'm sorry, maybe I shouldn't have phoned her, but she's not answering. I wanted to drop by, to see her. I want to make sure she's all right.'

Sally looked into the fire again, the light flickering on her face.

'She just needs time, I think,' Paul said, trying to offer comfort. 'She, well, she's done this before. She just wants to straighten out her head. I didn't want to tell anyone. I just want to let it sit for a while, you know. To keep the whole thing quiet.'

'I know, Paul. But this is Dublin, not Illinois. Dublin is a very small place, and things don't stay hidden very long.'

Sally looked into Paul's eyes.

'You should have told us, Paul. This is terrible. You need to see her, right away. You need to find out what she wants.'

'No, not yet,' Paul said. 'She'll call me when she wants to talk. I just want her to have some time. I think she just needs some time.'

Just then Harry and Hanna burst in the room. 'Daddy says to tell you Dinner is now being Served! It's time to eat, come on, come on, *come on*!'

* * *

Paul could not focus on dinner.

He wasn't hungry. He felt tired, fuzzy, slipping back and forth from the present into his past. Sitting with the four Sheehans, he remembered his own family dinners when he was a boy, those ordered, hierarchical gatherings: Dad at that end, Mom at this, steaming dishes passed carefully around the table, children speaking in turn, reporting about their day at school. They had learned from an early age to edit out of their accounts the real events of school life, and to present for their parents a clean picture, a picture of honest challenges and steady progress, a picture brushed free from the dirt, the anger, the fighting, the fear, the brutality, the sexuality, the dope, the embarrassment, the loneliness – all cleansed away during those family dinners, with chatter running around the table like ripples over a deep, treacherous pond.

In contrast, at the Sheehans' tonight, like every night, dinner was a wild, splashing, energetic, entertaining wash of food and words, a continuous attack of noise and activity. The twins never, *ever* stopped talking, like competing radio broadcasts filling the room, directed at each other, at Declan and Sally, at people not present – recounting, reciting, narrating, enacting their days, every aspect in an unexpurgated splurge of busyness, replete with underwear, bodily functions, obscenities from their little friends passed round in giggles, all the while grabbing, slurping, waving food around the table, dropping and fetching forks from the floor, drinking, filling, clinking, spilling, refilling glasses . . .

And throughout, Declan and Sally seemed capable of maintaining three or four streams of conversation at once, talking to Paul, to the twins, to each other, like stage comedians, with asides for the hecklers as the act continued unabated. In the midst of the chaos, Sally served melon, Declan served quiche with boiled potatoes, Declan poured wine, Sally served tea, Declan recounted a meeting with a health inspector, Sally joked about her mother, Declan said what he'd heard about Green Party protesters in County Kildare, Sally talked about arranging a choir rehearsal.

Paul ate half a melon, some potatoes, several bites of quiche. He apologised for not eating. He said his stomach wasn't right, said he had forgotten to bring his allergy pills. He agreed with everyone, said little.

In the midst of the noise, the food, the conversation, he remembered his days at school. He listened to the kids' description of the new equipment at the playground, and he remembered swinging, swinging on cold autumn days, in the dusty schoolyard, while children ran about below him shouting, and swinging above the stocking caps on their little heads, their calls falling below the surface of his thoughts, the sound of the cold air rushing in his ears.

An hour later dishes had been washed, dried and put away, and children had been read to and tucked in. Low jazz permeated the sitting room, punctuated by crackles from the fire, steamy snaps from coal dampened by the weeks of rain.

Paul sat beside the fire in a comfortable overstuffed arm-chair; Declan and Sally sat on the sofa that faced the fire. A bottle of Merlot, nearly empty, warmed on the hearth.

The conversation had carried on throughout the evening,

in jerky little pieces, comments, disconnected observations, interspersed by children, a phone call, a passed dish.

'Surely she gave some indication . . .' Sally resumed.

'She puts in far too much time at her work,' Declan noted.

'Has she anyone besides her mother to talk to?' Sally asked, distracted. 'I wish she would answer our calls.'

But now the three sat down together, finally. Not quite relaxed, but with a shared sense of purpose. Perhaps even a bit reluctant, but concerned. Adult. A bit tired but determined, finally, to explore this crisis, this tiring, unnerving crisis.

And for a few moments there was silence, a heavy, cottony silence in the middle of the room, a solid thing played upon by the flickering fire. Then Paul began to speak, staring before him, down, into the patterns on the rug, then off the fringes, then around the knots in the white pine floor.

'In Illinois, she always seemed to be alone,' he began. 'I'd noticed her even before we met, walking alone across the quadrangle, in the autumn, when it was still warm, without her jacket, holding her books with both arms. She had a look of concentration on her face, as though she was solving a problem, a problem with too many facets, with no solid boundaries.

'Then, when we met first, there were always groups of people around. Declan, you remember those crowds of people on Friday nights – half knew each other, half didn't. She was there one night in the midst of them, twelve or fifteen of them in the living room of some old wooden house, and I noticed her talking, or actually not talking, saying very little, listening, like a priest, an adviser. Everyone talked to her, and she had a look on her face that showed she was interested in all they were saying, but she never fully approved, nor disapproved, only listened, always carefully listened.

'I never intended to ask her out, not because I wasn't attracted to her, but you know grad school: it's not like college, it's focused and committed. It's an endurance test, really. I told myself I wasn't going to mess up, that I was going to concentrate on my work, that women were not part of the agenda, at least for the first year. And my research was going well. My supervisor was a very inspiring guy. You remember, Declan, I was in my poison phase, heavily into organic toxins: wild rhubarbs, poison ivies, nettles, foxgloves.

'Finally, just before the Christmas break, I saw Margaret one night in one of the cheap student restaurants in town, eating on her own. I ran through the whole debate in my head, I ate a whole salad and sat there, watched her order, and then watched her order arrive, thinking to myself that I shouldn't get involved, trying to convince myself that I didn't care that this Irish girl was having a lonely, miserable time in America.

'I remember sitting across from her, seeing her eyes for the first time. You know the way she can scrutinise you. Her eyes seemed to search me, as if seeking a motive, and she seemed to have such, I don't know, *depth*. She seemed to have the depth of a country that wasn't shallow and plastic, so far removed from the restaurant we sat it. She seemed a person rooted, rooted to something I didn't understand, something weighty, and her words, her soft accent, sounded something like wisdom.'

Paul paused, staring into the fire, remembering his surprise when they first kissed, surprise at the softness, the lightness of her lips, at her sweet breath, at the sheer pleasure of her mouth – surprise that her face, her small body, which had seemed so remote, so removed from their surroundings, could feel so warm, so present, so alive.

'I don't know when it happened, really, that I came to love her. I know we got married, and I know marriage implies devotion, and commitment, and whatever love is. But I didn't really love Margaret when we first married. Not because of any negative feelings. But I think I didn't love her because she didn't *believe* in love. We seemed to have reached an agreement in a wordless sort of way. I know this sounds stupid. It's as if we fell into marriage, without really talking about love.

'I began to fall in love with Margaret about two months after the wedding. I remember it was the first time we had ever slipped into a routine. She had a summer work-study job and was on a regular schedule, and I met her every evening when she finished work. We walked together through town to the apartment and every night we ate together, and I remember it was very hot that summer, and we ate salads and drank cold white wine.

'It must have been the routine, I don't know. I only know that I began to miss her during the day, every day. I started buying her little gifts – I'd never done that before we married – flowers, a fountain pen, a photograph album for her Irish pictures. And I felt so lucky, then, because I found myself married to a woman whom I, suddenly, could not live without.

'And shortly after that is when she left me, the first time. I woke up one Friday morning, just like this past week, and she was gone. She left a note . . .'

'Where did she go?' Sally asked.

'She never told me. She said in the note that she needed a break. She said not to follow her. She came back three days later. She never told me where she had been. We, well, we've never talked about it.'

'Paul, I shouldn't say this,' Declan began, with some hesitation, 'but she's not playing fair.'

'Okay, I know. But I just want her to do what she needs to do.'

'Yeah, but in the meantime you're biting your nails,' Declan insisted. 'This is a damned rotten thing to do to someone, especially since you're out in the cold.'

Paul looked down at the carpet.

'Look, Paul,' Declan said, 'I hate to see you stuck in this situation. But I can tell you what I'd do if I were you.'

Paul looked up.

'I tell you, I think I'd try to relax a bit. If she's going to go off on a holiday, I think you should too. Look, mate, right now she's calling the shots. Maybe it's time you took a bit of control here.'

'What do you suggest?'

'First thing *I'd* do is go to hear Fred Hersch and Tom Rainey this Friday.'

Paul considered for a moment.

Sally's disgust was apparent in her silence.

*   *   *

One hour later.

'So what do you think of our friends?'

'Hmph?'

'You're not asleep yet, Declan. What do you think of Paul and Margaret?'

'Both mad.' Declan rolled towards the wall.

'Would you ever do that to me?' Sally asked, pressing her body against his back.

'Do what?'

'Kick me out of the house?'

'Your father would kill me.'

'Do you think they'll get back together?'

'He loves her too much. Can't live without her.'

'Yeah,' Sally answered, drowsily. 'You know, I think that might be their whole problem . . .'

CHAPTER 12

*In which accounts are settled and Margaret
is resurrected.*

On this Tuesday morning, as on most days, Tony Dunne wore
black. Black designer jeans, a black T-shirt, a black padded
nylon jacket. He drove a black Volkswagen Golf with twin
exhaust pipes and he wore black glasses.

At ten o'clock he drove across Harold's Cross Bridge,
turning right just before the trim grounds of the Hospice.
He drove quickly down the short road to the security gate,
slowed, gave the nod to the security man, and drove into
Greenhills Industrial Estate.

The dreary estate consisted of several warehouses, a print-
works, a scrapyard, and a row of dark offices where visitors
were apparently not welcome. Trucks and small vans came
and went frequently in and out of the car park. None of the
drivers hailed one another as they passed.

Tony drove to the end of the estate, then swung down
to the left. Then he drove past two vacant warehouses and
stopped in front of Gray's Joinery.

Speciality Woodworks. Doors and Windows. Pub Interiors.

Tony parked the car and got out. He could hear the buzzing
of saws coming from inside the building.

He walked around the side of the joinery, past stacks of planks covered in black plastic, to a steel door that was flush with the wall. He knocked loudly, hoping to be heard above the rasping of the saws.

The door was opened immediately by a large man with a tightly trimmed beard and a gold bracelet. They nodded curtly to one another, and Tony walked in.

He entered a small dark reception area. The man closed the steel door behind them. He motioned Tony to sit down in a plastic chair, said nothing, and exited through another door. A few moments later he returned, motioned Tony to follow him down a narrow corridor. He ushered Tony into a small office, again closing the door behind them.

Tony stood before a balding, middle-aged man sitting behind a tidy desk. He wore a white shirt, a plain blue tie and thick, black-framed glasses. In the corner of the desk was a little glass paperclip holder with a picture of what looked like Venice.

The man looked up at Tony as he entered the room, his sagging features creased with an expression of boredom. His hands were folded on the desk. He looked like the headmaster at a school.

'Good morning, Mr Dunne,' he said in a quiet voice. The buzzing of the saws could be heard around them.

'Hiya, Mr Gray.'

'And how are things at university?'

'Not a bother, Mr Gray.'

'You heard, of course, about Mr O'Neill's little mishap?'

'Yes,' Tony replied. 'Sad bastard.'

'A competitor, Mr Dunne. One of your nearest competitors. And one should always learn from the mistakes of one's competitors.'

'Yes, Mr Gray.'

'And I'm sure you've some thoughts on why Mr O'Neill was so unfortunate as to have been arrested for dealing drugs, Mr Dunne, at University College Dublin?'

'He was too bloody obvious about it.'

'Oh?'

'Look, Mr Gray, those students – they're not like me or that O'Neill fella. They come from Ballsbridge and Foxrock and those places. O'Neill lived in Ballyfermot and got a fake student ID and hung around the bar selling drugs like it was nobody's business. Anyone working UCD from the outside like that doesn't stand a chance. They won't trust him. And they'll turn him in without a thought. That's what happened to O'Neill.'

'But, Mr Dunne,' Mr Gray interrupted, 'why is it that you expect these same students to trust *you*?'

'Because I'm a student, just like the rest of them.'

'Oh? And does this matter?'

'Yes it does. I've told you all this before. I'm out there every day, I'm in the library, in the lectures, in the tutorials. I know the people out there. I even know my tutors, personally like. They didn't take to me at first but now they're well used to seeing me around. I'm a small-time dealer and the students are okay with that. Anyone who tries to barge in from a dodgy neighbourhood and go big out there's going to get caught, because somebody'll get scared of them. It's all about trust, Mr Gray, and they trust me.'

Mr Gray did not smile.

'I thank you for your explanation, Mr Dunne. For now I'll have to accept your analysis of the situation. But I want you to be careful. It's not the money, Mr Dunne, that we're after here. My superiors are concerned simply to make a reasonable living from their business by operating in safe markets. And if they suspect that UCD will become a dangerous market for them, they'd rather let the revenue go than continue to trade there. Any uncertainties on the part of my superiors would mean that we would have unfortunately to part company, Mr Dunne. Do you understand?'

'Yeah, look, I know that, and that's the last thing I want to happen. It's perfectly safe, right? I'm keeping my head down, I'm studying hard, and it's all going grand. So can we get down to biz? I need some extra E this weekend for a party I'm supplying on Saturday night, right? As well as the usual order.'

'Very well, Mr Dunne. Mr Garvey, would you please accept Mr Dunne's cash payment and issue his supplies as we discussed? And good day to you, Mr Dunne.'

A few minutes later Tony Dunne left the building with a small pouch stuffed into the inside pocket of his jacket. Only after he had got into the car and grasped the steering wheel did he become aware of a slight clamminess in his palms.

On that same Tuesday, just after lunchtime, Margaret Boyle was finally discharged from St Vincent's Hospital.

She had presented a strange case. When she was admitted on Friday morning she was severely run down, dehydrated, and running a slight fever, which gradually worsened during the day. By Friday night she had broken out in a heat rash and her temperature had reached 102. She did not respond to standard antipyretics, and all day Saturday the fever remained high. Her blood tests revealed the presence of an infection, probably viral, and very low iron levels.

By Sunday a diagnosis of viral infection had been confirmed. Hardly life-threatening, but the severest case they had seen for some time. She had very low energy levels but slept little, even at night.

By Monday the fever had abated and some colour had returned to Margaret's features. Flu had reached epidemic proportions in Dublin over the weekend and hospital beds were needed for the influx of elderly victims. On Tuesday morning Margaret assured the nurses that she was well enough to return home.

'Yes, Mrs Boyle,' said the ward sister. 'We believe you are on your way to a full recovery. I trust you will be looked after by your husband when you arrive home?'

'Yes, sister. I expect him home shortly.'

'Very well. Why don't you gather your things and I'll bring you down now?'

A few minutes later Margaret found herself dressed in her own clothes again – charcoal-grey trousers and a black polo-necked jumper she was wearing on Friday morning when she arrived at the hospital. Her trousers were still dusty from her fall to the floor of the classroom. She had lost even more weight since being admitted, and her clothes hung loose and baggy.

Outside the hospital she climbed into the back seat of a taxi and gave the driver directions to Eglinton Terrace.

The taxi sped down Nutley Lane, and then slowed behind a queue of traffic. Light rain was falling and the wipers passed back and forth at intervals across the windscreen.

They were stalled for several minutes behind a double-decker bus. The back of the bus displayed a large photograph of a woman in a yellow bathing suit, an advertisement for holidays in the sun. The picture stretched the full height of the bus, starting just above the woman's knees and finishing at the sunglasses perched atop her head. The bus's rear window blocked out her stomach.

Twenty-five feet of voluptuous body exposed to the dirty rain.

The taxi driver chortled, leant forward, gestured towards the bus, was about to make a comment, but then caught Margaret's eye in the rear-view mirror, coughed nervously, settled back into his seat and said nothing.

It was 2:30 when Margaret finally paid the driver and walked up the path to her empty house.

The key felt stiff as she turned it in the hall door. Inside she glanced at the house alarm unit, which displayed the date and some sort of error warning. Still not working. Beside the alarm was a panic button, presumably for use if someone tried to attack you when you opened the door.

Good thing I'm not in a panic, she thought.

The hallway was cold. She walked into the kitchen, but

the heating had been off for some time, so the air was chill and damp.

The kitchen had obviously not been used since that day, last Friday, when she had left the note telling Paul to leave. The note was gone. The dishcloth hanging over the sink looked dry and stiff.

She glanced at the answering machine on the counter beside the phone, but the batteries had worn down, so there were no recorded messages. But just then, as if on cue, the phone rang. Margaret jumped nervously to answer it.

'Hello? Oh, hi Mum.'

Margaret's heart raced. She was not prepared for this conversation.

'Grand, fine, and you? No, I'm not teaching today, so I thought I'd work at home . . . Away? Yes, well, no . . . Oh, *you* were away! Of course, your trip! We missed you. How was London? . . . Yeah? Any good? Pity . . . Oh, he's grand, not a bother . . . Yes, yeah, maybe at the weekend . . . Okay, love to Dad . . .'

She put down the receiver. She noticed she was shaking. She bent down to peer into the small refrigerator and pulled out a carton of stale-smelling orange juice. She opened one of the presses above the counter and reached in for a glass, but then it slipped from her fingers and fell, bouncing off the counter and shattering on the floor.

Margaret's mouth was dry and she felt dizzy. Telling herself she was just tired, she went out of the kitchen and stumbled up the stairs. The phone began to ring again, but she kept going, breathing hard. She reached the top of the stairs and then entered the bedroom, where Paul had left the bed unmade and the wardrobes open.

Without undressing she fell onto the bed, face down, and then pulled the duvet up around her shivering body. She felt cold.

She lay quietly for a moment, listening to the rain blowing against the window. She still felt weakened, annoyed at her lack of strength. She wished someone were there to look after her, to bring her a cup of tea.

She thought about Paul, how he acted when she was unwell. He was dreadful in those situations, worrying constantly, fretful and indecisive. She recalled the last time she had a tummy bug and asked him for a hot-water bottle to warm her in bed. He was so concerned to get it right, just couldn't seem to take charge, kept running up and down the stairs from the kitchen, she counted, four times: Did she want the red one or the blue one? Was he supposed to boil the kettle all the way? Did she want a towel wrapped around it? What sort: a tea towel or a hand towel?

Poor Paul. He was only trying to help. But if only he were more, well . . .

Some time later she woke from a heavy sleep. She was lying on her front, her head pressed deep into the pillow. She shook herself awake, climbed out of bed, pulled off her clothes, stepped into her dressing gown and went downstairs.

She swept up the glass that she had broken earlier, and then put the kettle on. She knew she would have to go out eventually, get something to eat for later. Get the place organised. Plan her classes for the rest of the week. Sort out her career. Save her marriage. Take charge of this mess that she had made of her life.

But for now, just for a few minutes, she wandered into the sitting room with a cup of black coffee. She turned on the stereo, put on her Paula Cole CD, curled up on the sofa, allowed her mind to go blank, let the music wash over her.

Where have all the cowboys gone, ah oooooo . . .

Five minutes later the doorbell rang.

The bell shocked Margaret out of her reverie. She didn't know whom to expect, and in the few seconds that it took her to turn off the stereo and rush from the sitting room to the front door, she allowed herself to hope, for just that brief moment, that Paul had returned, that things would get back to normal.

But when she opened the door, there stood Tony Dunne, carrying a shopping bag in each hand and wearing an impish grin.

'Tony. Jesus Christ – sorry, I mean, what a surprise!'

'And the Blessed Virgin Mary to you. Can I come in, or are we going to eat this grub standing at the front door?'

'Yes, of course, come in, come in.'

Margaret squeezed herself against the wall while Tony walked into the kitchen. She tightened the belt on her dressing gown and followed him inside.

'Now, missus,' Tony said, setting the bags on the table. 'I used my extensive powers of reasoning to deduce that, since you only left the hospital this afternoon, you probably came home to find no food in the house.'

Margaret steadied herself against the counter, tried to appear welcoming.

'How do you know I was discharged today?'

'Easy enough. I phoned them. I told you, they think I'm your husband. So anyway, as I was trying to tell you, I've brought you two types of grub. In here, I have some bread and milk and orange juice for you to have for your brekkie tomorrow morning. And in here, something for your tea tonight, courtesy of your local Chinese. And finally, just in case you're so inclined, a bottle of vino to wash the whole lot down.'

'Tony, this is very kind of you. But really . . .'

'Now Margaret – you don't mind if I call you Margaret? – you've been through a bad patch, and you need to get your strength back, and besides, what's done is done, and you might as well sit back and enjoy it. I'd like you to plant yourself there, just there, that's better, and if you'd be so kind as to point me towards where you keep your plates and all that gear . . .'

Within a few minutes the table was set with white china plates on cotton, burgundy-coloured placemats. Wine and water glasses were on the table, and Tony was removing the covers from the aluminium containers of Chinese food, allowing steam and the scent of flavourings to escape into the air. He used a large spoon to serve portions of boiled rice onto each plate, followed by rich red sweet-and-sour chicken with large slices of pineapple.

Then he sat down, reached across the table, and poured just enough red wine to fill the bottom half of each glass.

'Now, Margaret. As my mother would say, let's see you get to the far side o' that.'

He raised his glass to her, and Margaret nodded in response.

'I love Chinese food,' Tony said as he began to eat. 'A few years back a Chinese meal meant a journey into town, a real treat, you know what I mean? Now there's a Chinese on every corner. There's so many of them, there's even a Chinese for the Chinese themselves.'

Margaret ate slowly, her appetite still weakened from her illness. But she was happy to have company, even enjoyed watching Tony eat with such gusto. He had hung his leather jacket on the back of his chair and was wearing a black T-shirt. She noted the faint trace of a scar along his left cheek.

'So, Tony. What do you think of UCD?'

'Me? I have to say, I love it. There's very few people from Dolphin's Barn would ever think of going to university. But I'm telling everyone I know that it's absolutely brilliant.'

'What's so good about it?'

'Oh, everything. The facilities, the lectures, the lot. I'm learning an incredible amount every week. Your tutorial is especially good, by the way.'

'Oh?'

'Yeah. Everybody says so. We don't know how you do it every week.'

'Do what?' Margaret asked, sitting back in her chair.

'Get so much out of those books. Get so much out of *us*. There's days that I walk into that tutorial not having a clue what we're supposed to take away from the stuff on the course. But then you go to work on us, and you just open the whole thing up. It's brilliant.'

'Surely the other tutors do the same?'

'They try all right. But maybe you don't understand my situation, Ms Boyle. I'm a mature student, as you know. This is the last chance I'll ever get to do this, to read these books, to discover what these writers were getting at. And you're making this very valuable for me. Really you are.'

'Good. I'm very glad you're enjoying it.'

'I really am. Totally.'

She looked into his face – so artless and eager he seemed.

'And what about the other aspects of campus life? The students. How about the girls?'

'What, at UCD?'

'Yes.'

'Oh, they're grand, I'm sure.'

'What do you mean, "they're grand"?'

'Well, to be perfectly honest with you, Ms Boyle, I find your average UCD first-year bird to be a bit on the, shall we say, fluffy side.'

'Fluffy?'

'Yeah. Very young, very sheltered. Mummy and Daddy's girls, if you know what I mean. And besides, if they ever took the likes of me home to meet the parents, I'd be flung out on me ear.'

Margaret studied Tony for a moment.

'Tony?'

'Yeah?'

'Do you mind my asking: why did you come here tonight?'

Tony's smile faded, then, as if drained of colour. And then Margaret watched as that direct, hard expression crossed his face, an expression that disturbed her momentarily with its intensity.

'I came here tonight because you've been sick and I thought you could use a bit of hand. That's all. That's the only reason.'

'I'm sorry, Tony. I just thought . . .'

'Maybe all that reading has made you a bit cynical. Maybe it's hard for you to see the simple things any more. Like, wanting to help someone out who's in trouble.'

Margaret flushed.

'I'm sorry, Tony. I didn't mean to imply . . . I'm just not used to this sort of, well, attention. And I appreciate your concern, very, very much.'

Then his face lightened again, and his impish grin returned.

'All right, I confess. Actually, I came because I want you to write my essay on Virginia Woolf . . .'

She laughed. And Tony laughed too, watching Margaret closely all the while.

'Now, Margaret,' Tony said, rising. 'I would love to stay and provide you with your evening's entertainment. But I'm afraid I have another appointment to keep. So I'm just going to stack these dishes here by the sink – no, stay where you are – and I'll put the kettle on so you can have a nice cup of tea when I'm gone . . .'

And a few minutes later Tony had grabbed his jacket, swung it over his shoulder, left the kitchen, and let himself out of the front door, waving away Margaret's thanks as he left.

'Not at all,' he said. 'You'd do the same for me if you had the chance. Toodle-pip, then, Ms Boyle . . .'

Later that night, Margaret lay in bed, listening to the vague sound of traffic passing back and forth at the end of the terrace on Eglinton Road. As she sank slowly towards an exhausted sleep, her mind wandered, drifted over the events of the evening. She recalled the arms of Tony's leather jacket as he entered the house, dampened by rain. She recalled his cheerful demeanour, his conversation: so sycophantic, so transparently flattering, and yet so earnest and pleasant to her in her current state, where so few events in her life seemed to support her or validate her existence.

And she thought of Tony's energy, his cheerful, innocent self-confidence: coming to her door, bringing food, expecting to be allowed into her house, assuming there would be no husband there to contend with.

And what else had he assumed, she wondered, as she greeted him downstairs in her dressing gown? What else had he expected, as he flung his jacket over the chair, poured the wine into her glass, and looked at her with those eyes, those clear, those steady, those hard blue eyes?

CHAPTER 13

In which Desperation enters the Garden.

Martin Walsh sat in his office at the headquarters of East Coast Ergonomics on Tuesday afternoon, scratching with a silver fountain pen onto ECE headed notepaper.

Fifty thousand fucking pounds, he thought. Fifty now will yield fifty profit next year. At ten per cent per annum that will double in seven years, again in fourteen, for two hundred grand when I'm – what's this I'll be in fourteen, fifteen years? Fifty-seven, not too bad, still have some life in me yet if I can make it through next week . . . Mortgage payments down this year but still at three grand a month. Three fucking grand! Why in God's name did I let her talk me into buying that house with no trace of a down payment to our names just so as her mother can impress her fucking luncheon crowd? If rates go up two points we're bloody crucified, so we are.

The telephone on his desk rang.

'Hiya, Charlie, how's the form? Where are you? Right, what's the story, are you closing at Sinex today? What? . . . But I thought you explained that to them already. Rosewood takes six weeks minimum . . . Look, we've been through this before, I thought he was all signed up to accept beech? He can have that in three . . . Fuck him, look, try some flexibility on the pricing, it's four complete boardroom sets for God's sake; don't fucking lose him . . .'

Mother of God, Martin thought, do I have to go out there and sell it for him? Stupid bollix has missed his targets three months in a row now. I should bloody fire him – what would it cost me to pay him off, train in a new guy? Two months, three months' sales down the Swanee . . .

He picked up the phone, dialled a familiar number.

'Tommy, Martin here, how's the form? . . . Not a bother, the house is absolutely spot on, Deirdre loves it, best move we ever made . . . So listen . . . really? Tell us more . . . Kildare? Re-zoning? Jesus, Tommy, nice one . . . Who's in it with you, if you don't mind my asking? . . . Right, of course, keep it nice and quiet . . . Look, mate, I'd love to get in on a deal like that myself, I really would, but to be honest I'm actually onto a very good thing here . . . yeah, property deal, three houses up in Stoneybatter, rock bottom price, it's a no-brainer and I'm just about to sign on the dotted line, but I tell you, Tommy, I just need a wee spot of cash upfront . . . Now look, Tommy, no lectures, it's only fifty grand, and we'll make it back in less than a year . . . yeah, I know all about the overdraft, and I know, I know exactly what you went through to swing our mortgage, but Tommy . . . Tommy, if you'll just give me a moment . . . Yeah, Tommy, but you know I've never missed a payment before now . . . But I explained to you, it's always a bit slow over the Christmas season . . . Tommy, it's simple, right, nobody buys fucking office furniture in December . . . Right, Tommy, look, I hear what you're saying, I had to give it a try . . . Right, right, I'm with you, okay, yeah, I *hear* you . . .

Okay, mate, righty-o, let me know how you get on with that Kildare thing, right? All the best now . . .'

He put down the phone.

Brilliant, he thought, fucking brilliant. Little shite does nothing all day but put margins on bank loans and he thinks that entitles him to play Lord God Almighty. Jesus, what I wouldn't do to be able to buy and sell that little fucker. Now where in the hell am I going to dig up fifty grand in the next three weeks . . .

Wonder how Auntie Mamie's feeling this weather?

Five years ago you could get a gorilla with a gun for a hundred quid in any pub off O'Connell Street. Even now, the gangs are out there running amok – Veronica Guerin. The General. That poor fecker on his way to work last week. Drive up, bang bang, off you go, no witnesses, at least none that would ever talk. Right, what am I thinking? I'm her only nephew, and I stand to inherit the house when she goes. How much is it worth this week? There'd be fingers pointed at me before the blood had dried on the pavement.

Martin scratched some more on his notepad.

What's his name again doing that decorating? Paul Boyle. Probably making a right balls of the room. American. Maybe he'll do all right. Wouldn't take it on if he didn't know what he was doing. But still, different buildings over there. Different styles. New. Wooden.

Paul Boyle. Wonder who he is when he's at home.

Martin turned to his computer, brought up the Internet, began a search.

PAUL BOYLE, dum-de-dum, anything here at all? Christ

of almighty, there's two hundred of him. Singer/songwriter, lawyer, another lawyer, too many fucking lawyers. 'Our family photo', hardly, nothing here, wait, what's this? *Atropa bella donna*, *Digitalis purpurea*, *Taxus baccata*, Organic Garden Quarterly, June 1996, John Baker, PhD, and Paul Boyle, MSc, could be him, he's supposed to know something about plants. What's this? 'Toxins and Homeopathy: Deadly Poisons in Common Garden Remedies.'

Interesting fellow, our Paul.

Martin scrolled through the article on screen, thought for a moment, and then sent it to the printer. He clicked a few times on the screen, cleared his browser's history list, cleared memory cache, cleared disk cache, cleared out the whole thing. These little tricks, he thought. Cover me old tracks. No one would ever know I've read this very, very interesting article.

It was Tuesday night, eight-fifteen. A small radio in the corner of the room eased forth a Mozart string quartet.

Paul stood on a ladder holding a new metal scraper with a yellow handle. He reached up to the top corner of the wall, where the wallpaper was beginning to peel. The corner seemed to be a damp patch, where the paper had bubbled and come loose.

Paul had never worked with wallpaper before. He had seen it, of course: pink stripes in his grandmother's kitchen; the floral paper in Margaret's bedroom at her parents' house, during those first weeks back in Dublin, before they had their own place. He remembered the insomnia, studying the patterns, looking for repeating flowers, wondering how he came to be with her, in that room, in this city, on this island.

Here, now, was plain cream on textured paper, an embossed pattern of acanthus leaves painted over with heavy magnolia, the raised patterns still visible through several coats of old paint.

He reached up, grabbed a corner of the wallpaper that was coming free, and pulled it away from the wall. A large patch of paper came away in his hand, surprisingly heavy. He ripped off the sheet and let it drift to the floor.

Beneath the cream was green – heavy green stripes separated by thin white lines. Using the scraper he pried a corner free, then pulled a two-foot section from the old wall, ripping it away, then letting the sheet float to the floor.

A third paper appeared: dull-coloured ivies, creeping for sixty, maybe eighty years up these sunless walls. This paper stuck hard, and Paul used the tool to scrape away, bit by bit, little patches of lifeless greenery, the pieces falling to the floor like autumn leaves.

Finally the underlying plaster was revealed.

Paul pulled and scratched and scraped for another few minutes, looked around the large empty room, and came to the realisation that this was the wrong approach to the job. Descending the ladder, he left the room and then returned in a few moments with a plastic basin of warm water, a heavy cloth, and a bottle marked 'Clear-all Wallpaper Remover', which Mamie had bought for him yesterday.

'You'll need this, Paul,' she had said, handing him two

bottles of the heavy brown liquid. 'You've a thick lot of paper to get through before you'll get at those old walls.'

He poured half of one bottle into the steaming basin. Soaking the cloth in the liquid, he proceeded to wet the walls, a patch at a time, allowing the soapy liquid to soak in through one, two, three layers of old paper, all the way through to the plaster. Then, while the paper was still wet, he slid the scraper in behind the first layer, and separated the wet paper from the wall.

Square by square the sodden paper fell to the floor, and square by square was revealed the old, clean, pink-grey plaster.

With the music in the background – first Mozart, then Bach, then something ceremonial – Paul proceeded to work as if he was restoring a fine painting, bit by bit dissolving the caked varnishes, the reparations of later, lesser artists, to reveal the true history beneath.

As the original surface of the room came to light, the walls showed their own mixed experience of domesticity: cracks, gouges and stresses; cheap filler smeared unevenly over rough patches. Holes drilled, then papered over, then drilled again. As more and more of the original walls was uncovered, Paul discovered that a picture rail had once hung about eighteen inches below the cornice, circumnavigating the room. Someone in a rage of modernisation had pulled the rail down, its one-time existence now evidenced only by a ribbon of dried adhesive.

In one corner, Paul uncovered two human remains in the form of signatures: a swirly 'Jimmy Murphy' from '1898', and a straight-up-and-down 'Robert Camden' six years later, apparently recording an interlude in the room's decorative life: Jimmy Murphy hung his wallpaper, which only a few years later was judged horrendous by the room's new occupants, who bade Robert Camden remove the offensive wall covering and replace it with something more to their taste.

Broader and broader expanses of wall appeared. He washed the walls down with the heavy cloth, then gently scraped away all traces of paper, glue, and old flaking paint. He ran his hand along the cool plaster, and it felt for a moment like skin, like skin suddenly freed from heavy clothing after a long, oppressive journey, skin that welcomed a rush of cool, refreshing air.

'You'll be sorry you started that, now,' Mamie said, entering the room. 'Once you start taking down the paper, you can't stop until it's all come down.'

She wore an old dressing gown and held a mug in either hand.

'Oh, hello Mamie,' Paul said. 'I'm sorry – I hope I wasn't disturbing you.'

'Not at all, I've just finished watching the news and I thought you might like a cup of tea. You're working very hard at this, Paul.'

'Thank you,' Paul said, descending the ladder and taking a steaming mug from her hand. 'These walls are in pretty rough shape.'

'You'll be in rough shape too if you don't take a break once in a while. Martin was here today, and I told him how hard you've been working.'

'Oh? Did he come in to check my progress?'

'No, he didn't seem concerned in the least about the room. Funny fellow, Martin. He rushed into the house, nearly knocked me down in the hall. Out of the blue he starts asking me about the garden, as though it was the most important garden on God's earth. He went out the back, took the old mower out of the garden shed, fiddled with it for half an hour, then came back inside with his hands all black and green, mumbling something about a mechanic to get the mower going again.'

'That's strange,' Paul said. 'That grass hasn't been mowed for months. It's far too wet to try to mow it now. He should wait until the weather improves.'

'Don't talk to me about Martin,' said Mamie. 'I've long given up trying to guess what he'll do next.'

A few minutes later, having admired Paul's progress, she took his empty mug and went to the door.

'Now don't work too late, love, or you'll be worn out entirely in the morning.' Then, pausing in the open door, 'That's lovely music. You've lovely taste, Paul. Lovely music altogether.'

CHAPTER 14

In which art meets agribusiness, and cheese meets intolerance.

Music emanated from the glassy boardroom of Spyral Multimedia.

When Paul arrived late on Thursday morning, he could hear muffled New Age tones wafting from the office, seeping through the warren of cubicles, around corners, past Jack's office and all the way down the corridor to where he stood in the reception area.

Jacinta, behind the desk at Reception, looked up from her newspaper without a smile.

'Ah now, here he is,' she said. 'Swanning in at ten o'clock. You're getting more Irish than the Irish.'

Paul shook out his umbrella and placed it dripping into the umbrella stand.

'And a pleasure to see you too,' he replied. 'What's that noise?'

'Dunno,' Jacinta said, returning to her paper. 'I think it's Dee in the boardroom. He's been making that racket all morning. Everyone's giving out. Oh, and he's been looking for you since nine o'clock.'

Paul walked briskly down the corridor, into the office and

towards the boardroom. When he opened the boardroom door he was engulfed by mood music: weird, electronic sounds of waves and wires, building in volume, but strangely soothing. In the darkened space Paul could make out a crowd of young programmers standing around a computer screen surrounded by speakers, with Dee hovering behind them.

Dee wore his shirtsleeves rolled up, looking businesslike and confident for the first time this week.

'Ah, here's Sleeping Beauty,' Dee shouted over the noise.

'What's the music?' Paul said.

'*California*,' Dee replied. 'We wanted something that would appeal to a laid-back bloody Californian.'

'For what?' Paul shouted.

'The MountAgro demo – don't tell me you forgot? Lads!' Dee shouted, turning down the music. 'Can you clear out for now? I want to show Paul what we've cooked up for his American friends.'

The young men filed out of the room, leaving Paul standing at the far end of the table, his mouth agape.

'What's wrong with you?' Dee asked. 'You haven't even seen the demo and you're ready to criticise.'

'But I thought . . .' Paul said. 'I thought you were so against this thing?'

'I am. I hate this shite. But look, never mind all that, just give this a gander and see what you think.'

Dee set the demonstration running, images beaming onto the large silver screen at the front of the room.

It started slowly, with multicoloured waves, aurora borealis flickering across midnight blue. Then, with the music building, the bottom of the screen began to sprout small shoots, and these grew with the music into luxurious fronds, and then the world appeared in their midst and the plants transformed themselves into the letters of MountAgro, and then the letters joined to become a cornucopia overflowing with fruits, and laughing twin babies climbed over the melons and grapefruit, and the babies clasped their hands and stood and grew into strong nude adult male and female figures, and they held their joined hands up to form a graceful arch over video footage of wheatfields, and then thick shoals of fish in an endless school, and then African children laughing and eating bananas, and all became the world again surrounding the words 'Genes means Growth' as the music reached a final compelling high note, and then all faded away, and the room returned to darkness.

The lights came on. 'So, Paul, what do you think?' Dee asked, unusually excited.

'God,' Paul said. 'Stunning. Good enough to brainwash the whole country.'

'Ah Jesus, stop, will ya?' said Dee, collapsing into a chair and pulling a cigarette from a pack on the table. 'I'm sick over this fuckin' project.'

Felicity came into the room wearing a blue suit and carrying a chequebook in her hand.

'What are you sick about?' she demanded.

'The whole fucking lot, that's what,' Dee said. 'But the demo's finished and that's all I care about for now.'

'It's brilliant work,' Paul said.

'I know it's brilliant work,' Dee replied. 'I can't believe it. We've managed to pull together some of the kinkiest graphics we've ever produced, all in support of an absolutely *evil* project. It's like packaging rat poison.'

'Now Dee, this is going to be an *educational* project,' Felicity objected.

'Yeah,' Dee said. 'Teaching your kids how to raise mutants. When the kittens start to pop out with six heads, then we'll figure there was something wrong with those beans.'

'Okay, you two,' Paul broke in. 'Has Jack seen this?'

'No – he's at some meeting,' Felicity replied. 'Something in Kildare. He'll be out all morning. He wants you to have a draft of the proposal ready for him when he gets in later this afternoon.'

'Okay,' Paul said. 'The proposal is nearly ready. Dee, I want to run through a few figures with you before I put the final touches to it. Are you free at lunchtime?'

'Yeah, I can do it over lunch. But right now I have to do a final review of the accounting project. I'm up to me eyes. There's enough work for two of me.'

'Talk to MountAgro,' said Paul. 'They might be able to help you . . .'

At one o'clock Dee came into the boardroom, where Paul sat at the table typing on a laptop computer, surrounded by papers.

'Did you want me to go through your figures?' Dee said, sitting down.

'Yeah, I'm just about done here,' Paul said, typing continuously.

'I brought you a sanger and a coffee.'

'Thanks,' Paul said, standing up. 'I just want to sanity-check this proposal. Let me get a printout.'

Paul left the room, returning in a moment with two copies of the proposal, one of which he slid across the table to Dee.

Dee flicked through the sheets, munching on his sandwich.

'Looks good. You do all this this morning?'

'No,' Paul replied, unwrapping his sandwich. 'I worked on it at home last night.'

'You look wrecked.'

'I wanted to get this out of the way,' Paul said, opening his sandwich. 'What's in this?'

'Ham and cheese.'

'Shit,' Paul said. 'I can't eat cheese.'

'Why not? What's wrong with you?'

'Dairy products. It's called "lactose intolerance". Oh well, nothing serious. And I'm starving,' Paul said, biting into the sandwich before taking a swallow from his coffee. 'Now if you flick over to page twelve, here's the effort estimates. I've costed labour at our standard rate, put a thirty per cent margin on the contract staff, put twenty per cent onto what ConceptDesign will charge us for usability testing, and added fifteen per cent contingency for fixed cost. Here's the total so far.'

Dee looked to where Paul pointed at the bottom of the page, and then raised his eyes to Paul's. 'You think they've got the dosh?' he asked.

'I wasn't sure until an hour ago,' Paul replied. 'I took the liberty of phoning our MountAgro friend at his suite in Paris. And I told him what I figured this thing would cost, just to make sure we were still in the game.'

'And?'

'He said that, subject to the approval of his finance people, we were just within his budget.'

'Ah now, me old son,' Dee said, breaking into a smile, 'very nice work for a Yank. Course that's why old Jacky boy hired you . . .'

Felicity, on her way back to her office, stopped at Ruth's desk.

'Howdy, stranger,' Felicity said.

'Oh, hiya,' Ruth replied. Her straight, brown hair was tied back in a long plait.

'Hate to interrupt a daydream.'

'Actually, I was watching Paul and Dee through the window of the boardroom,' Ruth said.

The two men could be seen hunched over a document, both chewing sandwiches.

'Just look at them,' Ruth said. 'Get two men working on something together and they bond like snails in heat. Totally oblivious to the world around them.'

'What do you mean?' Felicity asked. 'They're just reviewing Paul's proposal.'

'Yeah,' Ruth said. 'But two days ago Dee was dead set against this project. Since then he's had a little chat with Jack. Then he went to work with his toys on the demo. Suddenly his scruples are gone, he's wholeheartedly behind the project.'

'What's wrong with that?' Felicity asked. 'I thought you were backing the project as well?'

'Maybe I am, maybe I'm not,' Ruth said. 'But it will be *my* decision. Based on *principles*. You know, what I really feel. I won't decide on account of some masculine positioning game.'

Felicity looked at Ruth, who continued to look through the boardroom windows. She could sense a new anger, a new mistrust in Ruth's eyes.

'Look, Ruth, nothing's been decided yet. We're still only pitching for this work. The final decision will be based on all of our inputs.'

'I know, I know,' Ruth replied. 'But people's true colours are showing. And I don't think I like what I see.'

Two hours later, Jack called Paul into his office.

'Now, Paul,' Jack said from behind his desk, 'what have you got for me?'

'Here's the proposal as it stands,' Paul said as he laid the document on Jack's desk. 'I went through the costings and the project plan with Dee over lunch. Ruth hasn't proofed it yet.'

'Lovely stuff,' Jack said, leaning back and looking at the front cover. 'I'll just give this a little run through while you're here . . .'

Paul knew the process well. Jack was a very good reviewer, critical and astute. But he hated writing anything. So Paul sat with Jack during the review, taking notes as Jack threw out his comments, feeling like a junior clerk in a Dickens novel.

'Lovely, hmm, yes, good. You see here, now, I'd change that to "We would *recommend*" rather than "We would *suggest*". Stresses the consultancy aspect of our service, don't you think? And here, I think we've gone into too much detail over staffing. No need to include all this at this stage in our proposal . . .'

Paul was reminded of his days at school, sitting with an impatient English teacher, wondering if the session would ever end. But Paul knew the process worked, and it ensured that Jack approved of the route they were taking with the project. Indeed, the further Jack read into the document, the more Jack believed he had written it himself.

'I think we've done a *marvellous* job of describing these modules . . . Yes, my God, this is really the business, what?'

Jack was obviously pleased, and Paul was feeling that he'd got through the first hurdle. But then something began to interrupt the flow.

Was it? Did I? . . . Oh dear, yes I did. I certainly did.

Paul was suddenly reminded of lunch. That inner warmth, just a general sensation at first, not unpleasant: a slight pressure, an abdominal glow, a feeling of fullness. But Paul knew these signs, signs of a problem that had steadily worsened these past few years.

As Jack continued his slow progress through the twenty-page document, Paul became aware of a shifting, a motion, a transferral of sensation from one inner quadrant to the next, little shivers running from upper right deep down into lower left. And then the glow became insistent, pushing outwards in pockets, first here, then there, accompanied by muffled sounds of digestive turmoil: gurgles, a squeeze, a series of soft clicks. Then he felt his heartbeat in his nether regions, an insistent thump thump thump as the burning intensified, feeling, Paul thought, like the start of Brahms' first symphony: *boom* boom boom *boom* boom boom – oh, damn this anyway!

'Now Paul, I wonder could you have a little look here at the way you've structured our charges. I'd like you to rework this section to emphasise . . .'

And as Paul leaned forward to study the figures, his intestines succumbed to implements of torture: first scratchy wool, then a tennis ball seemed to pass to and fro, and then finally a hard hot tool, not sharp, but poking, scraping slowly through, down, deeper into his lower regions, and then the stab of it, the bloated insistent stab as he stood up, painfully, as Jack finally finished, handing Paul the document and Paul thanking Jack and walking, quickly, out of the room, closing the door behind him and hobbling, quickly, to the men's room at the end of the corridor.

Ten minutes later, emerging from the green steel cubicle, Paul felt weakened, drained and dehydrated. He stood before the sink in the men's room washing his hands with the liquid soap, breathing in its sweet perfume. His insides glowed from the ordeal, feeling like a hand that had been slapped.

He looked at himself in the mirror. Then he scooped the running water in his hands and washed his face once, twice. He walked blindly to the side of the sink, rubbing his face vigorously with the rough institutional towelling.

And then he returned to the mirror, examined his reddened

skin, the sleepless dark rings under his eyes. His hairline seemed higher than he remembered, the furrows now forming so easily on his brow.

He smiled a pathetic smile at the tired face confronting him.

'Jesus, Paul,' he said to himself. 'What are you doing to yourself?'

CHAPTER 15

In which Tony turns up and a figure from the North descends.

A dark, wet, wind-torn Friday morning.

Margaret Boyle sat in her dressing gown at the kitchen table. She used a wooden-handled knife to cut herself a slice of wholewheat bread. Setting the slice on her plate, she buttered it and then covered it with Wicklow Home-Farm Marmalade. Beside her plate was a glass of fresh-squeezed orange juice. Beside the orange juice was a steaming cafetière of black coffee, just plunged.

Have to get your weight back up, the nurse had said. Margaret licked the marmalade from her fingers.

She had not eaten the breakfast things that Tony Dunne had brought her when he had visited on Tuesday night. When she woke on Wednesday morning, refreshed after a good night's sleep, she could not bring herself to face Tony's white loaf wrapped in plastic, the carton of 'made from concentrate' orange juice. She told herself it was the quality of the food. But maybe it was something else, something more. Something in her that refused to accept charity from a student. Some little hint of mistrust.

Or was it simply pride?

She glanced at her watch, breathed deeply, and rose to clear the table. Time to get dressed and face UCD again, for the first time in a week.

She could hear the rain against the windows as she walked upstairs. The house had been so quiet all week without Paul. So many times she had convinced herself to phone him, but so many times she had lost faith, turned back. Nothing had changed, she told herself. Nothing had improved.

If she asked him to come back, what had she to offer?

She dressed slowly. She pulled on a pair of woollen trousers, a burgundy cotton polo neck and a black jumper. Her weight was still down from her bout of illness, and her clothes still felt loose. She returned downstairs, struggling to maintain a sense of control as she gathered her books and stuffed them into her briefcase. She slipped on her coat and then stopped for a moment, to inhale deeply, to breathe out slowly.

Outside the house she bent her head against the misty rain, felt the wind cut across her face. But then, just as she was about to step onto the footpath, a black car parked across the road flashed its lights to catch her attention. And then she recognised Tony Dunne.

'Bloody hell,' she thought. 'This is the last thing I need . . .'

She approached the car.

'Would you like a lift, Ms Boyle?' he shouted from his open window.

'Tony, good morning!' she shouted across the wind. 'Really, I'm actually quite comfortable walking . . .'

'Don't be silly, you'll get soaked in this rain,' he shouted. 'Get in!'

And so, reluctantly, she climbed into the front seat.

'Tony, what a surprise! What are you doing here?' she said, trying to keep the mistrust from her voice.

He raced out of Eglinton Terrace and out onto Eglinton Road.

'I was on my way into college,' he began, 'and I knew you teach on Fridays, and I saw how dire the weather was, and I thought I just might catch you before you left the house.'

'But Tony, I walk in, every morning, rain or shine. There's no need for you to go out of your way . . .'

'I'm telling you, it's not a problem. How are you feeling, by the way?'

'Much better, thanks.'

'That's great. Everyone's looking forward to having you back.'

Tony looked straight ahead, that impish smile playing at his lips. Margaret shifted in her seat, as if she had been forced into a compromising position. Neither spoke for a few moments.

They stopped behind a bus, the entire back of which was covered by the figure of a woman with large teeth wearing white pleated trousers. The text proclaimed that her tampons gave her the strength to face her day.

It's all about confidence . . .

'As long as we're here,' Tony said, breaking the silence, 'there was one or two things I wanted to ask you. You know, about the course.'

'What's on your mind?'

'I'm thinking that I might be a bit behind, you know, with regard to my studies.'

'Oh?'

'It's the reading. I can't seem to keep up. That George Eliot is very long. And I haven't even started the American gear.'

'There's still plenty of time before the exams.'

'But you see, Margaret, I work. I do the odd job here and there, you know, to pay my way. And I'm worried that I'm going to run out of time. Very worried, like.'

They arrived at the gates into UCD. Tony accelerated up the avenue to the campus.

'I was wondering if we could talk, you know. To plan what I should do. I was thinking maybe tomorrow, you know, in the afternoon. I could drop by.'

'Tomorrow? Saturday?' Margaret asked.

'Yeah, I was thinking later in the afternoon, like. I could drop by, say five?'

'No, tomorrow's not good for me, Tony. But I do have office hours on Monday, two till four . . .'

'No, Margaret, with respect, that's not really what I had in mind. You see, I need a bit of a session straight away. You know, a one-on-one. To get this sorted out. I was hoping to use the weekend to get started.'

'Right, I see. Maybe I could squeeze you in this afternoon in my office?'

They had arrived at the Arts Block. Tony pulled off the road and stopped the car.

'Look, Margaret, I need some help here. I'm telling you, I've been doing as much work as I can, but I really need to have some time with you to focus on what I should do next. If I could just swing by tomorrow, or Sunday even . . .'

'Tony, I'm sorry, but that's not possible. You'll have to try to make it during my office hours.'

His anxiety was beginning to show. She saw, once again, that hard expression cross his features, the expression that she had noticed for one tense moment the other night in her kitchen.

'I'm not looking for any special treatment,' he persisted. 'But just this once I need a bit of support. I need to get this sorted, fast, or I'll just get further and further behind.'

'Tony, I . . .' Margaret hesitated. There were students walking around the car. She didn't want to risk a scene.

'Okay, look. Phone me. Tomorrow. Any time. We can talk about it then. We'll find a time to get together. Just phone me.'

Tony faced her, his jaw tensed, trying to assess whether he was being brushed off. But just then his mobile phone began to chirp.

'Hello?' Tony answered. 'Really? That's great. Yeah, sure, this afternoon is cool, like we planned . . .'

Margaret whispered, 'I have to run, Tony – thanks for the lift.'

He kept talking, didn't turn towards her. She opened the door, climbed out of the car, and slammed the door shut behind her. Then she ran through the crowds of students in the windy rain up the steps to the door of the Arts Block.

'Ah there you are, Mrs Boyle,' shouted the security man as she walked through the door. 'You're welcome back. We thought we'd lost you altogether. But look at you, you're all out of breath. You need to take care of yourself now, mustn't push yourself too hard on your first day back . . .'

Later that day, on a cold, dark Friday evening in January, Elaine McAlister walked out of the door of the stately Georgian Customs House building on Customs House Quay in the centre of Dublin.

She passed through the imposing cast-iron gates and smiled her goodnight to the security man. As she crossed Customs House Quay she held her imitation fur collar snug beneath her chin. With her other hand she held a red overnight bag containing toiletries, underwear, an outfit for tonight, trousers and a jumper for tomorrow, and a document she intended to read some time during the weekend before returning to the office to continue her negotiations on Monday morning.

She walked along the Liffey towards O'Connell Street Bridge. The wind made the air bitter; the lights of the pubs, the gaudy signs and the cars were reflected in the cold, inky black of the river, running so high, so fast.

Her bag was too heavy for comfort and she was aware that she had a run in one stocking, but she pressed on. It wasn't far enough to take a taxi. Her blonde hair blew freely in the cold, gusting wind, sometimes snapping painfully into her eyes.

She had arrived in Dublin from Belfast that morning. She had been well-briefed by the senior civil servants in Northern Ireland's Department of the Interior. Her job was 'to draw up broad heads of agreement with her counterparts in the Republic of Ireland concerning cross-border co-operation on environmental matters of mutual interest'. Her report back to the Department would serve as the basis for the negotiations to be carried out between the two governments in the formation of cross-border bodies as agreed in the Good Friday Agreement, signed in April of 1998.

Her visit today, therefore, was considered by her direct superiors to be of vital importance to the future peace and prosperity of the island of Ireland.

As it happened, very little had been achieved so far. She had of course been treated well, perhaps even better than usual. Mr Courtney, a senior civil servant in the Department of the Environment, had met her at the train first thing this morning. Hardly necessary, as Connolly Station is only a few hundred yards from the Customs House – but protocol must be observed.

And Mr Courtney's staff were friendly and attentive – especially the three younger men in the room – and they had displayed a thorough knowledge and understanding of their country's Acts, Statutes, Bye-Laws and Regulations on all matters pertaining to the headings under discussion.

Unfortunately, though, they had not been sufficiently briefed regarding equivalent legislation in Great Britain and Northern Ireland. As Elaine had expected, her Southern Irish counterparts were quite uneducated as to the institutions, laws and procedures that applied in Northern Ireland, and seemed perfectly content to hear it all from her, for the first time, which took up most of the day. As happened regularly when she visited government buildings down South, she noted that their willingness to welcome her to Dublin did not imply any willingness on their part to prepare for the meeting, or clarify their objectives, or suggest any innovative way to move towards one another from their respective positions across the political divide.

And so, Elaine sighed, the day was a bit of a waste, as far as work was concerned. But sterling was worth more down here, her expenses for the weekend were generously covered, and she might as well make the most of it.

Elaine reached O'Connell Bridge, crowded at this busy hour: masses of workers finally released from their shops, their offices; people in a hurry, moving quickly, driven to enjoy this time, this precious time of escape and freedom. Office girls in short skirts, oblivious to the cutting wind; young men with cigarettes and dark, well-groomed hair; silver-haired men in suits and long coats, bowing their heads as they faced into the wind.

She crossed O'Connell Bridge and walked up the river along the South Quays. She felt the cold penetrate her skin as she worked her way down the dirty pavement, relentless traffic buzzing on her left, the cold air stale with exhaust fumes. Then she crossed the quay into the quiet pedestrianised region of Temple Bar, where still more throngs of people in grey and black clothes were congregating in small groups, meeting, huddled against the cold, preparing to laugh, to gossip, to taste that long-awaited first pint; to be courted, and pursued, and kissed.

She walked to the brassy entrance of Bloom's Hotel. The elderly man at reception recognised Elaine, took her registration card, handed her her keys, gave her a wink and wished her a pleasant evening. She looked at her watch, entered the lift, and went up to her room on the fourth floor.

Inside the room, she threw her case on the bed, went into the bathroom and turned on the taps. Then she returned to the bed, took a few things out of her bag and hung them up in the wardrobe.

It felt good to get out of her high-heeled shoes, her jacket, her blouse, her woollen skirt: the dull trappings of officialdom. Moments later, lying back in the hot bath, she thought through the day: pompous, pudgy, attentive Mr Courtney, trying so hard to be in control, debonair; prissy little Miss Murphy with her dyed black hair and her little notepad. And then young Jimmy Byrne, so obsequious during their meetings, so scathing in private!

She lay back in the hot water, feeling warm for the first time that day. She looked forward to the night's activities with the Dublin office crowd: dinner at 8:30, then a night on the town, a good night getting to know these people, these lucky, young Irish twenty-somethings, so free from the politics, so fully relieved of the tension, the sheer tension of living a hundred long miles north in her beloved, her damned Belfast.

Four hours later Elaine sat upstairs in Whelan's on Camden Street at a small round table covered with empty glasses.

She shared the table with two couples – Sharon from the office, plump and earnest, wrapped in close conversation with her thin, spotty boyfriend, as they had been in the restaurant, almost oblivious to Elaine, to the surroundings, to everything except their own earnest selves.

And then there was sharp Jimmy Byrne, perhaps twenty-three, and his very young girlfriend, skinny, leggy and sulky. They weren't getting along, and Elaine suspected that she (Elaine) was the problem. By this hour, after this much Guinness, Elaine was very tired of his tedious 'witty' asides, and of her open, angry stares.

Down below, all around, were Dublin's cool new trendsetters, making it in software, in marketing, in property – in the pink, in the money, in the know. Everything calculated to look so casual: hair looking just tossed; lithe, slim, gymnasium-styled bodies; cigarettes, jeans with Italian labels; a man in his forties in a pinstriped suit wearing a forties-style hat; a very tall girl with very tight black trousers reaching just to her ankles, her legs and thighs and hips so openly displayed, so high and smooth and round.

And there was drink, no end of strong Irish drink, streams of young men carrying two, three, a trayful of pints of Irish stout and bottles of German and American lager and long, thin, straight glasses with the clean smell of gin, tonic and lemon, and tasteless concoctions of spirits mixed with diet minerals.

Elaine looked over the balcony to the small stage below, where jazz was happening, where two Americans and an Irishman, looking so ordinary, so casual, made jazz happen that night: big Tom Rainey with his clean, American face, his look of clarity and control behind those drums, those simple, dirty-looking drums, those lustreless cymbals, playing round and round, each bar a new melody of rhythm, a new shape of sound built on a steady, subliminal beat, pulling the music together like a plan, like a map in the making with each passing moment – and Fred Hersch, small, thin, bearded, behind that stubby black baby grand, music like water pouring forth, music like nature growing, wild, tumbling and organic – and Dave O'Malley, so young, so naïve-looking with his round glasses, standing by that big bruised double bass, so alive, moving so smoothly up and down that massive animal, through those tunes, those old Bird and Ellington and Gershwin tunes, tunes sometimes lost completely in the fractured harmony of late-century jazz, then surfacing again like a mountain in mist, those tunes stated and dismantled and recovered, played by those three, ordinary, beautiful men.

Elaine watched them move, listened, tried to lose herself in the music, felt alone, drank deeply from a new glass that materialised on the table, but felt alone again. She was tired from her early train journey to Dublin that morning, tired from her frustrating discussions at the office, flashes of which kept coming back to her during dinner, and even here, in this oak-beamed haven, this sensuous and smoky escape.

Then the music stopped, and the applause rose, and rose again in waves, but the musicians had stopped entirely, were packing their gear, and the lights came up, and then Elaine could see clearly the tables beside the stage, and she could see the top of a head, the side of a face, a face that looked distant, but so kind, and suddenly yes, so familiar and alone.

Elaine stood up quickly, said goodnight quickly, made her way quickly through the crowd in the balcony, pushed her way down the back stairs, worked through the drinkers down below towards the now glaring, unfriendly lights at the stage and up to his table, where she stood beside him, until he looked up and saw her face, and said her name.

When Paul arrived at Whelan's the bar was already crowded. Declan had saved him a seat right up at the stage.

Declan seemed more than usually excited about the night, the music: he was already on his second pint, smoking a cigar, talking rapidly.

'Paul, old mate o' mine, sit down here and rest yourself, I was getting worried about you there, did you walk it? Sit down, sit down! What can I get you? I'm telling you, boy-o, we're in for a show tonight, they've arrived anyway, I was talking to one of the roadies, you know, the fella I met in New York when I saw Rainey and Hersch last time, only the bass player's out with the flu, would you believe it? But Dave O'Malley's standing in, d'you remember when we saw him at the Norseman? And you know he might just do for tonight . . .'

He sat at a low table in a low chair too close to the stage, but the music was good, and the lights were low, and the women all round seemed to float on a cushion of confidence and familiarity, and by the time Paul noticed he'd had too much to drink Declan had disappeared, probably met someone at the bar, and Paul was there alone in this crowd, with this music, and he kept thinking about Margaret and wondering, wondering when he wouldn't be able to stand this separation any longer and when he would go back to the house and see her and start to piece things back together again, and tomorrow that's what he'd do, he'd phone her, no, he'd go straight there to the house in the morning, they could at least talk and figure out what was going wrong, and then the lights came up, and he looked up, and there was Elaine.

Her sandy blonde hair curved round her small, round, girlish face. She was probably thirty, though she looked younger, more open than thirty, never entirely in control, a hint of vulnerability: the sadness of a survivor.

She carried her coat in one arm, the strap of her small black bag was around her other shoulder. She wore a short grey blouse that ended just above the waistline of her black jeans.

She stood beside his table. Paul looked up past her legs, past the silver button on her black jeans, up quickly to her neck with the little beaded necklace and into her face.

'A gentleman always returns a lady's calls,' she said in her rising Northern accent.

'Elaine, I've been trying to call you . . .'

'And what's more, any businessman worth his salt follows up on a new prospect, no matter how remote.'

'I told you, Elaine, I was going to phone . . .'

'Now, Paul, if you're going to make excuses, please try to make them interesting. Are you going to ask me to sit down?'

'Yes, sorry, please do, can I get you a drink?'

'No thank you, I've had quite enough already, I'm sorry to say. I know we have only a passing acquaintance, Paul, but I hardly took you for a jazz fan.'

'I am, a little, I suppose. A friend of mine is seriously into this stuff. We used to go to gigs together in the States.'

'Oh I see, a friend. Perhaps I'm a bit superfluous here. Where is this mystery friend anyway?'

'I'm not sure, he seems to have disappeared . . .'

'Look, Paul, I know you think I'm just a nuisance, some waif you met on a train, and you probably meet lots of lovely girls on your travels, and the shine from that ring on your finger is hitting me right between the eyes, but I'm deadly serious that I want to talk to you, and I think it would be worth your while if we could have a wee chat.'

'Yes, I'd like that, yes. Should we go? I'll just see if I can find my friend . . .'

'No, Paul, it's too late.'

'But Elaine, I'm so sorry I didn't phone . . .'

'No, Paul, I mean it's too late right now, at this late hour. I'm absolutely shattered. And besides, some of us poorly paid public servants have work to do in the morning while yous in the private sector enjoy the pleasures of your warm beds.'

'Tomorrow night,' Paul blurted. 'Please, could we meet tomorrow night?'

'My word, Paul. You've been drinking, haven't you? I didn't think you Americans ever sunk so low. I'm positively flattered by your invitation, all the same, but Paul, surely Mrs Boyle would have something to say about your plans for Saturday night, would she not?'

'Elaine, please, tomorrow night. Dinner. I'll meet you for dinner, and we can talk.'

'Okay, but it's your funeral, dearie. Meet me at eight. Can you call for me at Bloom's Hotel?'

'I will. Yes, tomorrow night!'

'Lovely. You'll remember this tomorrow morning, now, won't you? We Northerners don't take kindly to being stood up.'

'I'll be there. I'll see you . . .'

Then she waved goodbye, and turned to walk away.

Paul watched her walking away, turning, lifting her hips to slide between the backs of two chairs. And our Paul was suddenly aware that, for the first time since Margaret had left him, that very long week ago, during which time he was convinced his sensations had all become quite dead to the world, he was now experiencing the haze, the warmth, the first tingling rush of a confusing arousal.

CHAPTER 16

In which a day of labour leads to a restless night.

Saturday morning, 9:30.

The room returned a hollow echo as Paul entered and closed the heavy door behind him. It was ragged and untidy, the surfaces flaked and rough. Stubborn patches of wallpaper and wrinkles of dried paste still clung to the walls. Cracks in the plaster formed a crazy map, and patches of old red filler, bearing witness to a century of repairs, stood out like islands scattered across the sea. The walls were punctuated with holes where pictures and shelves had once hung.

The meeting place between the walls and the ceiling was pockmarked like a musical score. The cornice, which was not the original, had been installed and repaired so badly over the years that Paul had decided during the week to pull it down. Now the edge where the walls met the ceiling was naked and torn.

Even the skirting boards looked injured. Paul had taken away the new square-edged boards that had been tacked in over the years, and what remained of the original skirting, now denuded of paint, looked like grey camouflage in a war zone.

Outside the morning sun struggled to enter the garden, now

tossed by bitter winter winds. Paul stood for a moment looking out of the rattling window, sipping coffee from a blue mug, taking in the deep winter greens, watching the leaves shaking and dancing in the wind as if sending a signal of warning. A tiny goldcrest flitted in and out of the tall green yew, where one branch hung down, savagely broken by last night's wind.

Paul set his mug on the window ledge. He ran his hand over one wall to feel the roughness of the patches, the depth of the bumps and the gaps. As he moved his hand along he felt the stretches of the original plaster cool and smooth between the breaks and cracks.

He had not reached the bottom yet, he thought. There was still plenty to be cleared away before the real restoration could begin.

He set the ladder up with a sharp metallic clang in the corner beside the window. He pulled a sheet of heavy abrasive paper from a pack, folding it over, then over again to make a small square. Then he climbed the ladder and began to sand down the wall with a tight circular motion.

A haze of dust soon hung in the air. His sweatshirt took on a pasty whiteness as he proceeded along the top of the first wall, moving quickly when the plaster was clean, but pausing over old patches, at holes, around cracks, sanding away the imperfections. A thin, powdery stream of plaster cascaded down the wall below where he worked. Then he descended the ladder and sanded the lower half of the wall, slowing his efforts again at those awkward repairs, sanding down bumps and rough patches, smoothing the edges of violent scrapes and chips.

An hour later, when he had finished one wall, he stood back to look at his work. He went down on one knee, placed his face against the wall and looked up along the surface. To the eyes of anyone else, he knew, little had changed: the cracks remained, the holes still needed to be filled.

But he felt a sense of discovery, looking at this smooth, bare wall, staring at this clear, rejuvenated space. As if now a process of rebuilding could begin.

'There now, one wall's stripped bare,' Mamie said as she entered the room. 'Like a woman with a fresh clean face. Now she's ready to be made up again!'

By six o'clock Paul had sanded down the entire room. He used an old broom to sweep the heavy plaster dust from the floor into a dustpan, then poured the dust into a plastic bag to bring to the bins outside. His hands felt dry and rough from the sandpaper and the powdery dust.

Mamie, who had been monitoring Paul's progress, came in as he was folding the ladder away.

'Dirty old job, isn't it, Paul?'

Paul smiled. 'It's satisfying, though. It feels like the walls can breathe again.'

'Yes, I suppose that's right, though they'll have a hard time of it with all this dust. I've sausages in the fridge, would you care to join me for tea?'

'Oh thank you, I'd love to, but I'm afraid I'm going out tonight.'

'Oh? Seeing anyone I'd know?' Mamie said.

'Just a friend,' Paul said, a bit curtly. Mamie walked around the room, as if inspecting the work. Then she paused and turned to face Paul directly.

'Paul, have you phoned Margaret?'

'No.'

'It's been a week now, Paul. Surely you should phone her, just to make sure she's all right?'

'I can't, Mamie,' Paul said, not looking in her direction. 'She'll phone me when she's ready to talk.'

'Well, I suppose you know best. But I don't want to see the two of you drift apart over time. You'll start to develop lonely habits. And maybe the time to talk to her is now, when she's had a week to sort herself out.'

'I will, Mamie. I'll phone her. But not tonight.'

'I hate to pry, Paul, but I am a bit worried about you. You're taking this redecorating far too seriously.'

She continued her stroll around the room.

'Martin was in yesterday. He gave me a lovely packet of tea, and brought me some sort of a cake in a box. It's still fresh. I haven't opened it yet. I was going to have it tonight. Are you sure you want to go out? You've had a very long day.'

'Yes, I'm sure. It's an old friend. We've been trying to see one another for some time.'

'Right,' Mamie sighed. 'Well, I suppose you know best.'

Paul's muscles felt tired as he sat down on the bed to take off his shoes. Glancing up at the clock, though, he could feel his heartbeat quicken. 6:30. Meeting Elaine at 8:00.

Elaine.

He stood in front of the sink in the cramped bathroom.

The overhead lamp gave off too little light, and he squinted into the mirror as he shaved, once, then again. Then, running his fingers around the corners of his mouth, he decided he needed to use a fresh razor, and he shaved again, this time nicking his neck and just below his nose.

He soaped himself in the hot, steamy shower, washing twice behind his ears like a dirty schoolboy. He scrubbed his hair, hoping the last bit of plaster would rinse out. A little nervous shiver ran through his abdomen: vague memories of a high school dance, a college date.

He stood in the cold bedroom, a towel wrapped around his waist, working through the underwear in his top drawer: checked boxers, spotted boxers, old briefs. At the bottom, a pair of designer shorts, bought on sale last summer.

Yes, he thought. Why not. No reason not to wear them, rarely wear them. Perfectly good underwear. No particular reason. Have to wear something, now, don't I?

Elaine. He didn't even know her, really. Met her on the train, such a chance thing. The train was empty, she asked the time from across the aisle. He recalled her pulling her hair from her face on that train, that slow train. So friendly.

Yes, okay, there was an attraction. Nothing – a little flirting, just for fun. And then her voice on the phone. And then her face last night. And her pale skin beneath that blouse, standing over you, standing by your chair, inches from your face.

Right. This is absurd. You're still married, it's just dinner, you're not going to sleep with her or anyone else. Stop shaking. Get dressed.

Black jeans. No, wore them last night. Can't show up in

the same clothes two nights in a row. Suit? No, God no, too formal, she said she hates guys in suits. EU bureaucrats, she told me on the train.

On the train.

He finally chose navy trousers, a blue shirt with a designer crest. Standing before the mirror in the bathroom, struggling with his necktie, a gold tie with a blue fleck, too long, now too short, can't see in this mirror. Back in the bedroom, navy tweed jacket. In the drawers again: socks, long or short? Plain socks, argyle? Hole in the toe, better not, just in case.

Black shoes.

Bathroom again. Aftershave. Hair, brushed once, wetted, brushed again. Deodorant, Jesus, forgot. Sweating already. Reach in, there, there, button up. Right.

Keys. Wallet. Money – shit – credit card – no! – bill goes to Margaret, just what I need. It's only dinner. Concentrate. Just dinner. Need money. Cash machine. In town. Beside the chemist. For condoms? No, definitely, we're not. But what if? Yes. No.

God, this is a lot of work.

He put on his grey woollen overcoat, ran down one flight of stairs, tripped, flew forward, caught himself noisily on the banister, walked carefully the rest of the way down to the ground floor.

Pangs of conscience. He knocked on Mamie's door.

'Yes, Paul?'

'I'm on my way out. Just checking to see if everything is all right.'

'Yes, Paul, lovely. Have a lovely time. If you see my light on when you return, please call in and we'll have that cup of tea I promised . . .'

'I will, Mamie. Good night now.'

At Bloom's Hotel, Paul asked the man at the desk to ring Elaine's room to tell her he had arrived.

Then he waited in the lobby for fifteen minutes. He stood, then he sat. An attendant asked him if he'd like a drink from the bar. He declined and she walked away, and he immediately changed his mind and called after her, but she had disappeared. He stood again.

His hands were cold, clammy. He wanted to go into the men's room to warm them before Elaine arrived. He hesitated, in case he missed her. Then he walked quickly down the stairs to the lavatories, ran his hands under the hot taps, and then held them under the hot-air dryers till they were warm and dry.

He looked at himself in the mirror. He'd always looked young. Tonight, though, he looked tired beyond his years. He rubbed his face with his hands, trying to smooth away the bags beneath his eyes.

He returned upstairs. She hadn't arrived. In a few minutes his hands were cold again.

And when she walked out of the lift, his nerves worsened. As he walked towards her, smiling dumbly, he was overcome with fear that he would be seen, here, with Elaine, seen, with no explanation whatever.

Who was she, anyway, Paul? That blonde woman in the

coat with the fur collar, stepping out of the lift, kissing you on the cheek like an old friend . . . who was she?

'I'm sorry I'm late,' she said. 'Did you order yourself a wee drink? No? Right, shall we be off then?'

The blustery wind had continued all day and now a light rain was rushing from all directions. Elaine had booked a restaurant on Essex Street, a new restaurant she had read about. They threaded their way through the damp, shining laneways and courtyards of Temple Bar.

Lots of people about. Restaurants, people eating in the windows, laughing. Wine on every table.

'It's amazing,' Elaine said. 'This whole city is so laid-back. Years ago you'd come down here and it was all just pubs and too much drink. There'd be tension on the streets on a Saturday night. Now, I swear, they're all acting so relaxed, like a whole country of bloody millionaires!'

They found the restaurant, hurried inside to get out of the rain. A slim, dark-haired girl in black jeans and a tight black T-shirt greeted them. She had big eyes and a wide mouth and an expression of infinite contentment.

'McAlister? Table for two? That's lovely, just lovely. Please come this way.'

She led them to a small black table and took their coats. They sat in tall, slim black chairs beside a window looking onto a cobbled street.

Seated, they looked at each other for the first time.

'So,' Paul said.

'So,' Elaine replied. 'Your Dublin restaurants aren't short on style, now, are they? What are those things – bits of antique cars, are they? And look at the size of that chandelier! If that falls half the place will be dead.'

'There's a moose over your left shoulder,' Paul said. 'He's wearing earrings.'

'That painting there,' Elaine said. 'No, that one. Is that really what I think it is?'

'Not sure,' Paul said, studying. 'No, it couldn't be. Ah, look, it's supposed to be the bottom of a foot . . .'

'Good evening, folks.' A thin waiter appeared beside the table, again in black, wearing a white apron and a nose ring. 'Can I take you through tonight's specials? First we have medallions of Turkish lamb sautéed in red pepper and olive oil, served on a bed of saffron rice and lemon spinach. Then we have salmon with fried goat's cheese and couscous with raspberry and lime sauce. And finally we have roast quail wrapped in bacon with sage and olive stuffing. I'll leave you a few moments to look over our menu . . . Perhaps I could bring you something from the bar to warm you up? A glass of champagne, or a kir?'

'Yes, kir for me,' Elaine said.

'Right, yes, a kir would be fine,' Paul said.

Alone again, they studied the menu. Lurking beneath perky descriptions of starters and main courses were erotic images of oriental couples, their frank copulations strategically covered by weird floral motifs, pictures of fish, Japanese fans.

The waiter returned with the drinks. Elaine ordered the lamb, Paul decided to try the quail. A bottle of Argentinian red was ordered. Soon the first course arrived, and they were both hungry.

'So,' Paul said, setting his fork on a small plate.

'You said that before,' Elaine replied, wiping her mouth with her napkin.

'Yes, but it led us nowhere.'

'Nowhere indeed,' Elaine said. 'Let's try another tack, then: what are you doing here, anyway?'

'Didn't we go through this on the train, you know, when we met? Illinois and all that.'

'I'm not talking about your distant past. I'm talking about right now. What brings you here, to this restaurant, tonight?'

'I thought it would be nice to have a chat?'

'I know that, Paul. But to what fortuitous set of circumstances – I won't be able to say that after another glass of wine! – what's going on in your life? Look, I'm trying to ask about your *wife*. Where does she think you are tonight?'

'Probably the same place that you told your beloved David.'

Elaine smiled. 'My David is at his favourite pub, ten minutes' walk from our little house, watching Manchester United football club play Everton. As long as I phone him to ask him the score at some stage he'll be perfectly happy and our relationship will continue on its steady, blissful path. And besides, we're not married. And it's all very casual. But you *are* married, Paul, and I have a very, very good memory, and I don't recall that yours and Margaret's is in any sense a casual relationship.'

'No, you're right. I wouldn't use the word casual.'

'Okay, then, what word would you use?'

'To describe our relationship?' Paul said, pouring wine into Elaine's glass. 'Right now? I'd call it "non-communicative".'

'Oh dear,' Elaine said, putting down her glass. 'I'm sorry. I didn't realise I'd come in on a bad patch. Is it serious?'

'I don't know. We're, well, apart. For the moment.'

'I see. And are you all right?' Elaine asked.

Paul drained his glass. 'Elaine, I don't really know where Margaret and I are at right now. I'm living alone, and we haven't spoken in a week. It was all very sudden. But frankly I think it's a temporary thing, you know. A sort of trial separation. Like you read about in the women's magazines.'

'I don't read women's magazines.'

'You should. They're fascinating.'

'I rarely have time,' Elaine said.

'Lately,' Paul said, 'I feel like I have all the time in the world.'

She didn't like the spinach. Paul wasn't too impressed with the quail. They traded meals and got tipsy. They talked about her work, about Spyral, about Ireland, about new money and new values and new attitudes. Paul listened as she talked, listened to her stories about London, about the office, about corruption in the Department, North and South, about announcements that would be made, all very hush-hush, that would ruin men, big men, and how she'd be so happy to watch these men go down, these rich men without a thought for the land, for the environment, watch them go down, burning, down.

The waiter in black was most attentive. He told them he was just back from two years in New York. He said life was far better in Dublin, and so was the food. They asked for coffee, and he suggested Irish coffee, on the house, and they said yes, and then they had another one: hot rich black coffee, heavily sweetened with brown sugar and topped with cool white Irish cream.

When they stood up they both recognised that they'd had too much to drink. They walked through the cobbled streets of Temple Bar, and Paul knew he was not fully in control of himself, and his senses seemed alive to Elaine's voice, to her face in the city lights as they walked. She turned to look up at him, and even though they didn't touch, he could feel her warmth, was drawn for this one night to the life that was Elaine.

And they reached the hotel, and he felt he should pause, he didn't want to pause but he felt he should pause, to wait, for the slightest hint of an invitation.

'So,' he said at the front door.

'So again! You Americans need to widen your vocabulary.'

'It's been a great night.'

'It has, Paul.'

'I'm sorry it has to end.'

'Does it?'

'No, it doesn't have to end. Not yet.'

'Are you sure, now?'

'Positive.'

He moved to kiss her.

'No, not here. Wait, just wait until we're alone.'

They stood together in the lift. She shifted her weight from one foot to the other.

When they entered her room he closed the door behind them and he watched her as she hung up her coat. And then he moved towards her and kissed her, kissed her as she stood with her back against the wall, her hands pulling his shirt out from his trousers and grasping his bare waist as they kissed and they moved their bodies together, bodies warm from the walk, from the wine, from desire.

And everything was perfectly aflame between them as they made their way to the bed, except something was happening as he laid her back and kissed her mouth, there was something awry as he kissed her throat, as he began gently to loosen her blouse and feel her skin with his hands, and he wanted so much to please her this night, to feel wanted and needed and to hear her voice as he pleased her, and he moved lower on the bed and unbuttoned her blouse feeling so warm and so ready.

But something was amiss.

And then he became aware of that feeling coming to him as he kissed her, that growing warmth, that growing, urgent pain coming upon him from below as he remembered the cream sauce, the Irish coffee topped with cream, and his abdomen was suddenly hot, cramping and insistent with pain. And he paused, and he felt the knives within him, and he lifted his head saying, 'Elaine, my love, I'm so sorry, my love, but I can't, I'm sorry, I'm so sorry . . .'

He emerged from the bathroom a few minutes later, his face white, his desire depleted utterly.

She sat on the edge of the bed with her back to him. She had rebuttoned her blouse, which was still untucked from her jeans. Her hair was tousled. She had opened the curtains and was staring out the window at the ugly backs of the grey buildings.

Paul sat down in a chair across from her.

'I'm so sorry, Elaine,' he said. 'It's my stomach. The cream. I can't . . .'

'Don't, Paul,' Elaine said. 'Don't apologise. Please. I'm so confused. I don't know what I'm doing here.'

She put her head down into her hands, and began to cry.

'Paul, I'm so sorry, I'm sorry I've brought you here. You don't need this. Please go, Paul. Go now.'

He looked at her, surprised at her sudden distress.

'Elaine, what's the matter? Have I hurt you?'

'No, Paul. No, it's not you at all. It's me.'

'Elaine, what is it?'

'I'm sorry, Paul. Since October. Since my sister died. I'm just so lonely.'

She cried heavily, and Paul went to her, and put his arms around her awkwardly, and sat with her as she cried. When she stopped crying she was silent for a while. And then she told him about the bomb, about her younger sister who had been shopping on that Saturday afternoon when the car bomb went off. About how they had been so unlike sisters, so like friends, especially since they had left school, when Elaine had gone to work in London, and then Jenny had come to live with her. And Elaine told Paul how Jenny had always been there when things had gone sour, and how Jenny had always been the plain solid one, while Elaine, flighty, pretty Elaine, had always attracted the wrong guys, exactly the wrong type of guys, and how Jenny would be there to help her out with advice, and how they would feign illness, and tell lies, and do dreadful things together to get out of the binds that Elaine always seemed to get them into.

And then she told Paul about himself, about meeting him that day on the train from Belfast when her memories of Jenny had been so strong, and how Paul had been so kind, so quiet but a bit of fun and so caring, just on a day when she had been feeling such hatred, such anger and hatred for the evil bastards who had done that to Jenny and to her, the evil bastards who had taken Jenny away and ruined Elaine's life, Elaine's entire life.

And she was sorry, sorry that she had involved Paul in all this, and sorry for him and his wife, but mostly, maybe, just sorry for herself.

Paul held Elaine as she cried that night, and listened, and ordered tea for them in the room, and listened some more. And then they stood and held one another once again, just for a moment, and said goodbye, at 5:30 on Sunday morning. And Paul felt so close to her that night, and so intimate, and yet he did not know if he would ever see her again, and thought perhaps that he should not.

He walked down George's Street at that black hour, down Camden Street past the Arabic foods and the Oriental medicines, down the canal, then past the tall, red-brick houses of Ranelagh. He walked past the taxi rank and the public toilets where a group of men smoked cigarettes and huddled against the cold, down the empty street past the quiet shops, where each passing car, driving so fast at this hour, broke the heavy silence with violence and without shame.

The wooden flap at the base of the door made its usual scraping announcement when he entered the quiet house. He could see light coming from under Mamie's door. He paused to listen, but he guessed she was asleep in her chair before the television.

He opened the door to the room, now stripped so bare. He switched on the bare bulb overhead, sat down on the dusty floor. And he listened to the silent walls in that hollow room, listened to the years within them, listened to the emptiness of that space, which was now so void, but which could be brightened, warmed, filled, made meaningful. Made beautiful again.

He crept upstairs to his room, and undressed in the cold, feeling grey and empty. And as he drifted off to sleep, he thought of Margaret, and how cold and empty and strange the world had become since they'd been apart.

CHAPTER 17

In which we hear silence and the music of God.

An hour before dawn broke, Mamie McDevitt was awakened by the sound of the front door. She heard what she interpreted to be a slow, too-careful rasp as the wind panel slid across the wooden saddle, and then back again as the door was eased back into position. The latch issued its hollow report as the lock clicked into place. Controlled, deliberate footsteps entered the back room, and then ascended the stairs, progress suggested only by wooden creaks, at intervals, emerging from beneath the damp carpet.

Paul had just returned home.

Mamie sighed, rolled over, pulled the covers up to block out the cold morning air. But she knew she wouldn't return to sleep.

At this bleak early hour, she was comforted in a way to sense Paul's presence, two floors above her. Even at this distance, the silence was so heavy that all sounds carried clearly as if through a misty haze. She could hear him open his kitchen door, move a chair, remain still for a moment – reading yesterday's newspaper? Then she heard the bathroom door, waited for the almost human whinge – there it came – as water rushed through the ancient pipes. Finally, she could hear his bedroom door closing, and then nothing, nothing as, presumably, he slumped exhausted into bed.

No use lying about, she thought. She pushed back the covers, stood, reached for her dressing gown hung on the back of the bedroom door.

She knew this house, its sounds, its silences, so changed as the years passed: almost as if time itself had a sound, or a collection of sounds, different for every passing year. Like an aural photograph album.

When she and John had first moved in, they slept on the middle floor in the big bedroom at the back. In those days the house sounded of expectancy: three empty bedrooms, a sitting room downstairs with hardly any furniture: all clean, waiting to be used, filled up and occupied. It was like a perfect story, that time: pregnant with Sean, herself and John papering the kitchen, the baby's room, never quite getting round to the sitting room (never actually did, in the end), and then the delivery men from Clery's carrying the cot up the stairs, palpably transforming the house into a picture-perfect home!

Mamie stood in the kitchen, made herself a cup of instant coffee, spilled a bit of milk. Hated turning on the light, but still so dark outside!

Then, for four years, there were Sean's sounds: waking in the night, those little cries, as she crept across the landing to lift him, carrying him back into bed with her while John slept. Her two boys, mother to them both it seemed, protecting them from the world outside . . . Then later, the kitchen: little Sean seemed to take over the kitchen, constantly hungry, pursuing her everywhere as she tidied up, banging pots and pans on the floor with a wooden spoon, singing his little heart out.

When he was about three the sitting room became his territory, and they were glad they'd never completed the decorating. Such a mess at the end of the day! She remembered washing crayon off the wallpaper, mopping up spilled drinks. Entering the room, struck dumb, seeing him surrounded by broken glass, the vase she had foolishly left within reach shattered all around him, her begging him not to move as she panicked, afraid to leave him alone, afraid to fetch the brush.

But now, on this cold January morning, as she stood in the kitchen, sunlight only now filtering into the garden, washing up her cup, her plate, her knife, she knew, deep down, it was the silences that would always remain with her.

The sound of the house when they returned from the hospital, without Sean. Neither of them speaking. John pacing the floor, going out for messages, returning. Mamie crying, without stop, for she didn't know how many days: empty, silent days.

The times, at night, when she lay awake, beside John, their marriage now so close in many ways, but only a shell in others, Mamie so afraid, so unwilling to cross that divide, to enter that pain that was Sean and Sean's loss from their life.

John wanted to move house, to get away from the memories, but Mamie refused. She saw the whole thing as such a failure, the only failure, and she determined she would get over it, just get on with life, she felt so guilty and consumed with the thing.

They took in the lodgers – it was her idea – to fill the space, to break the silence. And at times it was a comedy itself, the characters: the succession of travelling salesmen, boxes in the corridors – birdcages and pipe fitting and carpet samples. The two Misses O'Reilly – were they sisters? No one knew – the teacher from Longford, at least he was nice. And throughout, the procession of lovers, so ineptly smuggled inside: as if the walls did not transmit the low talk, the giggles, as if she would ever have the heart to interrupt the fleeting pleasures of these lonely souls!

She completed her make-up for Mass, fastened her dress, shivered a bit.

And now the new sounds, just lately. The traffic, now so noticeable. And of course, the sound of Paul, the new sounds emerging from the sitting room, through the walls into her flat: deep sounds, not just the scraping, or the echoes from the naked floors, but deeper sounds still, as if the sounds of *time*. Since Paul had begun his work Mamie found herself overwhelmed with long dormant memories. It was as if by removing the carpet, tearing down the wallpaper, Paul were releasing the time hidden in the very fabric of the room, the house, her life.

Mamie pulled her coat from the wardrobe. She thought to herself that today, in town, at Mass, she would pray for Paul. She felt that time was speeding up for her, that so much energy of the past was being freed up by Paul's work, and even though she knew him so little, she felt the changes happening around her might, unless she intervened, harm Paul in some way that she could not yet understand.

And so she would pray, and pray hard, for something to happen, something that might finish the room, and resolve Paul's lonely life, and bring just a bit more joy into her days.

The darkness had lifted by the time Margaret woke on Sunday morning. Grey light filtered into the room through the half-shut curtains. A Jilly Cooper novel lay face down on her duvet, open on the page she had been reading before falling asleep late Saturday night.

She turned lazily onto her side to face the window. She listened to the wind outside, an unsettled pattern of wet gusts against the panes.

She drifted into memories of Sundays when she was a girl. Her mother was a lapsed Methodist, her father a strict Catholic. He was responsible for Margaret's and her sister's religious education which, when they were young, he took quite seriously, saying their prayers with them at their bedside at night, quizzing them on the religious teaching they had received from the nuns during their days at school.

But then, shortly after Margaret had made her First Holy Communion in the church on Beechwood Avenue, something happened, some falling out with the parish priest, and her father's attitude to religion began to change. He became cynical, leading the girls into difficult and confusing discussions about the nature of their religious beliefs, and the power of the priest at consecration, and the real nature of papal infallibility.

For a time they continued to go to Mass, her father, her sister and herself, but no longer at the local church in

Ranelagh. Now they drove into Dublin to the Carmelite
Friary on Clarendon Street.

She remembered vividly those few months, perhaps a full
year, before they stopped going to Mass altogether – those
depressing Sunday mornings, driving through the deserted,
dirty streets of Dublin, parking on Grafton Street, walking
into that cavernous, cold, musty-smelling church. Because it
was a friary rather than a parish church, the Mass was never
well-attended. Only a handful of poor and elderly residents
of the inner city came each Sunday, most of them living
in the Corporation flats on Mercer Street. She remembered
the priests, sweet-seeming men, performing their rituals as if
largely unaware of the scattered congregation before them.
And she remembered the organ, a wheezing thing, gasping
through its familiar renditions of hymns with forced, meaningless rhymes and few voices to give life to the tired, empty
tunes. And the choir, reedy-voiced pensioners, there every
Sunday, in the worst wintry conditions, to add their breathy
tones to the ancient rite, as if sending forth their spirits at the
moment of death.

There was some comfort in these melancholy memories,
perhaps because they were confined to a short period of time,
a time before God stopped entirely, and before her father
got his new job which took him away for so many weeks
on end. A time when the three of them shared that part
of the week together in a safe and predictable environment,
old-fashioned and strangely comfortable even then, when she
was nine years old.

And she thought of herself here in this empty bed, facing

a dark winter's day of loneliness and uncertainty, and she experienced that strong pull of pungent memories, almost believing that, if she went into that church once again, the past, or something like the past, might be there still, something palpable, something real.

Soon she was walking up Ranelagh Road, past the newsagents selling their papers, past the triangle, where a group of young men smoked cigarettes. She walked past the tall, red-brick residential buildings on the way to the canal, past the Barge Pub with its gaudy exterior, its now tired bunting shivering in the wind.

She walked past the new, unfamiliar offices on Harcourt Street, coming to Stephen's Green, where traffic was building up even now, alive even at this hour with tourists and couples.

She walked down Grafton Street and turned into Bewley's, remembering suddenly that it was gone, that the old smoky, mahogany interior was gone, replaced by its new, weird 1950s kitsch decor and foreign staff.

She looked around briefly but felt alienated from this strange new space. She walked back out of the front door, then walked around to Wicklow Street. Cars were lined up along the pavement. She entered a new-looking coffee shop, hoping it would be a quiet place to catch her breath.

She went straight to the counter, looked into the glass case filled with almond danishes and fruit squares and cream cakes. She opted for a large fresh raspberry scone from a basket on top of the counter. A young girl who seemed to be from

Eastern Europe handed her a steaming, bowl-shaped cup of coffee.

The coffee shop was noisy, with most of its small tables occupied. Tinny jazz loomed over the sound of conversation and clinking porcelain. She had to thread her way carefully between the crowded tables to find a spot, way back in the far corner. As she sat down she suddenly felt tired, confused by this mass of people here on a Sunday morning, young couples who should still be in bed, here, showered, dressed in clean shirts and designer labels, reading newspapers and being together like grown-ups: so many young grown-ups in town on a Sunday morning!

Above the noise Billie Holiday sang with nasal vulnerability: *Don't explain* . . .

She sipped her coffee, buttered her scone. Nearby a couple sat across from one another, scanning different sections of the *Sunday Times*. She was thin with very straight, very black hair. She looked up from her paper, stared openly at Margaret, and then returned to her paper.

Damn, Margaret thought. What am I wearing? Oh, damn her anyway.

She remembered last night at eleven o'clock when, overcome with loneliness, she tried to phone Paul. I shouldn't have phoned him, she thought. What would I have said? Hi, it's me, where are you? Sorry I threw you out. Sorry I brought you five thousand miles from home, sorry you've had to give up everything to come to this mess, sorry I'm such a disaster, hope you're having a lovely time.

Maybe he *was* having a lovely time. And why shouldn't

he? Could you blame him for trying to make the best of things?

She suddenly felt relieved that he had not answered.

She looked around the coffee shop. Couples, so many couples. Women talking, men listening, or not listening, or talking, just talking, about the rain, about last night. Two young men across from her, both wearing round glasses, talking animatedly about something political, something vitally important that had to be done to prevent something terrible from taking place.

Waitresses carrying breakfasts, large plates of bacon and eggs and toast and black pudding.

I phoned because I wanted to make sure you were all right, she thought. I was worried about you. Are you sure you're okay?

What if he's running a fever in a saggy bed in some cheap, dire, awful B&B?

Margaret felt nervous, unfocused. She finished her coffee, stood up, left half her scone on the plate, fumbled in her bag for change, paid at the counter and walked out of the coffee shop.

She walked down Clarendon Street, stopped to look in the window at Brown Thomas. A promotion – House of Comfort. Rugs. Low puffy chairs. A small, silver-coloured stereo system with miniature speakers. Four thousand pounds.

She continued down Clarendon Street and into the courtyard of St Teresa's. She hadn't been in this spot for twenty years. She walked through the courtyard, past the old pieta where Jesus still bled and Mary still comforted. Then she passed through the door to discover that the small, dark entrance to the church had not changed.

She walked through the next door and into the church proper, the church she expected to remember vividly, the church she had been picturing to herself all morning.

It had retained its size, its shape, its expansiveness. But the musty air was gone, the feeling of gloom, the darkness. The church smelled of flowers. There was brightness, openness.

Clean wooden flooring. Walls freshly painted in cool green. Fresh gilding on the tall, pink-marble, Corinthian pillars. Beautiful, yes, beautiful high white ceilings – no cracks, no peeling – pure, clean, smooth white vaulted ceilings. Strategic lighting – up from the walls, down from the ceiling, shapes of light, bright spaces surrounding pictures, streaming from on high.

The altar had been moved forward, its white marble clean, almost joyous.

She took a seat in the middle of the church, blessed herself, and knelt down. But she couldn't pray. People were walking into the church. Couples, middle-aged parents and adolescent children, gay couples, well-dressed people who had driven in from the suburbs.

She moved into the middle of her pew to make room for more people coming into this old city-centre church on this winter morning.

And then the organ began, loud and confident, and the choir, up high in the loft behind the congregation, began to sing. She couldn't see them there behind her, couldn't force herself to turn round to see this new, young choir singing first in unison, then breaking out into complex harmonies as three priests processed up the aisle, priests in bright green vestments, one swinging the censor smoking with incense, one stopping at young couples to bless babies with papal generosity.

And then the celebrant welcomed the congregation from the pulpit, and the congregation actually responded 'Good morning, Father,' as if happy to be there, happy to be at Mass on this Sunday morning, this winter morning.

Then there was more music, and then a young woman came from the back of the church to sing, to lead the congregation as they sang their responses, a proud, confident, smiling young woman singing to the congregation, smiling to them and singing as they responded, singing to the Lord a New Song, for He has given Joy to his People!

Margaret couldn't pray, even as the congregation filed up to the altar at Communion and she knelt, she couldn't pray, couldn't pray with this music, this beautiful, sensuous music issuing from this old church, where she had spent those timid, quiet Sundays as a girl so long ago.

Mass ended as it began, with a flourish, a loud, modern, ringing organ piece that filled that cavernous space and made it shiver, made it alive, before it stopped dead, leaving only an echo and the sound of conversation as they talked and laughed on their way out of the church, these people who had once known the drudgery of a million Sundays now coming, freely, to this Mass, this brilliant production that was now Mass at St Teresa's on Clarendon Street.

As Margaret walked out of the church she wanted to tell

Paul, she wanted to tell him all about this morning, about the people, about how strange this all had become just this week, how she was living in a new land, this new Ireland, and how it wasn't her country any more, it was something new, someone else's Ireland, and that maybe they could discover it together, if only they could talk.

But she knew he wouldn't want to hear this just now, that too much had happened, that she couldn't expect him to listen to her new feelings, her new discovery. She had gone too far, she had done this unthinking thing to him, she cared about him too much to be able to ignore everything that she had done to him by bringing him here and then, now, abandoning him, there was too much guilt there to talk to him any more.

And to add to her troubles, when she got home that afternoon she found a note lying on the floor, a note that had obviously been shoved through the letter box. It was on a sheet of paper ripped from a notebook. The handwriting was a jerky scrawl, as if written in haste. Impatiently.

Margaret,

I thought you said we could talk. I phoned you yesterday, three times. You weren't in. Your answering machine wouldn't take my message. I need to speak to you. About the course. Right away. I might drop in tonight.

Could you please give me a ring as soon as you get in? Thanks.

Your student,
Tony

CHAPTER 18

In which we observe Martin Walsh on the Lord's day.

It's a curse this, I tell you. This waking. Every single night, or rather every single morning. Early, when it's still black outside, this waking, at four o'clock, sometimes half past three in the morning, wide awake when there's absolutely nothing to be done in the house only lie here, listening to the rain, staring into the darkness wide awake, shaking, heart racing.

Nothing to do only lie here and wonder what in the name of God I've done to get myself into this state.

Goddamn jar of bloody liver pâté.

Basically I'm screwed because there's no options here, not this time. If the lads are going in for this Stoneybatter property, and I told them I'm in, well then by Jaysus I'm in. If I back out now it will be the end, the absolute final end for them and me. It's been on a downward spiral these past months but this would be the nail in the coffin altogether if I don't deliver the goods.

Sneering goddamn superior fuckers, so they are.

It's in everything lately, this money. I keep seeing it, *hearing* it even. In the park, walking the dog, I keep thinking – under the next bush, there it will be a briefcase: some poor drug-dealing bastard, the guards in hot pursuit, throws the stash into the hedgerows, hoping to come back tomorrow to collect the drugs money, the used notes, the fifty thousand pounds in used notes that I'm going to tuck under my shirt and calmly walk away with . . .

It's destroying my peace of mind, I'm telling you. This house, this bloody house, our dream home, what an impressive bloody pile on the outside, with our bloody winter-flowering jasmine creeping around the door, and the view of the city's Southside gaping outside the picture window – it's suddenly nothing but chains, nothing but a big ledger book with that fucking loan shark's name scratched across the front, the same fucker who got me into this mess in the first place, and now won't lend me the extra fifty grand to buy myself into freedom.

But the worst of it is knowing the dosh is right under my nose, and I can't do a blessed thing to get at it.

Auntie Mamie. Liver pâté. What a disastrous state I'm in.

Sitting there, on her own, in that massive great chunk of Dublin 6 property. One breath away, one little heartbeat away from my salvation. She'll be seventy years old come November, she won't last much longer no matter what I have to say about it. And so what if the worst happens? A bit of mouldy French pâté does her in. Is it any harm? Save her a few years – what am I saying? A few months! – save her a few months of miserable old age. Send her off peacefully, for God's sake, and doesn't she deserve a bit of peace after seventy years?

But in the meantime, I'm lying awake every night of the week.

And I've tried everything, I can tell you. Deirdre is after me to go easy on the gargle, but a few pints is the safest remedy I know for insomnia and I've got to do something or I'll lose it entirely at this rate, I swear I'll lose my marbles altogether. She gives out that I'm in dire form all the time but sure what does she care at the end of the day? She only wants me around to put on a show for her relatives and her choir mates and the bloody Parent–Teachers Association, and on and on and on.

And in the background she's no earthly idea about this bloody awful endless bloody suffering I'm going through.

Lying there wondering. Did the old dear open the jar? Did it give off a pong? Did she cop on that it might have gone off? Did she try the stuff anyway, thinking maybe that's the way it's supposed to be?

Roll over, try to sleep. Useless.

So Sunday comes along and all the plans have been laid for a lovely day at home, and I'm to be on my best behaviour for the day, says she. So I haven't slept more than ten minutes all night, and thanks be to Christ I'd got my hands on that old fireplace on Saturday. Brilliant excuse, that, to get out of this blessed house and away from these curses of women and children.

Sunday morning started off grand, you know, when I went down to the Goat to have a quick one before the dinner. Willie and Jack were there in their usual form and Willie was all chat about his trip to Frankfurt, and the time he had of it with the lads when they went out on the tear, and the eyes popping out of him when he was telling us about the showgirls in the pubs – it was only priceless, I can tell you.

So I suppose I had two or three pints and I know I should have gone easy but the thoughts of those dreams last night and going back there now with Deirdre and that screeching harpy that goes by the name of my mother-in-law, and that little Ella one, who is becoming a rare old expert at getting on my nerves. I walk in the door and the flesh of my flesh, my own beloved daughter is there sitting on the floor talking on the phone in the hall and I give her a kiss on the top of her head as she yaps away and I ask her how's the Queen of Sheba and she only glares at me, you know, really nasty like, looking down her nose at me like I'm some class of a servant in the house, in my own bloody house!

So Deirdre and her mother are in the sitting room on the new settee with their heads bent close together and their voices low as if some terribly important bloody conspiracy were being hatched, you know, to save someone from buying some bloody awful hat, or to measure the impact on the world if the desk were moved from the landing down the stairs to the hall. So of course the mother-in-law asks me how I am and before I have a chance to answer she remembers something that she had forgotten to tell Deirdre and launches into yet another bloody story leaving me with my gob wide open and feeling like the king of shite.

But I do my duty and go into the kitchen to open a bottle of wine and there they are, same as they've been for the past two weeks: the jars. It's Deirdre, with her job with that sleazy Marketing crowd. Lately she's been bringing home these bloody awful-looking containers from work. Some new client, some sad bastard trying to import disgusting food from the continent.

And the jars are lined up across the kitchen counter. Gherkins, from Romania, with unpronounceable names. Olives stuffed with anchovies. Polish eel in brine. Horrible, grey-looking mush in squat little jars – mushroom and pig's liver, from Brittany. *Mousse de Lapin. Terrine de Foie. Pâté de Canard.*

A smiling Dutch boy standing there with a platter of dead rolled-up herrings.

And the whole lot made me feel sick, I can tell you: sick-looking yellow labels, and sick-looking mush-coloured contents. Knowing what I'd given Auntie Mamie. Knowing that I'd taken a jar, unscrewed the cap, let it breathe.

Prayed for bacteria to grow, fucking grow. And then delivered it to her, like a kind and caring nephew!

So with those bloody jars staring me in the face, I breathed deep to stop the sweats and I opened the first bottle of wine, and then very soon I was back to open the second, and I suppose I was knocking it back fairly handy but sure am I not entitled to enjoy a glass of wine of a Sunday especially when I bloody well paid for it and the food on the table as well?

Now I must say it was a grand dinner altogether with the pork and roast potatoes and the works, only I had to sit there quietly smiling the entire bloody time thinking about those infested jars from those miserable countries and listening to herself go on about her useless sister with her phone bills and her rattling windows and her rising damp and all the while suggesting that we all pitch in to pay for her bloody sister's bloody house renovations, why the hell couldn't she just take a lodger to pay for it herself? Whole house on her own, it's bloody ridiculous. All these old ones sitting around in their bloody houses worth a fortune!

Of course it would've been so much better if her husband, Deirdre's dad, had lived. Most decent bloody chap I've ever met, would've given that harpy of a wife someone to talk to and kept her out of my house on my Sundays off. Didn't he have the patience of our Suffering Lord to put up with that woman for thirty-three years of marriage?

So by the time we'd finished off the pudding I'd have to admit I was well-enough bladdered and I don't know how I managed to get on her bad side – oh yes, it was her bloody useless friend Maura who happened to marry Liam Keating who owns half the insurance agencies in the country and who's on the board of the bank and who sent his kids to bloody Clongowes and set them all up with cushy jobs with the estate agents and the PR firms. She can't seem to stop going on about who bought this house and who's going on this holiday and I swear to God I was going to burst and I asked her when dear Maura and Liam would condescend to invite her over for Sunday dinner? And Deirdre had a look on her like she was going to ram a steak knife through my prick.

So eventually I said I had to get this fireplace over to Auntie Mamie's house and she looked at me like she always does when I mention my relatives as if they were some species of fungus and I tipped back the rest of my wine and found the keys and got the hell out of there thanks be to Christ.

Of course I didn't know what I'd find when I got there what with the redecorating going on and I suppose I was a bit shaky knowing I had delivered three jars of sick-looking gunge to Mamie during the week in the pathetic, misplaced, evil, drunken hope that the stuff would send her to her maker. But when I pushed the doorbell I could hear her feet shuffling as she came and opened the door looking hale and hearty as ever God bless her.

So she takes me in to see that American chap who's standing in the middle of the grey sitting room totally stripped of wallpaper, and him looking black and white and grey like some workman out of an old comedy film. And I ask him if he knows anything about fireplaces and he looks at me kind of strange I suppose because I might not quite have been fully myself, and so I explain to him that this chimney breast here used to be a fireplace and if you take a hammer like this and whack it good and hard you break through the wall and in a minute I've opened the thing up and there's the original iron backing still in place and he just stands there looking a bit like a frightened dog.

Then I tell him to come out to the Range Rover to see what I brought him and we dig that old iron fireplace out of the back that I got for a hundred quid and we bring it into the house and the penny drops for your man and he figures out that he can break out the rest of the old plaster and put the new fireplace in and fix the walls up around it and I tell him he's a genius and to keep up the bloody marvellous work.

And then I shout into Mamie did she enjoy the cake and the tea and, of course, the pâté that I left her during the week, and she says she hasn't eaten it yet and I start explaining to her all the lovely stuff that Deirdre's been bringing us home from work. And then I tell her it's all foreign stuff and supposed to be very healthy and keep her going for another seventy years. And then I tell her about the companies that make the stuff in France, La Maison Salmonella and Château Clostridium, and of course I remember the names of a dozen bloody bacteria that can grow in these things because I've been thinking about them for so long at night for so many bloody nights, and there's our great American *omadhaur* standing there when I'm telling all this to Mamie and then I'm walking out the door and the two of them watch me get into the Range Rover and I swear at that moment I'd just like to hire some bastard thug off the street to go in and get rid of them both and get my hands on that house and wouldn't life then just be worth bloody living thank you very much.

'My God,' Paul said to Mamie. 'What brought all that on?'

'I'm telling you now,' she replied, 'that fella could be dangerous. It all goes back to his mother, you know. Spoiled him rotten as a child. Gave him everything he asked for and then some.'

'I think he was a bit drunk,' Paul said.

'Isn't that a fine way for a man to be on a Sunday afternoon?'

'What was he saying to you, anyway?' Paul asked.

'Nothing I could understand,' Mamie replied.

'Those French names. They were names of bacteria.'

'Were they?'

'Yes, if I heard correctly.'

'You're a wonder,' said Mamie.

'So why was he rattling off bacteria?'

'I haven't a clue,' said Mamie, pondering. 'But I would like a cup of tea after all that.'

Paul smiled. 'Yes,' he said, yawning. 'A cup of tea would be very nice.'

'I'll put the kettle on, so,' Mamie replied, walking back into her flat. 'Don't know how you keep going at all after the late night you had last night . . .'

And Paul followed her, striving to keep the rush of blood from his face.

Later that evening Paul continued to work.

Martin had left a large hole in the middle of the chimney breast, and the old cast-iron fireplace was leaning against the wall. Paul had never tried to install a fireplace before and wasn't immediately sure how to approach the job.

It was clear, however, that a fireplace had once been there. Paul could see from the hole in the wall that the old fireplace had been blocked up hastily, with only a thin veneer of plaster spread over the gap in the wall. He easily pulled the rest of the patch away to reveal the iron inner cavity leading up the chimney. The plaster around the original fireplace was still in good shape, and Paul began to see that the installation of the new fireplace would not be difficult.

The fireplace Martin had delivered was cast iron and badly rusted, the designs obscured through what might have been years of neglect sitting in an abandoned building. When

Paul touched it his hands were immediately covered in red dust.

First he set to work with a towel to remove the loose flakes of rust. Then he used a small wire brush to remove the deeper layers of rust and grime and reveal the ironwork beneath. As he worked the brush gently over the individual panels and into the iron ridges and crevices, an elaborate decorative motif began to emerge: two elegant flowering plants creeping up on either side, and above, two panels with birds picking berries from a bush, surrounding a central panel with a Grecian muse, her face expressing calm and serenity.

And before long the fireplace was a gleaming black. The figures were perfectly unharmed from the restoration, freed from a century of rust and decomposition, new and solid and real once again.

And as Paul lay in bed that night, he thought about those figures, so lovingly crafted in Victorian times, preserved in that intransigent medium: those plants, those birds, that face, so serene, looking out at a room warmed by her fires, with adult conversation, and children's games, and pots of tea warming on the hearth.

And botulism.

Now what brought that into his head?

CHAPTER 19

In which the firm hand of righteousness sows the seeds of destruction.

The next day, Monday afternoon at 1:00, Kevin Connolly sat in the front row of Theatre P at University College Dublin, as the third-year lecture in Legal Studies came to a close.

The black-robed lecturer rushed from the podium and through the back door like a crow fleeing the roadside. Students broke into noisy conversation, gathered their notepads, filed up the steep stairs and flooded out onto the concourse.

As the room emptied, Kevin adjusted his round bifocals and bent down to retrieve his burgundy leather briefcase. Placing it on the wooden ledge before him, he snapped the latches, opened the case and carefully placed his notebook inside, beside his diary, his legal dictionary and his calculator. He unzipped a leather pouch where he kept pens, pencils, an orange highlighter, rubber erasers, pencil sharpeners and a small extendable ruler. He inserted his pen inside the pouch and zipped it shut, replacing the pouch in its original position.

He opened his diary, the leather cover of which matched his briefcase. Oh dear, he thought. Lunch with Cousin Gerry today. He glanced at his watch. Better dash.

The lecture theatre was empty when he climbed the stairs. He threaded his way through the crowds of students on the concourse, walked out of the Arts Block into the cold air, and ran stiffly across to the grey college restaurant.

Such crowds, he thought. Never would his father have predicted that such crowds of young Irish people would attend university. In his father's day, only the eligible few were granted the privilege of spending these years studying, their work overseen by the nation's great minds. Standards were more easily maintained then, Kevin thought. Back then, resources were concentrated upon those who had real talent, and could reasonably be expected to make a material contribution to society.

Kevin entered the restaurant building, squinting across the crowd to see if Gerry was waiting for him in the foyer. He sighed. Perhaps Gerry's forgotten. Disorganised, as usual. Don't know how he manages to keep on top of his studies.

He joined the queue that stretched from the base of the stairs to the dining area on the upper level.

Kevin tried to meet Gerry at least once each month. Gerry was his cousin on his mother's side, from Carlow, now a First Arts student. Kevin took it upon himself to look out for Gerry, to hail him whenever he met him in the corridor, to try to make Gerry feel welcome. Kevin was concerned to ensure that Gerry didn't lapse into the lonely habits of so many young men from the country living up in Dublin for the first time. Kevin did this out of consideration for his mother, whose people (it must

be admitted) were simpler than his father's, country folk
who would never became fully *au fait* with the habits of
the capital.

Ever since he was a boy, Kevin had been aware of a
tension between his father and his mother's people. Mad,
his father contended. They were all wild and mad. Friends
and neighbours dropping in any time of the night or day.
Carrying on till all hours.

Pigs in the kitchen, he said.

Kevin's father was in the Department of Public Prosecu-
tions. He was a man who met regularly with Government
Ministers, High Court Justices. The men who ensured that
the new Ireland stayed on course. The newspapers were
filled with stories about businessmen and the country's new
prosperity, but Kevin knew that it was the civil servants like
his father who made it all possible. They maintained control,
Kevin thought. Without them, Ireland would never be freed
from its ancient habits. Dishonesty. Underhandedness. And,
it must be said, petty corruption.

As he picked up his tray and selected his lunch, Kevin
pondered the English question once again. Like his father,
he was enamoured of the British legal system, the rock that
formed the foundation of everything great in Irish law. And he
wondered, as he often did, looking out over this steamy dining
hall – a sea of girls in tight-fitting clothes, ill-kempt young men
– Kevin wondered once again whether the continuation of
English rule would have been as bad as all that, so bereft of
good qualities.

So much disorder. Such lax attitudes.

Paying for his meal, he scanned the crowded room – ah, there he was, Cousin Gerry, today, as always, surrounded by that gang of Arts students, some of whom, Kevin surmised, did nothing to enhance his (Gerry's) reputation on campus, and some of whom may have even lowered him in the eyes of his lecturers and tutors.

'Virginia Woolf,' Gerry teased, 'would never have eaten what you're eating.'

Gerry beamed mischief. He was good-looking, with red hair and a round face and an alert expression. He liked people, he liked good fun, he liked Susan, and he especially liked everyone around him to enjoy themselves.

'Of course she would,' Susan replied, from her position across the table. 'She was a crusader, and crusaders have always loved beef.'

'I think it's disgusting,' said willowy Mary at her right, picking at a salad and pushing her long hair behind one ear. 'Gorging yourself on dead animals.'

'Nothing compared with what you gorged yourself on last Saturday night,' Susan replied.

'Oh dear, who let the cats out,' Charlie said, laconically. Charlie was tall and thin, with sharp, angular features and an ironic expression.

'I don't think Virginia Woolf ate at all,' Gerry said. 'She looked awfully thin to me.'

'Self-punishment,' Susan said, pointing with her fork. 'Women internalising male values. Down with the old order, I say. Let's put some pleasure back in our lives.'

'Speaking of pleasure, Gerry,' said Charlie, 'I think I see your lawyerly cousin.'

'Bloody hell,' Gerry said. 'I was supposed to meet him below. Sorry, lads – be decent now.'

'Good Lord!' Charlie shouted above the crowd. 'Gerry, it's your good cousin Kevin! Shove over there, Susan – let Kevin squeeze in beside you.'

'Kevin can squeeze in beside me any time he likes,' said Susan, with an urbane half-smile.

'Let me take that case off you there, Kevin, so you've space to put down your tray,' said Gerry, standing.

'Make way for Senior Counsel!' said Charlie in an English drawl.

Kevin set his tray down awkwardly and sat down amidst the group.

'So how did your lecture go today?' Gerry began.

'Very well, very interesting, as always,' Kevin replied.

'Interesting, was it?' Charlie asked. 'What did you cover today? "Maximising professional fees"? "Obfuscating issues with pleonastic verbiage"?'

'Sorry?' Kevin asked. 'Oh, no, of course not. State arrest. Your rights, you know, when you're arrested.'

'You mean, "How far can they go to make you talk?"' Charlie said.

'Yes, that's it,' Kevin agreed. 'A very interesting topic.'

'I heard the gardaí can keep at you for ages,' Mary said, 'as long as they give you a break every four hours.'

'Four hours?' said Susan. 'I'd lose interest after four minutes.'

'Most criminals say nothing,' Kevin said. 'That's the problem – all that wasted time. The gardaí have no powers to enforce co-operation.'

'So you'd prefer the old-fashioned way, Kevin?' Charlie asked. 'The old rubber hose job?'

'I believe the State has the right to know what detainees were doing when they were arrested,' Kevin said.

The others exchanged bored glances. There was silence for a moment.

'Well,' Gerry said in an effort to be cheerful, 'our English tutor finally returned today.'

'Is this the one who fainted during the tutorial?' Kevin asked.

'Yes. Now *that* was frightening,' Gerry said. 'But she seems to be all right again.'

'She's a wonderful tutor,' Mary said. 'It was lovely to have her back.'

'You're not the only one who thinks so,' Charlie said, suggestively.

'What do *you* mean?' demanded Susan.

'D'you see that fellow over there?' Charlie indicated across the hall. 'The tall fellow in the black jacket?'

'Yeah,' Gerry said. 'That's Tony Dunne.'

'He's gorgeous,' said Susan.

'He's not my type,' said Mary.

'What about him?' Gerry asked.

'He's a man of many talents, they say. And I think he's riding your tutor,' Charlie said.

'Get off!' Gerry replied.

'I saw them on Friday morning,' Charlie continued. 'It was early. He pulled up in his black Golf GTi over by the Arts Block. And then she got out of his car. I can draw only one conclusion.'

'Ah Charlie, you're making this up,' Gerry said. 'She's a grown woman. There's no way she would shag a student.'

'And why not?' Susan asked. 'Aren't women allowed to enjoy the virility of young men, the same way middle-aged men use young women?'

'Maybe he's her brother,' said Mary.

'Wouldn't say so,' said Charlie. 'He's from Dolphin's Barn or Ballyfermot or one of those places. And she's very West Brit.'

'I'm sure there's a simple explanation. Maybe he saw her on the road and gave her a lift,' said Gerry.

'Perhaps,' said Charlie. 'But I noticed that she didn't thank him. You'd always thank someone for a lift. Though not necessarily for a shag.'

'So how do you know so much about Tony Dunne?' Gerry asked.

'You know that party in that big house in Mount Merrion last week – the one with the body paints?'

'Yeah, I was there with you, remember?' Gerry said.

'Do you remember all the cannabis?'

'Yeah, bucketsful of the stuff. Go on . . .'

'It was all his gear,' Charlie said. 'He supplied everything. He's a pusher. Small-time, but a real pro. And he's not a bad student, so they say.'

Kevin had been listening silently to this conversation. Suddenly he coughed, dropped his fork.

'Are you all right there, Kevin?' Gerry asked.

'Yes, I'm grand,' Kevin replied, reaching under the table.

'So you're saying our Ms Boyle is having an affair with a drug dealer?' Mary said.

'That would appear to be the situation,' agreed Charlie. 'There's a bit more to your little Ms Boyle than meets the eye.'

'Amazing,' Gerry said.

'It's like a Bertolucci film,' Susan said. 'Tough guy meets middle-class girl for joyless sex and inane conversation.'

'I personally don't believe it,' Mary said. 'I wonder if there's anything written on drugs and contemporary women's fiction?'

'I can't take this excitement any longer,' Gerry said. 'I'm going up – would anybody like a coffee?'

'Yes, please, darling, I'd adore one,' Susan said. 'Hot and black, if you wouldn't mind . . .'

Kevin Connolly was shaking.

As he walked out of the restaurant his body was wet. His muscles were sore, as if they had contracted too suddenly. As though he had been thrust without warning into a situation of raw terror.

The casual attitudes, he thought. The casual, joking manner in which they accepted this behaviour – nay, these behaviours, here at University College Dublin. Fornication between a student and a teacher. The abuse of drugs at a student social event. And finally, the toleration of a drug dealer in their midst!

And his own cousin amongst them. This was grave, very grave indeed.

Kevin had to be alone, to think, to decide how to act. He walked quickly back to the Arts Block. He pushed his way through the crowds downstairs to the lower ground floor. He walked past the unsavoury characters in the games room, coming finally to his locker. He undid the padlock, opened the door, and stared, simply stared at his coat, his umbrella.

He had seen that face, that hard, dangerous face. Even before he had heard the story he had sensed the evil of Tony Dunne – yes, the name stuck with him, thank God. Ballyfermot, they said. Or one of those places. Golf GTi. Black.

As his breathing subsided Kevin moved from horror to resolution. Yes, now that this thing had been discovered, it must be dealt with. Brought up from the depths, dragged to the surface and outed, eradicated, cleansed from this place, this privileged place.

Can't allow this to go on, he thought. Cannot let this thug pollute our university, he thought. Father, he thought. Must, simply *must* tell Father.

CHAPTER 20

In which Paul's problems worsen.

Paul sat in the boardroom at 2:00 on Monday afternoon, drinking coffee, staring at his computer screen. He was surrounded by papers. He looked pale, worn from lack of sleep. And today, all day, he was getting nowhere.

The MountAgro proposal was stalled. He was waiting for information from Ruth and Dee, he was stuck over final costings. Jack had disappeared from the office, as if retreating from the staff. When he did appear he wasn't communicating.

In fact, everyone in the office seemed as dismal as the weather.

And Paul knew that, deep down, he was beginning to feel lonely, so lonely. He had hoped that work today would stimulate him, give him a challenge into which to pour his nervous energies. But instead, everything was on hold, it was wait-and-see, all so empty and grey.

At that moment Felicity peered into the boardroom.

'Paul, do you have a minute?'

'Sure, come in,' Paul said, suddenly jolted back from his empty reflections. 'Did you have a good weekend?'

Felicity wore her black hair tied back in a spartan bun.

Usually she was fastidious about her appearance, but today Paul noticed her make-up was hastily applied. He could see dark rings under her eyes.

She entered the room, sat down across the table from Paul, stared out of the window, and said nothing for a moment.

'So,' Paul said, 'I take it the weekend wasn't any great shakes?'

'No, it wasn't the best,' she said, sighing. 'In fact it was absolutely dire.'

'I'm sorry. Anything I can do to help?'

'No. At least, I don't think so.'

Felicity stood, somewhat dramatically, and walked to the window.

'What do you think of this company, anyway?' she asked.

'Think of it? What do you mean?'

'Spyral. Do you think it's a good company? Do you like it here?'

Paul was not sure how to respond.

'Sure. Yeah, well I suppose it's a nice company. I haven't worked for many companies. But this one seems to be just fine.'

'And would you be sorry,' Felicity continued, 'if something happened?'

'Something like what?'

'You know what I mean, Paul,' Felicity responded, a sense of urgency in her voice. 'Paul, I'm asking how you'd feel if Spyral were to go under.'

'Go under? Why? What's happening?'

'Paul, I've been wanting to speak to you for the past week

about this. But you've been so distant, so wrapped up in this MountAgro thing. And I'm finding it hard to talk to anyone in here lately. Do you remember those lunches, Paul? The ones we used to have in the old office, back in town?'

'Yeah. They were good. We should do it again.'

'Paul, I don't know if you're noticing what's happening around here. But we couldn't just do lunch. Not any more. Not with the way things are going.'

'Why not? Come on, Felicity, what's all this mystery about?'

'Paul, I'm not supposed to be saying these things. But the others seem to know already. And even if they don't know, they'll find it out soon enough, and by then it might be too late. Basically, we're in trouble. Deep financial trouble. We'll never get paid for that program for Orbit – they've gone under, the company is being wound up. There's nothing left for them to pay us with.'

'I see . . .'

'We've got time, Paul. There's money in the bank for now, for the next few weeks. But if we don't win this MountAgro business, pretty soon the cheques will start to bounce. Spyral will go to the wall. And I think Jack would be happy to walk away and leave us here.'

'Okay,' Paul said slowly. 'But we *will* win MountAgro. They aren't talking to anyone else. There's no reason why we won't win this business.'

'But Paul, don't you see? It's over. I mean, between us all. Ruth and Dee are hardly on speaking terms. Dee is totally gung-ho to win this project, even though he hates the idea. It's like some weird death wish. But Ruth won't budge. We're

having to drag information out of her. She's ready to walk
over this. And if Ruth walks, well, as far as I can see, we're
history.'

Felicity walked to the window again, shaking.

'Paul, I know you'll get another job. But I'm too old for this
to happen. I don't have any money, my parents are both sick. I
just can't take this uncertainty. It's all just so uncertain . . .'

Paul stood, wondered whether to comfort her. He hoped
no one would enter the room.

'And Paul,' Felicity said, pulling a tissue from the arm of
her cardigan, 'the worst of it is, I won't be thanked. Not by
Jack, not by anyone. I'll walk away from this mess, having
given my all. And for nothing!'

She blew her nose, sniffled a bit.

'I'm sorry, Paul,' she said. 'I wanted to tell you, to let
you know. I hate this. I want it to be like it used to be.
I'm sorry.'

And then she left the room. Paul sat for a few minutes,
staring once again into his computer screen, as he had done
for most of the day, wishing, just wishing, he could phone
Margaret, and ask her what he should do next.

It was now nine o'clock Monday night. Paul was wearing
his decorating clothes – jeans and an Illinois sweatshirt, now
clotted with material scraped from the bare walls.

He struggled to position the heavy, cast-iron fireplace
against the chimney breast. He had finished polishing it the
day before, and the figures now stood out in high relief –
those tall, mythical flowers running up either side; those

black birds, so intent upon their black berries; and then her, that sylvan goddess, with her calm, beatific smile, casting her blessing upon the hearth.

Paul shifted the base into position, and then eased the fireplace back against the wall. It married perfectly with the hollow, and sat well against the wall of the chimney breast.

The fireplace had two small iron tabs sticking out on either side, each with a hole in the centre. He slid the fireplace to one side, and drilled two small holes in the wall. Then he repositioned the fireplace, slotted two screws through the holes in the iron tabs, and drove the screws into the wall.

He tested his efforts by trying to pull the fireplace from its position. It didn't budge.

Just then, Mamie appeared in her usual ghost-like fashion.

'Ah now,' she said, 'it's been many a year since we've been able to warm this room with a fire. And a fire brings such comfort to a room, don't you think?'

'Yes, it's going to be very nice when I've patched up the plaster. But we'll have to get someone in to inspect it before we light a fire.'

'So, Paul. Such a cold winter's night. Haven't you accomplished enough for today?'

'Yes, I think so,' Paul replied.

'Why don't you come in for a cup of tea, you know, to unwind a bit? Or maybe a wee glass of wine?'

'Yes, that sounds very nice. Let me just clear this mess away. I'll be in in a moment.'

'Righty-o,' she said, turning to leave the room.

A few minutes later, having changed his clothes, Paul stood

in Mamie's small, damp kitchen. The electric kettle was just coming to the boil as he entered the room.

'Now, Paul. What would you fancy? When Martin was in last week he brought me some nice pâté from France. His wife, Deirdre – she's a very busy lady these days. I don't know how the two of them cope, both working, both up so early in the morning. Anyway, she works for some fellow who imports foods, delicacies I suppose you'd call them, mostly from the Continent. And Martin brought me this pâté – I don't know if it would be my sort of thing, but I thought I'd give it a try. What do you think?'

She handed Paul the jar.

'*Terrine de Canard*,' Paul said, examining the jar. 'I think that means duck.'

'Yes,' Mamie confirmed. 'And I was in Gammel's today, and I bought some crackers to go along with it. Shall we give it a go? Here, you open the jar. My old joints get so stiff in this damp weather . . .'

Paul set the jar on the counter, twisted open the cap. It came off easily in his hand.

He inspected the contents.

'Looks authentic to me,' he said.

Mamie peered into the jar.

'Looks about right,' she said, sceptically. 'But, oh my, do you get the smell?'

Paul lowered his nose to the jar.

'Yes, I do now. Is it really supposed to smell like that?'

'I don't know,' she replied. 'As I said, I wouldn't eat much pâté.'

'Mamie, I'm no expert here, but I wouldn't eat canned meat that gave off such a strong smell. This should have been sealed during the cooking process. It shouldn't smell this way. And besides, the jar opened too easily. It wasn't airtight.'

'I see,' Mamie pondered. 'But what should I do? Martin's been asking me if I've tried it. He seems to want my opinion.'

Paul thought for a moment. Something in the back of his mind, couldn't quite place it.

Disease.

'Why don't you simply tell Martin that you enjoyed it,' he said finally. 'You know, tell him a little white lie. Tell him all about how great the French are with their pâtés and their sauces. Tell him it gave you a real lift. Tell him I had some as well, and that I really enjoyed it.'

'But Paul, maybe we should just try it first . . .'

'I'm sorry, Mamie, but this doesn't seem quite right. I studied this stuff in college. If canned foods aren't cooked properly, there's a risk of salmonella, and that can be very nasty. Please, Mamie, why don't I just throw this out, and we'll have a nice cup of tea, just like always, and you can thank Martin for his pâté, and he'll be none the wiser.'

Mamie sighed.

'All right, Paul, that's grand, if that's the way you want it.'

'Thanks, Mamie. You're a peach.'

'Thank you, Paul. But as my mother used to warn me, you Yanks aren't half fussy . . .'

CHAPTER 21

In which the fox is followed to the lair.

On Tuesday afternoon Tony Dunne walked from the Arts Block through the squally wind towards Car Park S. He walked quickly, a book bag hanging from one shoulder. As he bounded up the steps into the car park, his mobile phone rang. He cursed, dropped his bag onto the pavement, and pulled the phone from inside his jacket.

'Yeah? Uncle Dee. Grand, and yourself? ... Yeah, okay, not a problem. The usual. I'll have it for you tonight ... Not on the phone, mate. They can hear every word on these things ... I'm not fucking paranoid, it's just the way it is ... Yeah, okay. See you 'round nine, right? Cheers, mate.'

He slipped the phone back into his jacket.

Something in the air, he thought as he walked towards his car. I'm jumpy today. But any six-year-old can bug a mobile phone. The cops are doing it all the time. It's in the papers.

He reached his car, set his bag on the roof, fumbled for his keys. Then he stopped and stood, surveying the car park. After a few moments he deactivated the car alarm with his keyring and got inside.

Something, he thought. Maybe nothing. Maybe I'm just tired. Should get more sleep.

He turned the key, revved the engine. Doesn't smell new any more, he thought. Should get it cleaned. Used to be a serious motor. Now look at this car park. Students used to have bloody bicycles and Citroën Dianes. Now they drive Beamers. All Daddy's money, of course. They're not buying BMWs with their own dosh. Even the money they use to buy my gear is Daddy's money.

He pulled a small notebook from the glove compartment. It was his order book, written in code. Letters for numbers, numbers for letters. Backwards. Just in case.

Right, he thought. I'd better get over to Mr Gray. Due there at 3:00. He's not into dilatoriness, as he puts it. Not into excuses either.

Tony drove the black Golf GTi out of the car park, accelerating hard, slowing for speed ramps, and then accelerating hard again.

Something about today, he thought. It's like I'm uneasy about something. Everything. There's nothing wrong with this car. Nothing. Except that it looks suspicious, because now everyone is driving red Beamers instead of black Volkswagens.

He drove over the bridge at Clonskeagh, moving steadily with the traffic.

Except it's different, he thought. Their Beamers, and my GTi. Theirs are fucking legit. Mine is drugs money. That's it, pure and simple. I live in Dolphin's Barn. They live in Dublin 4. If I give up dealing, I've got fucking nothing. And they've still got their Beamers, and their big houses, and their parties in the back garden on Daddy's dosh.

He turned on the radio, flicked around the stations. Dance

music. Ella Fitzgerald on Jazz FM. The Frames on Phantom.

This being different, being on the outside. It's getting to me. The way they look at me, like I'm a bit of a joke. Or no, maybe a bit of danger. Very safe, but danger all the same. I'm their fucking little exotic. They call me, I appear. Come on, Tonzer, give us some more o' that good gear you brought us last week. Give us what we need to go on the tear Saturday night.

And then back you go, into your corner, you fucking scum.

And then there's Margaret Boyle. That's the big one. *That's* why I'm so fucking nervous. I'm not getting anywhere with her. She's not helping me out at all. Shouldn't have left that note at the weekend. I'm probably making her suspicious.

But I don't care. I still need to see her. I need to get her on my side. I need to get someone in this fucking place on my side.

I wonder what would happen if I came on to her. She's so fucking cold, so in control. Imagine, though, if she cut loose. I'd say that underneath that cold exterior she could be a madwoman, a real tiger. And with her husband away – if there is a husband at all. She's probably just nervous about coming on to a student. She might just be waiting for me to make the first move. Here I am, hassling her about the course, when all the while, underneath, she's dying for it.

Christ, what am I thinking? Fucking stupid, so I am. I wish I could just fucking relax!

He drove into Harold's Cross. He passed the park, then

turned left down Greenhills Road. He stopped at the entrance
to the industrial estate. The security guard looked out blankly,
raised the gate. Tony drove in.

Something is wrong, he thought. I shouldn't have come
here today.

He drove past the paint factory, slipped between the two
warehouses, parked in front of the printers.

He got out of his car, reached into his pocket, turned off
the phone. He walked, then stood for a moment in front of
the joinery. He surveyed the car park, looked behind him
where he drove in.

He walked across the front of the building, then around
the corner and down the side to the steel door. He could
hear the buzzing of saws coming from inside.

He knocked once. No response. He knocked again. Then
louder. He lowered his head, listened. The buzzing stopped.
Then started again. He looked down at his watch. Then he
kicked the door, hard, but again, with no response.

Bastards, Tony thought. Five minutes past three and the
fuckers won't open the door for me.

He kicked the door angrily. I've got real dosh here, he
thought, and I need fresh gear. Couldn't they give me just
a few minutes?

Bollix. I'll have to set something up for tomorrow. And I
hate walking around with this amount of dosh.

He retraced his steps down the side of the building towards
where he had parked his car.

This is bullshit, he thought. Now I'm totally out of gear and
I've got nothing for Dee. And then there's those fuckers for

the Law Society party tonight. Plenty of cash, and I've got no fucking gear.

Mr Gray doesn't like to take calls. I'll have to wait for him to bloody phone me. I'll have to bloody explain to him that I was delayed, and see if he'll allow me back into his bloody inner sanctum before Thursday, so I can at least get some gear for Friday.

I'd better not bring the dosh to college. Suppose they find it on me. They'll wonder what I'm at. Or worse, they'll probably guess exactly what I'm at.

He walked towards his car. Then he noticed two tall men walking away from him at the far end of the car park. He could hear the sound of their hard shoes against the pavement, even above the hum of the saws. And he saw their grey trousers. And matching coats.

Oh Jesus, he thought, staring at the men as they sauntered casually away from him. Couldn't be.

He took out his keys, opened the door, and quickly got into the car.

His mind began to race as he reversed into the narrow car park. He stopped again to watch the men, who disappeared behind a delivery van.

No, he thought. You're only getting worried over nothing. They work in the printers.

He slowed as he approached the lane-way between the warehouses. He turned his head to look back, to spot the car.

Oh Jesus, he thought. There it is, staring me in the face.

His breathing increased, and he could feel the sweat break out on his forehead.

The two men were getting into a navy car. An Opel. The same car, he thought, that everybody and their granny would recognise. Standard-issue, unmarked Special Branch vehicle.

Fucking Special Branch.

Those fucking bastards, he thought as he drove through the security gate. They followed me here. I led the fuckers *here*!

That's why they didn't come to the door, he thought.

He drove hard, out of the estate, past the security gate, now wide open.

Fucking hell, he thought, accelerating hard into the afternoon traffic.

I'm bloody done for.

CHAPTER 22

In which the ladies take afternoon tea.

On that same Tuesday afternoon, Margaret glanced down at her watch on her way out of the Arts Block at UCD. Just gone three. Should be okay.

She recalled Sally Sheehan's message on her answering machine, delivered in Sally's professionally-chirpy telephone voice:

'Margaret, hi, this is Sally, it's been *far* too long, Declan and I have been thinking about you, wondering if you might be free to join me for afternoon tea at the Shelbourne at four on Tuesday next? Look forward to having a nice chat. Leave me a message if we're not in – byyyyyyye!'

Margaret phoned Sally back and left a message saying she'd be there, and that she, too, was looking forward to it.

Which was a lie.

Not in the mood for this, she thought. What am I going to say? Hate lying. Can't tell the truth. Hate this.

Still, she thought. Nice of Sally to make the effort . . .

It was another cold January afternoon – icy, suddenly very still, the air heavy with a dull, bone-chilling dampness. She walked across the green in front of the College restaurant, carrying her briefcase in one hand, struggling to button her coat with the other.

A bus rose ahead of her like a sea monster rising from the mist. She boarded and paid her fare. There were few passengers. She mounted the stairs to the upper deck, taking a seat near the front.

In a moment the bus pulled away from the stop and lurched into the afternoon traffic. From her vantage point at the top, Margaret looked out over the cold, damp streets, now wrapped in the early dusk of mid-winter. Huge, bare, craggy trees lined Morehampton Road, now black, shrunken shadows of their summer incarnations. Behind the trees, large red-brick houses, bastions of old money, stood poised like fortifications against the damp, asthmatic air. Above it all the sky was cloaked in the tired greys of winter, shot through with lurid pink emanating from the dying sun.

The bus struggled up Baggot Street and over the still brown waters of the canal. Margaret wondered if the day created her mood, or if in fact it just happened to match how she felt. She wanted to be alone, in the company of this dusk, this winter death, this Dublin. She felt drawn into the bleak cityscape, as if it were somehow a part of her, as if within herself there lay a primeval connection to her grey surroundings, to this city, to this deeply sodden island. She succumbed, on that stale-smelling bus, to a singular, unadulterated sensation: this afternoon, this dull day, this bleak, low light, this grey city, this being alone, this solitary mood.

She wanted it to last, this lonely self-indulgence, so high above it all.

Arriving in town earlier than expected, she alighted from the bus at St Stephen's Green and walked into the park. The tired dusk hung in the sky for a few final moments. As she walked through the manicured gardens, she revelled in the sunless death of this northern clime: the heavy, waxen greens of the hedgerows; the dark, steaming browns of flowerbeds, now as cold and lifeless as so many fresh graves. High above her, winter-fattened wood pigeons flapped in the bare branches. The ducks slept mid-pond, motionless. The songbirds were silent.

Ahead Margaret saw two girls who appeared to be in their late teens, their hair tied back in ponytails, pushing perambulators along the path. Cigarette smoke appeared like halos above their heads. They were inadequately dressed for the cold afternoon, wearing summer-time athletic gear, and no hats, no gloves, no scarves.

They walk with a certain pride, she thought. Young mothers, displaying the pride of those wounded in war.

As Margaret walked past the girls she glanced down into the prams, but plastic covers hid the babies from her view. The girls cast her a stony look, a mixture of boredom, mistrust, class hatred – and possibly, Margaret thought, triumph.

As evening seeped from the January sky, she left the Green, crossing at the traffic light. She was approaching the bronze lantern-bearers that flank the doorway of the Shelbourne, when she saw a familiar form walking on the pavement ahead.

Declan Sheehan, she thought. Must have dropped Sally at the Shelbourne. Gosh, he's dressed very casually for a Tuesday afternoon.

She stood before the entrance to the hotel. The Shelbourne, she thought. Can't remember the last time I was in the Shelbourne. Used to come here often, years ago, after shopping with Gran, when I was very young.

Typical of Sally, she thought. Wouldn't meet at Bewley's – not even the new Bewley's. Has to be afternoon tea at the Shelbourne. Spends her life spending money.

The concierge touched the brim of his hat as she entered the foyer.

'That's a cold afternoon, madam.'

'It is indeed,' she replied.

Inside, unbuttoning her coat, Margaret surveyed her surroundings. It was busy in the hotel, and she hesitated, a bit disoriented. Then she saw Sally, seated at a comfortable red settee towards the back of the tea room. Sally was just removing her scarf. Then she looked up, checked her hair in the mirror on the wall, and, finally spotting Margaret, waved.

The tea room, a throwback to the turn of the century, was filled to capacity. Margaret threaded her way between the low tables: tired tourists, confident business types, and several pairs of elegant, elderly women amidst their parcels.

Sally smiled reservedly as Margaret approached. She looks like a nervous bird, Margaret thought, in these relaxed surroundings. She was dressed older than her years, wearing a dainty little pink twinset and navy tailored trousers. Margaret realised once again how petite, how insubstantial Sally could appear outside of her home setting.

'Margaret!' she said, rising, extending her hand, kissing Margaret on the cheek.

'Hello, Sally.'

'I'm so pleased you could make it today.'

'Yes, it's so nice to see you. You were very good to phone me.'

'We've been trying to get you for ages, Margaret. We've phoned several times. I was delighted when I finally got your answering machine.'

'Yes, I'm sorry. It's been giving me such trouble.'

'Well,' Sally said, exhaling, 'shall we sit down? I've ordered tea. It's very busy here today. I'm sure the tea will be here shortly.'

Margaret draped her coat over the back of the settee and sat down next to Sally. They faced each other for those first few moments, hands in laps, knees almost touching on the low seat.

'Margaret,' Sally began, smiling sadly. 'Margaret, we're so sorry about all this.'

'I know. You're very kind.'

'What's happening, Margaret?'

Margaret tried to smile. 'It's all a bit of a mess, I'm afraid.'

An elderly waitress appeared, wheeling a trolley with a large pot of tea, delicate china cups, saucers and plates, a plate of scones, biscuits and cakes, milk, sugar, napkins. Margaret watched passively as the cups and plates were placed on the low table before them. The waitress poured the tea and withdrew.

'Mmm, how lovely,' Margaret said, removing a piece of fruit-cake from the plate. 'I haven't had fruitcake since Christmas.'

Sally sipped her tea, then set her cup down with a nervous clink.

'So, Margaret. Please tell me. How are you?'

'I'm fine, Sally. Really and truly.'

'But Margaret. Paul. You're apart. You've been alone now for how long? Is it two weeks? What's happening?'

Margaret picked up her tea, sat back in her seat, glanced over the room.

'I don't know, really,' she began. 'I mean, I don't know if I can explain what's really happening. I haven't spoken to Paul for so long. It seems such a long time. Sally, I don't actually know where he is.'

'He's all right, Margaret. We saw him. He came to us for dinner. He's been out with Declan. He's bearing up well.'

'Is he?'

'Yes, under the circumstances,' Sally said, a note of accusation in her voice. 'Margaret, why did you do it?'

'Do what?'

'You *know*. Send him away. Did something happen?'

'No, Sally, nothing happened. I, I wasn't well. I've been ill. I've been in hospital. I just needed to be alone. To get back on my feet.'

'Hospital?'

'It was nothing. I was so run-down.'

'But you asked him, told him to leave the house. Why, Margaret? What has he done? Margaret, love, is there another woman?'

'I don't know. There might be. Someone, I don't know. She leaves messages on his mobile phone.'

'Someone from work?'

'Seems to be. Not at work, but someone he met through work.'

'I'm sorry, Margaret. I didn't know.'

'No, Sally, look, I don't know if it's true. I'm probably making something out of nothing. It's just a suspicion. Maybe I'm lying to myself. Something, I don't know, to justify . . . You've seen him recently. Does he seem to you to be having an affair?'

'No, Margaret. Not at all. I think he's quite alone.'

Margaret paused, looked down at the table.

'So what *is* he doing? Is he going to leave me? Leave Ireland? What is he saying?'

'Margaret, calm down, he's all right. You're going to be all right.'

'Sally, is Paul talking about leaving Ireland?'

'I don't think so, Margaret.'

'Why? Why wouldn't he leave? Why does he want to stay?'

'I think he'd miss you too much.'

'Ah Sally, come on now. I want to know the truth.'

'Margaret, do you know what he's like?' Sally began. 'He's like a puppy. When I was a girl we had this puppy, and we had this tiny pen in the back garden where we locked him up at night, and I remember one Saturday we all had to leave early in the morning to go to a wedding or something down the country, and we forgot to let the dog out into the garden. And I remember worrying all day about him being locked up in that little pen, and thinking that he'd be terribly cross with us when we got home that night.

'But you know, Margaret, when we finally arrived home, that puppy was so happy to see us, and he wouldn't stop wagging his tail and following me around and licking my hand. And that was Paul the other night. He'll do anything for you, Margaret. Sure, you know that already.'

'Yes,' Margaret replied, 'I do know that. But you know, that's part of the problem.'

'Why? What do you mean?'

'Sally, I don't want a puppy. I wish he would just, I don't know. Take charge.'

'Take charge of what?'

'Everything. I feel like I'm always calling the shots, always making the decisions. I wish sometimes he would put his foot down and just tell me what to do.'

'But Margaret, that's the way Paul is. He's considerate. He wants to do what will make you happy. And these days, Margaret, you can't expect a man to dictate to you. It doesn't work that way any more. And deep down, you know that's not really what you want.'

'I know, Sally. Of course you're right. Maybe I'm just looking for an escape. Someone else to blame for everything. It just seems that he must resent me. This. Ireland. Everything. Sally, it's like this. I just want to have this inner space. Within me. To think. I need to think, Sally. I like to read, and to think. I don't care where I am. And I suppose I have other needs as well. And I'd like Paul to be with me. I really do like having Paul near me, Sally. But I can't seem to give him anything in return. I love Paul, but I can't think of a single thing that I give him in return for all he's done for me. And here I've set the agenda for our lives, dragged him all the way over to Ireland, and I just feel he must be feeling so resentful . . .'

'But Margaret, he doesn't feel that way in the least. He loves you. He loves it here. He doesn't need anything at all except to be with you.'

'But Sally, I dragged him over here so I could pursue my career – and that's a disaster, my work is going so poorly, I'm not getting published, and my parents are so tiresome, and the weather's been so dire, and I'm not making any money, and my studying is taking up so much of my time. And I can't be with Paul, knowing, knowing how badly it's all going, feeling like I owe him an apology for every little problem . . .'

Sally took a deep breath.

'Margaret, this is more serious than I thought.'

The two women sat, peering into one another's eyes.

'Margaret.'

'Yes, Sally?'

'Would we have a small brandy? You know, to warm us up?'

'Yes, Sally, I think that would go down extremely well about now.'

Sally hailed the waitress. A moment later two copper-coloured drinks arrived.

'Margaret, listen to me. I think you're making a serious mistake, and it's time you put your life back on course. You need to drop whatever it is you're doing and make contact with Paul, and arrange to see him, and talk. Tonight, Margaret. Please.'

'Right,' Margaret said, drinking slowly, then breathing deeply, as if to exhale all the foul air from her life. 'I know you're right. Okay. I'll phone Paul. I'll see if he wants to come and collect his damaged goods.'

She smiled an embarrassed smile. And then they embraced, awkwardly on their low settee, but warmly, a warm, open embrace.

'Sally, thanks for this.'

'You can thank me later, Margaret. When you're back together.'

Margaret settled back into her seat.

'You know, Sally, I do sometimes envy you your life.'

'Oh?'

'Being married to a good, solid Irish fellow. I mean, Paul is lovely. I can honestly say I've never felt for any man the way I feel for him. But I never know, you know, what he's thinking. If he's had enough. If he's longing for home.'

'You could ask him . . .'

'But Paul would never tell the truth. He's too good. He's too bloody good. That's the problem.'

'Okay,' said Sally, with resolve in her voice. 'So you need to set some ground rules.'

'Ground rules?'

'When you two get back together. No more politeness. No more half-truths. Honesty, Margaret. That's got to be rule number one.'

'Mmm. Maybe you're right,' said Margaret, glancing down

at the table. 'But I still think a simple Irish husband must be so much easier.'

'Ah Margaret, if you think it's all that simple, you've forgotten what Irishmen are like.'

'Oh? What do you mean?'

Sally smiled sadly.

'Now Sally, it's your go now. Tell us.'

'No really, it's nothing. Just lately. Declan just seems, I don't know. Distracted.'

'How do you mean?'

'He gets up very early in the morning. He dresses in a suit and tie every day, and then he leaves the house just as the kids are waking up. He phones me twice a day from the office, usually at eleven and then around three when the kids are home. He arrives for dinner around seven. He's usually tired. He does the dishes, helps me put the kids to bed, and then he reads a bit. I try to talk to him, tell him about my day. But lately, he just doesn't seem interested.'

'Is he working hard?'

'Yes, very. He's at meetings. Almost every time I phone him he's at a meeting.'

'And is his business going well?'

'I think so. He doesn't say, but I think it's going all right.'

'He's probably just tired, Sally.'

'Oh, I know. He does work hard. I felt so guilty the other day – I took one of his shirts from the wash basket, and well, I sniffed it, you know. For perfume.'

'And?'

'Nothing, of course. Just the usual man smells!'

They laughed. Sally looked down at her watch.

'Margaret, I must dash to collect the kids. This has been lovely . . .'

'Yes, Sally, it has.'

'And Margaret, you'll phone Paul?'

'I will, Sally. I promise.'

Margaret walked out into the cold, dark air, the streets now ablaze with the lights of heavy traffic. The dismal, quiet, reflective afternoon, she thought. So violently dissipated by the night, the rush, the evening exodus of city workers escaping to their homes, their partners, their families, their lives.

She didn't hurry with the crowd. She was feeling light-headed from the brandy that still warmed her blood, and softened her impressions, and simplified her life. She thought of Paul on this cold night, and she knew she would see him again soon, and that these cold, lonely nights would soon be over. And she thought of Sally, and how kind she had been to break through, to see her, to listen. And then she thought of Sally's husband Declan once again, as she had seen him, walking before her on the pavement outside the Shelbourne that afternoon, wearing his casual jacket, his jeans, his dark glasses.

That night, Margaret sat in the kitchen, alone, with the radio on, a choir singing softly, a series of long chords and continuities, so soothing on this winter's night.

Making plans.

And when the phone rang, she let it ring, and she let the

answering machine with its fresh batteries do its work, and she listened to Tony's voice, saying he needed to see her, with a rare note of pleading, a rare note of longing in that cool, steady voice. And she didn't pick up the phone, and decided to let him wait until she was in college tomorrow, when she wasn't too tired, when she was ready to take control, when she would see him, and make it plain that this nonsense had to stop, and begin to get her life back in order again.

Tomorrow.

CHAPTER 23

In which we peer into the manifold workings of a Wednesday night.

One tires of Dublin in January.

One tires of this darkness, this grey light. The sky that livens only to the dull glow of dusk. One tires of wet pavements, of ruined shoes, of the damp, leafless, mucky droop of dead winter gardens.

One tires of feeling one's skin burned by cutting, icy rain, and of bones deeply chilled and aching, and of the sensation that one's very breath is threatened by a rising bronchial rot.

One doesn't often read of these tiring things. In these days of Dublin's heady prosperity, it's so easy to gloss over the earthbound and ordinary. One may wish, indeed, on this dull Wednesday evening, from this high vantage point, looking out over these endless tracts of dull, semi-detached suburban houses – one may wish to escape it all, to pass by these bland exteriors, this uncomfortable climate, this boring, modern, pebble-dashed façade. So sodden and heavy, so mundane, so frankly unimaginative.

One longs for the South. Brightly coloured tiles. Succulence. Perhaps a return to Dublin in the summer, when the rock stars visit.

But perhaps, having got this far, we'll press on, tonight, on this ordinary January Wednesday night. We'll press on, and go in, to look into this cold, dark night, to uncover the warm plots and passions behind these dull surfaces, to gather together into one place events so tied together, yet so separated from one another, to expose the patterns that run so deep in the fabric of this city, even when soaked through with January's worst rains, and chilled with January's ceaseless breezes.

We'll press on, just like the inhabitants of this coldly contemporary city – or rather, like the valley dwellers who lived just north of here 4,000 years ago, the neolithic builders who pressed on through the winter, who placed rock on rock, sighing and complaining and tiring of it all through these bleak days, borne up only by knowledge deep within, by their inarticulate yearning for the warmth that would come, slowly, tentatively, and then fully, confidently, beautifully in the months, the not-too-distant months ahead.

Martin Walsh sat in his Range Rover parked before his house. 6:30. He stared through the streaming rain. It passed before him in sheets, yellowed by the streetlights, irregular, heavy and uninviting.

Truth be told, he was a bit jarred.

He had been to the Goat with his old mates, Richard and Johnnie. They had met for one and stayed for three. They had discussed Wales' performance last weekend, and Ireland's chances in the weekend to come. They had discussed the two legal tribunals currently under way: the tactics of the prosecution, the antics of the accused.

But mostly they had discussed their other mate, Peter, and Peter's property deal, and their respective readiness to hand over fifty thousand pounds to cash in on this rare opportunity.

Johnnie was flush. Had trebled his money in a year in software shares. Heard hard times were ahead for the company, sold out, cashed in. Feeling quite flush at the moment.

Richard was prepared to borrow the money. He didn't have the cash at hand, because he had a number of good things on, including a Northern Ireland deal that, if the Good Friday Agreement came through, would net him one per cent (gross) of up to sixteen million over three years. And for Christmas Richard had bought his bank manager a case of Bordeaux '92 from Grapes of Mirth, you know, that place in Rathmines, and so his bank manager had bloody well better come up with the readies when he needed them. And how long did Peter give us, anyway, wasn't it another three weeks?

Martin's third pint went down very easily and he brushed the matter of fifty thousand pounds aside with a reference to business being strong and cash flow not a problem and wasn't this a brilliant opportunity if only the property market holds, which it will, no question.

Then Martin returned to his car and drove towards home. The rain showed no sign of easing.

When he arrived, Martin threw open the door of the Range Rover, slammed it behind him, ran towards the house, remembered his briefcase, ran back to the car, fumbled for his keys to unlock the door, grabbed the briefcase, relocked the car and dashed up to the house. By the time he closed the hall door behind him he was soaked through.

'I'm home!' he shouted, without enthusiasm.

His daughter Ella came down the stairs, looked at him as if he were an insect, and squeezed past him to walk into the sitting room.

He hung his coat in the hall and went into the kitchen.

Deirdre was sitting at the kitchen table in a blue satin dressing gown, smoking a cigarette. Martin kissed her on the top of the head.

'Sorry I'm late, lads,' Martin said. 'Smells gorgeous. What's cooking?'

'Marks & Spencer's. It was ready half an hour ago. Where have you been?'

'Nowhere. Just down to the Goat with Richard and Johnnie. I phoned you. It was engaged.'

Deirdre ground her cigarette out in the ashtray, lit another with a red plastic lighter, and got up from the table.

'You're on your own, I'm afraid,' she said. 'I have to go to a do at work. We're launching the Fruit Pots tonight, and one of Boyzone will be in attendance, and Jimmy wanted everyone to be there looking beautiful. I'm supposed to be at Jury's for eight thirty.'

'Right,' Martin said, sighing, peering into the oven.

'My mother phoned,' Deirdre said in a tired voice. 'She said she saw you having lunch at Eden yesterday with a man and two women.'

'Yeah,' Martin said. 'It was the sales team.'

'She said the women were looking very glam.'

'When you're in sales, you have to look the part,' he replied.

He put on an orange oven glove, bent down, reached into the oven and retrieved his dinner. He placed the foil packet on the table and removed the cover. Then he walked back over to the fridge, took out a half-empty bottle of white wine, poured it into a large wine glass and returned to the table.

'So what else did your mother have to say for herself?'

'Nothing. Oh, she's flying to Majorca late on Sunday evening. I told her you'd drive her to the airport. So she's coming here for Sunday dinner.'

'Again? She was here last Sunday.'

Deirdre did not reply, breathing smoke out through her nostrils.

Then, 'Oh, I knew there was something else. Your Auntie Mamie phoned.'

'Oh? How did she sound?' he replied, drinking deeply from his wine glass.

'She was all chat. Went on and on about some pâté you gave her.'

At this news Martin coughed violently, spluttering his wine all over the table.

'Martin! Are you all right?'

'Yes, of course,' he said, gasping to catch his breath. 'So what did she *say*?'

'Sorry?'

'About the pâté! The *pâté*, for God's sake. Did she eat the stuff?'

'What pâté?'

'The pâté you just said she was talking about! What did she say about it?'

'Oh yes, the pâté. She *loved* it. She said she's been eating a bit of it every night. Said it was wonderful, never had anything like it. Martin, are you sure you're all right?'

'Yes, I'm grand, now what *else* did she say about it?'

'Right.' Deirdre assumed a reporter's monotone. 'She's finished the lot, wanted to know where you got it, said she'd never had such a perfect starter for a meal, that it was beautiful entirely, so full of flavour — I couldn't get her off the phone going on about this bloody pâté.'

Martin stared at her, wiping his mouth with his napkin, over and over.

'She told me to tell you you're marvellous, that the young American you've got living in the house with her is lovely, that she sends her love, that she'd love to see Ella again, and frankly, lovely woman though she is, by this time I was ready to throw the bloody phone into the washbasin.'

She ground the cigarette into an ashtray on the counter.

'Shit, I have to go or I'm going to be late. Don't let Ella spend the whole night on the phone with Jack.'

'Who's Jack?'

'I don't know, but he sounded a bit old for her the last time he phoned. I think she's trying to break it off. Could you get her to do a bit of study? Her mock exams start in three weeks. Right, I'm away.'

She floated out of the kitchen trailing smoke behind her, as Ella walked in.

'Where's she off to?' Ella said.

No reply.

'What are you eating? Looks disgusting.'

No reply.

'God, Dad, you're such a *zombie*.'

Paul was unusually tired on this Wednesday night.

He stood holding a mug of tea, wearing his decorating clothes, in the middle of the room, listening to the rain.

It had been a long day. Everyone was busily finalising their preparations for the MountAgro visit on Friday. Why top brass were coming to review a proposal for a multimedia training program, Paul could not imagine, but they were coming all the same. First there would be the presentation, and then the demo. There would be lunch. And according to Jack, a go-ahead would be given, on that day, for about half a million pounds' worth of software development.

As a consequence, poor old Jack was bouncing around the office like a wasp off a window. He was snapping at everyone, tearing down the slides for the presentation, rephrasing everything, giving out about the graphics. Paul ordinarily enjoyed cordial relations with Jack, and he had never seen him so peremptory and demanding.

Now, finally, it felt good to be here, alone, in this room, silent but for the rain beating its meaningless pattern on the black windows. The walls were bare, the skirting board sanded, the fireplace installed, the wooden floors ready to be varnished. There was a raw emptiness here now, such a calming space: unadorned, hollow, basic, and aged.

Paul finished his tea and set the mug down in the corner,

the ring of porcelain on wood magnified by the echoing walls.

He took a pencil from his pocket, walked to the far wall, and began to inspect the surface for imperfections.

The cracks were obvious, as were the nail holes. Old scrapes left a bit of a shadow, and gouges from the plaster knife, when he was removing the wallpaper, showed up like fresh wounds. With the pencil he drew a circle around all these flaws.

Then there were the less obvious imperfections. The dents, low down, from furniture, or ladders, or shoes. The pinholes, where a child's painting had been stuck to the wall. The evidence of old, hasty repairs, where a hole had been patched badly, leaving a bumpy, uneven surface, an imperfect mating between the old plaster and the new.

Paul found these with his sense of touch, running his hand over the wall, feeling the declivities. He marked them all with the pencil, his circles and swirls growing to a pattern, raising all these hidden imperfections into view, like a schoolboy's essay covered by a teacher's impatient markings.

He continued all around the room, working with care in the full knowledge that if he missed even the smallest of the dents, it would show up once painted, and disturb the smooth surface of the wall.

When he had finished, he rummaged through the pile of supplies at the end of the room, digging out a basin and box of patching plaster. He left the room, returning a moment later with the basin half-filled with water. He slowly poured the white powder into the bowl, stirring with an old pastry knife until it was smooth, creamy, and workable.

And then he started to patch.

He worked quickly, dipping the pastry knife into the plaster, scraping it gently across each declivity, leaving behind only enough plaster to smooth the surface. Hairline cracks were filled with a hairline of new plaster. The nail holes, once filled, bore up to close inspection. The new grey plaster was soon making patterns against the old pink surface – dots, spots, lines, crescents of cloudy white – as the walls became smooth, covered, complete once again.

He used the ladder to go around the edges of the ceiling, filling in the holes where the coving had been screwed in before it was torn down last week.

It was calming work, Paul thought, this progress, this renewal. Achieving this perfection, this humble, stretch of modest perfection in this quiet room. Leaving the world outside beating like frenzied souls against the window, as he worked this surface back to its original smooth texture.

The noise of delicate scraping. The soft grey patches. The glistening.

In two hours he had finished the walls. Tomorrow night, he planned, when everything had dried, he'd make one last pass over the room, patching any little dents before opening the paint and beginning the final recovery of these walls, these beautiful, smooth, calming walls.

The muse at the top of the fireplace smiled her wise, beatific smile.

Sally Sheehan was upstairs in the twins' large, airy bedroom. She sat on the edge of Harry's bed.

'Mummy,' Harry said. 'My finger is nearly better.'

'That's great, love. Do you think it needs one last kiss?'

'No, Mummy, I think it'll be okay.'

'Good night, Harry,' Sally said, kissing him on the forehead.

Then, as she did every night, she crossed the room to Hanna's bed and sat down.

'Now Hanna, what are you reading tonight?' Sally asked, looking through the pile of books on the bedside table.

'I'm going to read *Good Night, Moon* again,' she replied.

'Right, lovey, here you are.'

'Mummy?'

'Yes, pet?'

'Is Daddy okay?'

'Yes, I think he's okay. Why do you ask?'

'I dunno. He's a bit cranky.'

'He's just a bit tired, Hanna. He works very hard.'

'So do you, Mummy.'

'Yes I suppose I do,' Sally replied, sighing. 'Will I see you in the morning?'

'Yup.'

'Good night, lovey,' Sally said, bending forward to kiss her on the forehead.

Then she sat for a moment. Downstairs, she could hear Declan entering the sitting room from the kitchen. Dishes all washed up. Lovely. Then, through the silence, she could hear the sound of the CD cabinet being opened. Then closing. And, a moment later, the muffled tones of a jazz quartet rose through the floor.

She stood.

'Good night, you two.'

'Night, Mumsy-wumsy,' they replied, in unison.

As always.

Sally walked down the stairs and into the sitting room. Declan was sitting on the couch in a sweater and corduroy trousers. His eyes were closed as he listened to his jazz, his soothing, soulful jazz.

She sat down beside him, pulled off her shoes, and curled up against his shoulder.

'How are you, love?' she asked.

'Grand.'

'Dishes done?'

'Yeah.'

'What's playing?' she asked.

'Fred Hersch.'

'Gorgeous.'

'Mmm.'

'Like you,' she said.

No reply.

She ran her hand slowly up and down his arm.

'Just like you,' she said again.

But again, no reply.

Tony Dunne knew he was in trouble.

He was no longer afraid, as he had been yesterday. Yesterday, when he phoned Leo to ask him when he could pick up his gear, and Leo hesitated, and then said he'd come back to him, and rang off, Tony got scared.

Then last night when he went into the Glimmer Man and sat down next to Gerry and Gerry could hardly say a word to him, Tony got very, very scared. Because even though Gerry was a lousy prick, he always knew what was happening and he never stopped talking, even if half of it was shite, and if Gerry suddenly starts giving you the cold shoulder in the Glimmer Man, then you know something's up. It was the same as when everyone except Nicko knew that Nicko had fecked up when Gerry scarpered the pub the minute Nicko walked in. And two days later Nicko was on the boat for England, afraid for his life.

So Tony Dunne knew he was in it up to his neck.

And last night he'd had a rough old night of it. He sat at the bar trying to stop shaking and had a good few pints until Louise came over and she could tell he was in a bad way and he bought her a pint and he talked shite and really wanted to shag her to put himself out of this misery and he walked home with her and he tried to kiss her when they got to her flat and she pushed him off, laughing, and he nearly fell over and when he was alone again he was very jarred and very, very scared.

Today for most of the day his head was all over the shop and he couldn't focus, wondering when they'd come after him and thinking that since nothing had happened by midday maybe he was in the clear but realising that, when you bring the gardaí to their fucking hall door, especially when they had warned you to be careful and told you upfront that they didn't want any trouble from you, well then, you know they just needed a day or two to get organised and then they'd come looking for you, end of story.

So by the evening, when the rain had started again, his head was wrecked with all the gyrations he'd been through, between feeling raw fear and imagining vivid scenes of violence and the brief moments of forgetting and then that sweating rush when he remembered again that soon, very soon, they'd be there, facing him, no messing.

He thought about running. He knew Nicko was doing all right for himself in England but he didn't know where Nicko lived and he didn't think anyone would tell him now and he never liked England anyway or Nicko for that matter and besides, there was no guarantee they wouldn't come looking for you even if you went over there. And fuck them, anyway, he wasn't going to ruin his life for them. If they were determined to kill him then it was up to them to do it, he wasn't going to make their lives any easier by running away.

Pathetic cunts.

I just need a bit of time, he thought. I just need to lie low for a bit. I need somewhere to go. Somewhere to make a bit of a plan. Somewhere to hide out until I can stop this fucking shaking and get my head back to normal and plan how I'm going to get around these fuckers.

Just somewhere. Anywhere. Just somewhere, fuck this anyway, to clear my head.

At 8:30 on that Wednesday night, Margaret stood in her bedroom surrounded by shopping bags. She posed before the mirror, wearing a knee-length skirt of grey wool, and a black belt, and a black polo-neck jumper. And the boots – yes. The boots, the skirt, the jumper. The new bra. It all worked.

That afternoon she had walked home the other way, through Donnybrook, just for a change. Had noticed the sale signs in the boutique. Had called in, on a whim.

And the clothes fitted, fitted perfectly. For the first time in months, she was wearing clothes that fitted. A big step, she thought. Should have done this months ago.

I wonder, she thought. Is there time to get my hair done before Saturday?

The rain had worsened, was now quite heavy. Tony had to park some distance away out on Eglinton Road. And now he shivered as he pressed the doorbell to Margaret's house.

From the step he could hear Margaret running down the stairs.

'Tony,' she said, with surprise in her voice. 'God, you're soaked. Come in.'

He walked into the hall. She stood facing him, still wearing her new outfit.

'I got your call,' she said, hesitantly. 'I phoned you earlier today. I left a message.'

'I know. I got it.'

She looked at him, standing in the hallway. His short black hair, usually brushed straight back, was messed, untidy, dripping from the rain. His skin was blemished, he looked pale. He was shaking with cold.

Her impulse was to bring him right inside. To find out what was wrong, to comfort him in some way. But something in his demeanour made her cautious, held her back.

'I'm sorry to burst in on you like this,' he said. 'But I can't,

I can't seem to get the message through to you. I need some help. Could I, you know, sit down for a minute?'

'I'm sorry, Tony, I can't invite you in,' she said, glancing at her bare wrist. 'There's something on. Tonight. I'm on my way out the door. Is there anything I can do?'

'Anything you can do?' he said, smiling ironically. 'Is there anything Margaret Boyle, who won't let me into her nice little house, with her nice little Ranelagh address, can do?'

'Tony, I don't know what you've come here for. If you'd like, we can set a time to meet, some time when we can talk. But unfortunately right now is not good for me.'

'Look, missus,' Tony said angrily, 'I'm starting to get the picture. I'm getting the message that I'm just not your type of student. You're happy to help out that other lot, the ones with the posh accents and Daddy's bank accounts, but you're just not too keen on the guys who come from the wrong side o' the tracks.'

'Tony, I think that's a bit unfair . . .'

'Yes, it *is* a bit fucking unfair, isn't it? You can't be bothered with the likes of me. You just don't know what it's like. You stand there in your new clothes with the new price tags hanging off them, and you just want me to disappear so you can get on with your little Dublin six life.'

'Tony, there's no need to raise your voice.'

'I'll fucking raise my voice if I want to raise my voice. It seems to be the only way I can get you to fucking listen to me.'

Margaret breathed deeply.

'Tony, I want you to leave now.'

'I'm going fucking nowhere until you explain to me why you're treating me like shite, after all I've done for you, you lousy . . .'

He stepped towards her.

'Tony! Stop this!'

Her hand went up, for the button, the panic button on the wall, the button attached to the house alarm. Tony saw her arm move, saw the alarm and stopped, his face suddenly white with anger.

'Oh I see,' he said, with raw menace in his voice. 'You're going to raise the alarm on me, are you? Like I'm some kind of rapist on your doorstep? Think I can't control myself? What a laugh! I can control myself all right. And this husband of yours – wherever he is – looks like he's keeping his hands well off you as well . . .'

'Tony, I'm asking you for the last time. Please leave this house. Now.'

'Right, Ms Boyle,' he said, bitter irony returning to his expression. 'I hear you. I'll be off then. You can go back upstairs, try on some more new clothes. But I'm telling you, love, you don't know what you're missing.'

And with that he turned and left, slamming the door hard behind him. She could hear him kicking the railings, barking an obscene curse at her from outside the door.

Margaret stood for a moment, shaking. She waited until she could hear the sound of his footsteps fade as he walked away. Her breathing came in spasms. Her eyes filled with tears.

Right, she thought. What to do?

Call the guards. Okay. What will I say to them? A student

was here. He was angry. He seemed a bit unhinged. He's
gone now.

So what? So fucking what?

And then she covered her face with her hands, leaned back
against the wall, and let her tears flow.

It was a strange sound, like nothing the residents of Eglinton
Road had ever heard before.

A sort of hollow popping sound. Pop pop pop.

Mrs O'Donovan heard it and was quite puzzled by it, but
she was glad because she looked up at the clock and it was
just 9:00 on Wednesday, still time to enjoy the day before
going to bed, still time to recall the night before, when Mr
O'Donovan had displayed a passion so unexpected, so rare for
a wet Tuesday night, so unusual for him lately, so overworked
he's been, and so tired in the evening, and wasn't it a comfort
to know they still had it, the love they had shared for so
many years, and hadn't he left her feeling lovely and warm
and pleasantly tired, and hadn't she thought about it all day,
with that glow, a glow of love and a happy life?

Across the road, Sally Jennings, awkward and tall, had her
studying interrupted, lifted her head from her book, was
snapped back to the present by the startling noise, and she
looked with terror out of her window into the black sky and
saw nothing, but then cursed the noise and cursed the day,
feeling rise from within her stomach all the humiliations, all
the torment of those girls at school, those spiteful vixens
who every day, every single day took every opportunity to
snub her, to taunt her, to create torture out of her every

waking moment, to make her over and over again wish for a new life, with such intense and painful longing for escape, for a sweet, beautiful, young, peaceful death, anything to escape this endless taunting.

Up the road in number seventeen, young Danny Givens heard it from beneath his cowboy duvet, and felt confused, and rolled over, and wondered where it was, and why it happened, and what did it, and then he rolled over and wondered if it might— and then no, and then nothing as he fell back into his easy, warm, seven-year-old sleep.

Even as far as the end of the road the sound could be heard as Erica Williams yawned and reached down to turn on the taps for her bath, getting ready for bed so early, in order to get up early tomorrow to get into work in time to complete the proposal and bind it and send it for delivery before the deadline at 12:00, when life at the office would finally return to normal, though she had noticed that, for the past two years, it was no longer normal at the office, *ever*, only a continuing barrage of new and complex opportunities, more work, tighter deadlines, too few staff, less sleep, more worries, more grey hairs as the steam from the bath slowly clouded the blue-tiled bathroom.

And Donal O'Grady heard it too, sitting before the telly, as usual, as he would do from now until late into the night, with no reason to get out of bed the next morning, since his retirement before Christmas six weeks ago, not wanting to fall asleep too early, not wanting to wake too early to face a long day opening out before him, wondering how this deep sense of anxiety and unhappiness could possibly be settling in upon him after so many years, so many years spent yearning, dreaming of this time when he would finally escape the back office of that dusty, depressing bakery, yearning for this retirement, for so many years, so anxious.

But Margaret Boyle, undressing in her bedroom at the end of Eglinton Terrace, her thoughts so filled with the events of the evening, did not hear it, was oblivious to this sound from the neighbouring street, was hanging her new clothes in the wardrobe and stepping into bed, early, wanting to get warm, to drink her glass of wine and read that novel again, that Jilly Cooper novel to take her mind off what had happened, to get a good night's sleep and to start tomorrow fresh, and strong, if only she could, if only she could.

So many heard it, though, on Eglinton Road, such an unusual sound on this dark wet night, a dull, hollow *pop-pop-pop* sound right outside their windows, and none of them knew the meaning of the sound, or of the car door slamming and the engine revving and the peep-squeak of the tyres as the car raced away, but if they had leapt from their chairs and dashed down the hallway and flung open the front door at that moment they would all have seen, through the darkness and the heavy rain, by the eerie yellow light cast by the streetlamps in front of their houses, the body, Tony Dunne's body, on the ground beside his Volkswagen, with blood beginning to seep from beneath his torso, from beneath his head, another dreadful Dublin murder, so many dead lately, and this so close to home, dreadful business entirely, so close to home.

CHAPTER 24

In which Dee and Margaret are shocked.

Thursday morning at Spyral Multimedia.

'Jesus, Paul. Where's Dee? It's almost half ten. Jack is like a bear out there!'

Felicity bent over Paul's desk with fear in her eyes.

'I don't know where he is, Felicity. He's often a bit late. Why? What's the problem?'

'It's the demo, Paul. The *MountAgro* demo. We were looking at it just now and suddenly the colours went all wonky. All the reds have turned to blue. The programmer says the file has become corrupted, we need to use a backup file. And only Dee seems to have access to it. Jack is going to explode!'

Paul looked back at his monitor. 'We've been through the demo a hundred times. I'm sure Dee will be in soon. We'll just have to wait till he gets here.'

'And what about Ruth?' Felicity asked.

'What about her?'

'She's in such a state. She's hardly speaking to anyone. We're relying on her to explain the demo, you know, the *concepts*. But she's so cross. She's refusing to rehearse until we set the colours right!'

'Don't worry, Felicity. It's just nerves. Ruth is a great performer. She'll be fine.'

'Paul, it's worse than you think. MountAgro are coming in here *tomorrow*! At this rate we won't make it past the starting line. And everyone is at each other's throats. I don't know if I can take another hour of this.'

'Right,' Paul said, sighing. He took one more look at his monitor, then stood. 'Maybe I'd better introduce my usual calming influence to the situation . . .'

At that point the door at the end of the office opened and Dee walked in, dressed in a wet leather coat. He closed the door behind him carefully, then peered around the office with a puzzled expression. He walked to his desk with exaggerated care, taking each step slowly and deliberately, placing one foot in front of the other like a tightrope walker.

Paul and Felicity watched him cross the office.

'Dee,' Felicity said slowly. 'Are you okay? Where *were* you this morning? I thought Jack was going to send the guards for you. You're looking a bit wrecked.'

'No, I'm grand. Well, actually, I've been better. If you know what I mean.'

'You're very pale, Dee,' Paul said. 'Are you okay? Would you like a cup of coffee?'

'Yeah, thanks, a coffee would be brilliant, actually. Really brilliant.'

'Dee, look, you're shaking,' Paul said. 'Sit down. What is it?'

'Ah, fuck it, Paul – why are we doing this?' Dee said, collapsing into his chair.

'Doing what?' Felicity asked. 'What do you mean?'

'All this shite, you know?' Dee said slowly, waving his arm to indicate the office.

Just then Ruth appeared.

'Hello, traitor. Where've you been?'

'Ruth,' Felicity said. 'Something has happened. Dee's not well.'

'Not well?' Ruth said, approaching his desk. 'You look fine to me. What's the matter?'

The three stood around Dee, waiting as he sipped his coffee.

'I'll tell you what's the bloody matter,' Dee said. 'Those fucking cunts murdered my nephew. Fucking Tony. Dead as a post. That's what's the fucking matter.'

'Oh God,' Ruth said. 'Dee, I'm so sorry.'

Ruth knelt beside him.

'They fucking shot him,' Dee continued. 'In the back of the head, the bastards. And by the looks of things, they'll bloody well get away with it. Fucking gardaí were more interested in doing Tony for drugs than finding the fuckers who murdered him.'

'Drugs?' Felicity asked.

'Yeah, drugs, right?' Dee said defensively. 'He did a bit of dealing. Nothing serious. Recreational gear. Good stuff, always. Very good stuff in fact.'

'When did he die?' Paul said.

'Last night. Gunned him down on the fucking road. They phoned me. I was in bed. I had to go down there, to see the body. Bloody awful.'

Dee paused for a moment, studying the floor. Then he continued.

'It's the greed that really gets me, you know what I mean? They shot Tony because they wanted him out of their turf. They wanted to make a bit more dosh. A few extra lousy quid. And nobody gives a fuck about Tony because he's gone now, and we can all get on with the rest of our greedy pathetic little lives. It's everywhere. It's sickening. We've lost everything that used to be important in this country.'

'Dee, I think you need to get out of here for a bit, to clear your head,' Paul said. 'I can ring Reception for a taxi . . .'

'No, look, it's *all* of us,' Dee said, with sudden animation in his features. 'We don't care any more. We used to care here. We used to be a decent fucking country. But we just don't fucking care in this society any more.'

'Dee, you're very upset,' Ruth said, putting her hand on his shoulder. 'Maybe you should take the rest of the day off? I can run you home.'

'I'm sorry,' he said. 'It's just, I can't seem to see any sense in it any more.'

'Things will be a bit clearer tomorrow,' Ruth said.

'Yeah, fucking tomorrow,' Dee said bitterly. 'You and I and all of us will be here tomorrow, and we'll have to deal with these cunts from Mount Fucking Agro. And life will go on, won't it? Just the same, the same greed, the same fuckers allowed to get away with whatever they like.'

He paused for a moment.

'Right,' he said. 'Okay. I will. I'll be here. I'll be grand tomorrow.'

'I know, Dee,' Ruth said. 'You've had a terrible shock. Come on. Just let me get my coat.'

'Yeah. Right. Yeah. Lads, I'll see you tomorrow. Yeah. Thanks.'

'Brilliant – this is just brilliant,' Jack said angrily from behind his desk. 'Biggest contract to come along in four years and our chief designer gets locked and pisses off the day before the presentation.'

'He'll be okay, Jack,' Paul said. 'I'll call him later this evening to see how he's doing.'

'But the demo . . .'

'Jack, the demo is going to be fine. I got the backup files running. It looks great. The guys are doing the final coding now, there's time to retest it this afternoon. The presentation has been ready for three days, and we'll rehearse it again after lunch. I think we're as prepared as we can possibly be.'

'Right. I hope you're right.'

'If we don't get this contract, Jack, it won't be because of lack of preparation, or the quality of the demonstration. We gave them the figures last week, and they've decided to show up tomorrow, so money doesn't seem to be a problem. I don't want to be over-confident, Jack, but I think we're onto a winner here. By tomorrow this time I'm intending to be celebrating our big win.'

Jack shook his head. But then he smiled for the first time in two weeks.

'Right, Paul. Sounds good all right. But don't forget those slips, Paul. 'Twixt cup and lip. Anything can happen.'

'I know Jack. I know it all very well.'

'And Paul?' Jack said.

'Yes, Jack?'

'You know Felicity.'

'Yes, Jack?'

'Could you, well, keep an eye on her?'

'Felicity? Sure, Jack.'

'She doesn't handle pressure well, you know. Never has.'

'Right,' Paul said.

'If you could just keep an eye, if you know what I mean. Wouldn't want her getting too caught up in all this.'

'Right. No problem. I'll make sure she's okay . . .'

University College Dublin, 3:15 on that same Thursday afternoon.

Margaret glanced down at her watch. A departmental meeting scheduled for half three. She couldn't concentrate. She closed her book, looked out of the window at the grey afternoon.

So bleak, she said to herself. Such a dreadful day. Even the students seem washed-out today.

She looked across the familiar scene: the sea in the distance, the suburbs, the lake, the students milling about in the cold air, smoking, chatting.

It feels like a conspiracy, she thought. Some dreadful news that I've missed, that no one is going to tell me. All these small groups, all this whispered conversation.

Maybe it's just me, she thought. So tired, after last night, after Tony. So late. I don't remember falling asleep. Why did he threaten me? What have I done?

What will I do, she thought, if I meet him? What will we say? I wanted this to be over, I didn't want to have to speak to him again. I need, I need to close this chapter. I need something to get normal again.

God, I miss Paul. I really, finally miss Paul.

She reached for her diary, checked the time of the meeting once again, began clearing her desk. Just then a quiet knock.

Oh God, she thought. It couldn't be . . .

'Yes?' she said.

Professor Garland opened her door very quietly, stood in the doorway. A ghostly figure. Unhealthy, pale skin. Snowy hair. Clearly distressed.

'I am so sorry for this interruption, Margaret. But I've just had some disturbing news,' he said. 'May I come in?'

'Of course, Professor,' Margaret said, feeling a sense of relief. 'Come in, sit down.'

The professor sat. 'Margaret, I've just been on the phone. With the Garda Síochána. It appears that a student, one of your students, died, was murdered, last night. Murdered on the street.'

Margaret would remember the next events as if filmed in slow motion. Professor Garland looking at her, the rush of blood surging towards her cheeks, the sound as she inhaled slowly, her mother's voice coming to her, prompting her: in the face of startling news, be still, do not react, breathe, say nothing until you've had a moment to breathe . . .

'Tony Dunne,' Professor Garland continued. 'He was in your group. Fridays. Did you know him, Margaret?'

'Yes, I did, I knew him,' she said, her voice on the edge of control. 'Friday mornings. Ten o'clock.'

And then she looked into Professor Garland's face as he looked at her, so concerned, his concerned expression feeling like blades cutting through her skin.

'I am sorry, Margaret,' Professor Garland replied. 'Did you know him well?'

'I did, yes, I knew him. He came to the tutorials. Most of them.'

Breathe in. Breathe out.

'The gardaí will be conducting an investigation,' Professor Garland continued. 'A full investigation. I had to give them your name as Tony's tutor, you know, to help out, with their enquiries. I told them I would speak with you. I told them I would determine if you had any information that might reveal why, why this dreadful event . . .'

'Yes, Professor, I understand,' she replied. 'But I'm sure I know nothing, nothing that would be of value.'

'No, I thought not,' Professor Garland replied. 'But I told them that I would ask, you know, the staff, if they might have any information. And of course, if something does spring to mind, you would of course make contact with them directly?'

'Of course,' Margaret replied. 'If I can think of anything at all.'

'So sorry, Margaret,' he said, awkwardly. 'So very sorry.' Their eyes met once, and then he stood, suddenly seeming so tall, and, for the briefest moment, such a judgmental figure.

'On a more mundane matter, then,' he said. 'I believe I have called some sort of meeting?'

'Yes, Professor,' Margaret replied, looking at her watch. 'It should be starting now. In the staff room.'

'Thank you, Margaret,' he said, retreating from the room. 'Such bad business. So sorry, for this intrusion.'

That same evening, 8:30, Sandford Road.

Mamie sat in her armchair, reading the newspaper, before a dwindling coal fire. She heard the front door open and close again. She knew it was Paul by the rhythm of the action: the slow turning of the key in the lock, the gentle rasp of the windguard over the door saddle, the same rasp as the door was pushed to, the pause, the final click as the lock struck home.

She put her paper to one side.

'Paul?' she called.

'Yes, Mamie . . .'

He knocked quietly at her door, then peeped his head in. 'How are you?' he asked.

'Sure I'm grand. I'm exhausted. I was out all day. I had a meeting to organise – that charity concert, you know. And how those ladies can talk! And you?'

'I'm fine. Tomorrow is the big day at the office. The American company are coming in to see our presentation.'

'And are you prepared?'

'Yes, I think we are.'

'You look tired, Paul.'

'Yes, I am a bit tired. I don't think I'll do any decorating tonight. Want to make sure I'm fresh for the morning. We need to win this business.'

'Paul?'

'Yes?'

'Paul, I wouldn't get my hopes up too high. About tomorrow.'

'And why's that, Mamie?'

'Something in me says your meeting won't go as you've planned.'

'Oh?'

'Because, Paul, from everything you've told me about it . . .'

'Yes?'

'Your hearts, Paul. They're just not in it.'

'But we need this pretty badly . . .'

'But needs and wants, Paul. Two different things.'

'I see what you're saying.'

'Good night, then, Paul. Get a good night's sleep.'

'Good night, Mamie.'

CHAPTER 25

In which aspirations contend with righteousness.

Friday morning, 11:30, at the offices of Spyral Multimedia.

Felicity walked quietly into the boardroom. This room which, all morning, had been filled with animated discussion was now empty and silent, painfully silent, like a child shrinking from an angry parent.

It felt like a scene of punishment.

The remains of the meeting that had taken place that morning were still on the table. The good china cups with blue and gilt rims sat in their several saucers, each holding the cold dregs of milky tea or brown coffee. Paul's cup was still full. Felicity's cup was red with lipstick. Biscuit crumbs on three saucers only: Jack's, and the two Americans' from MountAgro.

Jack was right, Felicity mused, as she began to gather the cups together. Americans eat at meetings, the Irish do not. Jack had offered the biscuits around at the start, after the initial hellos, when everyone was a bit tense with anticipation. He offered biscuits again after the demo was finished, when both sides had loosened up, and it all appeared to be going so well. And both times the men from MountAgro took one chocolate biscuit each. And Jack took a Mikado on both occasions, to keep them company.

But no one else ate. Twelve biscuits left over. Limp, stale and rejected.

It had started so well! she thought. Jack at his most effusive and charming when they arrived. Then the formal business: Ruth talking them through the concepts, so clear, so confident and convincing – skinny little Ruth, so strong before these American executives! And then Dee, with his earring and his white shirt, going through the demo, no-nonsense, no signs of his recent troubles: their eyes lighting up, the smiles on their faces glowing, actually glowing as the images flashed across the screen – the fruit, the wheat, the healthy mothers and babies.

Then Paul with his project plan, step-by-step, as if we did this sort of thing every day, just another project to add to the list, no bother at all . . .

So proud of them, Felicity thought. This tiny Irish company, and all of us looking so well, so impressive. They loved us! They were about to sign!

Until, she remembered, Ruth. Her question. Out of the blue.

Felicity shivered as she arranged the cups on the tray, squeezing them over to one side.

Don't know where Ruth picked this stuff up, Felicity thought. About MountAgro. About the protests in India. The small farmers, displaced from their land. And the research, in America: the crops being contaminated with genetically modified seed. And here at home, the MountAgro farm in Kildare – where did Ruth learn all this? How did she know what they were doing on that farm? How did she know it was all illegal?

The looks on their faces.

Oh, they were cool all right, at least at first. Well used to this sort of thing. Ready to brush it all off.

But the more Ruth went on, and then Dee chiming in about the educational content of the program, and Jack trying to break in, and the colour starting to ooze from their faces . . .

The tray shook as she walked from the boardroom to the kitchen.

He nearly pulled it off, Felicity thought, as she filled the kitchen sink with water. Jack nearly pulled the meeting back to the centre. Ruth was willing to back off, to listen to their side, to come with them to visit their offices and hear their views. And it looked like the meeting, and the project, could be saved.

Until Paul reminded them of their promise, and then insisted on it: editorial control. Of the entire project. Paul, being a botanist. Knowing his stuff. And they refused. And Dee flaring up, and the whole room now so tense, such accusations!

Felicity remembered the silence, as the meeting concluded and they packed their cases and walked out of the boardroom. For ever.

Jack would never, ever forgive them, for what they did today.

Felicity washed a cup, the same cup, over and over. Her tears began to fall into the water as she recalled his face, Jack's face. His anger, his sheer rage, when he returned to the room, shouting, throwing his notes across the room, then stamping out of the room, out of the office.

This was it, she thought. Her job was gone. Security, her future, all washed away during one short meeting. She began to cry harder, leaning on the sink, unable to focus with worry.

She didn't hear Dee and Ruth entering the kitchen behind her. Dee touched her shoulder, and she turned, crying, to embrace him, falling against him with her tears. Then Ruth joined them, the three of them hugging one another, the tears swelling in their eyes as they held on tight and cried, harder and harder, together.

A moment later, Paul appeared at the kitchen door. He leaned on the door frame, folded his arms. They turned to him, Ruth and Dee and Felicity, each with wet, red cheeks, looking like children.

Paul stood for a moment, facing his three colleagues, expressionless.

'If you could see yourselves,' he said. And then he smiled.

And a moment later, grins, and then laughter, a rush of laughter in their desperation, at their predicament, feeling such a bond, such a strong bond, their arms around one another as they laughed in sheer relief.

Paul returned to his desk. The others, exhausted from the meeting, from the tension, had gone to the pub for lunch. Paul said he would join them later. He sat down, stared at the papers before him: notes, slides, the proposal, all the preparations he had made for the meeting. The big meeting. The one that had come, and had gone, and had left a blank where his future used to be.

He tidied the papers into a pile, put them into a file

folder, stood to put the folder into the cabinet beside his desk.

He sat down again, suddenly breathless.

Don't think, he thought. Just act. Just tidy up. Don't think about unemployment, and rent, and Margaret. Just clear your desk, just get out of here, just get over to the pub before you panic at this gap, this huge yawning hole that has opened up before you . . .

And then the phone rang.

'Hello, Paul Boyle.'

'Hello, Paul?'

'Yes. Elaine?'

'Got it in one.'

'Gosh,' Paul said.

'How expressive you Americans are.'

'Elaine, sorry, I wasn't expecting . . .'

'Of course you weren't. We Northerners rely on surprise. Now before you even ask me how I am – that is, if you really want to know – I'm at a bit of a loose end. I need to talk to you, because I've messed up rather badly, and you might be able to help me out.'

'Are you in town?'

'Yes. In bloody Glasnevin. I've just had a meeting cancelled, and I'm about to drive home, but I thought if there's any chance I might see you for a wee chat . . .'

'Elaine, I . . .'

'Now look, Paul, no seductions this time. This is business, real business. Could you free yourself up to see me this afternoon?'

'Yes,' he replied. 'As a matter of fact, I just happen to be free . . .'

Ten minutes later, his heart pounding, Paul headed out of the door and into the car park.

CHAPTER 26

In which the sun shines upon Paul and Elaine.

By 1:00 on that Friday afternoon in late January, the storm had passed. The clouds had cleared, the sun shone down, and for one brief hour Dublin emerged, refreshed, from its long hibernation.

In the city they poured into the bright streets with a feeling of release and freedom. Like prisoners emerging from dark cells, men and women in heavy winter clothes entered the sunshine that streamed into St Stephen's Green and Merrion Square and Grafton Street. They opened their winter coats, their eyes watering, dazed by this shining, this bursting forth, their garments flapping carelessly in the breeze. Well-dressed women from insurance offices, groups of young men from solicitors' firms stopped on the pavements, eased back their heads, let their hair fall back over their collars to expose their faces, their throats to the sun, feeling the warmth slowly open their pores and seep into their pale skin, so long sheltered from the outside air, covered, muffled, stifled beneath the woollens of a long and sunless winter.

As this emergence was taking place, as Dublin was awakening to this rare warmth, Paul Boyle drove into town. His driving seemed out of step with the new feeling in the air.

He felt nothing, thought nothing as he sped from traffic light to traffic light, through Goatstown and Clonskeagh and Ranelagh. As he drove he tried to forget the new, simple facts of his life: he had no wife, he had no job. He drove, uncaring, at speeds that shook his ageing Vauxhall, passing slower cars, speeding up George's Street, skirting round Trinity, his mind filled with vague, empty clouds: no wife, no job, no identity.

The sun, still low in the sky, shot brilliant rays between the buildings, through the trees, lighting up winter's heavy greens, creating a blinding sheen on the road before him as he drove north and entered busy Drumcondra, slowing for buses, slowing for old women walking across the road. Finally he pulled off the road and parked before the gates of the Botanic Gardens.

As he stepped out of the car he felt as if he were waking, suddenly aware of his quickened pulse, his accelerated breathing. He caught his breath, told himself to ease off, to relax, to forget what had happened, and to take what was about to happen easily, relaxed, with confidence.

God almighty, he breathed to himself.

Brilliant sunshine lit up the entrance to the gardens. As he walked along the path, the graceful frames of the greenhouses loomed before him, their steamy curvilinear windows gleaming in the sunshine.

A group of Japanese tourists moved through the gardens, quietly, comfortably. Such respect for their surroundings, Paul thought.

Then, Paul spotted Elaine on a bench, watching him approach, a sandwich on her lap, chewing, smiling ironically.

Paul stood before her, tried to return her smile.

'I'm just finishing my lunch,' she said in her clipped, Belfast accent. 'I was starving. I've been stuck in desperately boring meetings all morning. I couldn't face the conference buffet. And there's a bloody pompous dinner to attend tonight. Have you eaten? Would you like a bite?'

'No,' Paul replied. 'I'm okay. I'm not hungry. It's so nice to see you.'

Elaine smiled. 'Right. Here we are then.'

She stood, brushing crumbs from her lap.

'Such a fantastic day. Shall we take a wee stroll?'

Paul nodded his head in agreement. Moments later they were walking down the damp garden paths. They walked in the shadows of massive, silent trees, with wet bark and bare branches that glistened in the bright sun. At their feet the vibrant greens of ferns and mosses covered the lush soil.

And the birds were here, as if awakened by the sun: single, warbling wrens and robins. Peeping gangs of long-tailed tits. Fearless greenfinches flitted from tree to tree, noisy sparrows landed in the shrubbery. High above, in the ancient oaks and birches, tree creepers criss-crossed the broad trunks as if tickling the skins of mythical beasts.

At first Paul and Elaine spoke little, awed by this rich old garden. Elaine walked ahead on the path, her wool coat open, her pace steady. Paul felt empty of words, empty of memory as he watched Elaine, watched her shape beneath her coat as she walked, stepped over a branch on the path, or bent back to look up into the trees, into the sunny sky.

But before long Paul knew that it was gone from her, that feeling that they had once shared. She hadn't come here to play, to banter, to continue their brief flirtation. Here in this winter garden Elaine was distant, self-protective. Paul felt, even as they walked in silence, that Elaine had moved on, recovered herself from what she had been with him, changed the rules.

Grown up.

They stopped on a stone bridge to gaze down into a stream. Shadowy trout darted, then disappeared, then darted again, casting flashes of cream and silver.

'Paul,' Elaine said. 'Paul, I think we should talk about what happened last week.'

'Yes,' Paul replied hesitantly, 'I suppose we should.'

'I don't want you to take this the wrong way, Paul. I don't regret for a minute what happened.'

'No, I hope you don't,' Paul said. 'I certainly don't.'

'You were lovely to me, Paul. And I appreciate what you did for me.'

He forced a smile.

'But Paul, I think we both have some sorting out to do. Last week – God, for the past six months – I feel like I've been running away. I can't keep running away, you know. From her. From Jenny. Not by pursuing one-night stands. And as for you: look. I don't know anything about you and your wife, Paul. But I'm thinking you might try to work it out between yourselves.'

'Yes,' Paul replied. 'I know that.'

'Because, Paul, no matter how bad things might be, or

however bad she might be, she doesn't deserve to lose a fellow as lovely as you are.'

Paul stared into the water.

'Look, Paul,' she said, turning towards him. 'Don't go all morose on me. We have to be realistic. Last week we were both on a bit of a downward slope, don't you see? It's time to move on. For both of us. Recover our balance, Paul. Set things right.'

Paul looked into her eyes, sensed her earnestness.

'Because, Paul, I need a favour from you. And I can't go asking for favours if it means that we can't, well, cooperate, you know? But before I go on, I need to know if this is going to be too difficult. For you, Paul.'

Paul looked into her face again. And suddenly the mystery was gone. And she stood before him, now, as she had been all along: a bright girl, a bit flirtatious, full of energy – but nothing, nothing more.

'Okay, Elaine. Let's give it a shot.'

Elaine extended her gloved hand. 'Can I have your word on this one?'

He took her hand, there on that bridge, with the stream rushing beneath and the tall, protective trees for witnesses. He shook her hand, self-consciously, and smiled a brief smile.

'Right,' Elaine began. 'Now that's settled.'

She turned from him, continued to walk at a brisk pace. He caught up with her as the path widened.

'I know this is an inopportune moment to talk business, Paul. But I don't have much time. You're still working with Spyral, aren't you?'

'Yes. Well, sort of.'

'I checked your website. It says you do educational materials.'

'Yeah, that's us.'

'Multimedia and all that carry-on, right?'

'Yes, we do. I must say, Elaine, this is a helluva spot for an interview.'

'Never mind that, Paul. I'm in a fix. I'm on this committee. We're looking for educational projects. About the environment. And so far we're making an almighty bags of it. We advertised for proposals last month in the *European Journal*, just before Christmas. We left it wide open – anything at all, as long as it was educational and had something to do with the environment. The problem is, because the advert came out over the Christmas break, we've had very few responses. And most of the proposals we've received are rubbish.'

'Oh?'

'Absolute crap. And the deadline is next week. Tuesday, in fact. And frankly, Paul, if I don't have any decent proposals to work from, I'm going to appear, shall we say, *less than productive,* before my superiors.'

'Okay. So how can I help?'

'Could you get some sort of a proposal into my office? Something educational. It has to be on some environmental issue, and it has to be bloody relevant to people north and south of the border.'

Paul's mind began to race.

'Elaine, is this some sort of a joke?'

'Paul, do I look like I'm joking? My head's on the block here.'

'Okay. How about genetics and the environment. You know, genetically modified crops. Disease control. That sort of thing.'

Elaine thought for a moment.

'It can't be too technical now. It has to be suitable for schools.'

'No problem.'

'And it has to be good. And it has to have something Irish in it. And it has to be in to me on Tuesday.'

'I think we can throw something together.'

'Right, Paul, can you do that for me please? I just happen to have the tender documents here with me . . .'

She drew a large envelope from her bag, pulled out a sheaf of papers.

'For God's sake follow the format, to the letter, or we won't read it. If you submit anything decent at all you'll have a good chance of winning. And you'll have our decision within a few weeks.'

They found themselves back at the entrance to the car park.

'Look, Paul, I'm sorry for dragging you all the way out of town for this. But I'm in a real fix, and I thought you might be interested in the opportunity . . .'

'Yes, Elaine, yes,' Paul stammered. 'I'll have a proposal into you by Tuesday. Look, thanks.'

'Right,' Elaine said as she walked briskly away from Paul towards the gates. 'Let's talk Monday.'

And then she stopped, standing beneath the arch. She turned around, walked back towards Paul, and stood before him.

'Now Paul,' she said, the sound of traffic suddenly infringing on their conversation. 'I can't leave you here looking like a hurt puppy. You're going to be all right. Phone Margaret. Get yourselves sorted out. It's for the best.'

Then she reached up with her gloved hand, stroked his cheek, and kissed him. And then she turned and walked briskly away.

Paul walked slowly out of the gardens with the envelope in his hand. He could feel his heart beating. When he reached the car, he rested his elbows on the roof, ripped open the envelope, scanned through the document.

It was perfect. It was exactly what they had wanted to do for MountAgro. It was objective, educational, high-quality, high budget. Jack would be over the moon – must phone him.

Right, he thought. Phone Jack. Get into the car and phone Jack, before he shoots himself.

But before Paul could unlock the door, he felt a sudden heaviness in his limbs.

Come on, buddy. Get into the car and phone Jack.

And then everything became a bit fuzzy in the winter sunshine. He looked down to the damp ground.

For a few moments, the world seemed to stop turning, there, as he stood on that street in North Dublin. The ground was so bright with sunshine that his eyes stung. He could hear cars racing past him on the road into town. But everyone and everything that he knew seemed so distant, so far away. He didn't care about Spyral at that moment, he didn't care about living or working, he didn't know who he was, or why he should continue being.

And he felt foolish about his desire for Elaine, foolish to feel the wet warmth under his arms, the cold sweat in his palms, the remnants of a pathetic desire for a woman he didn't love, who was merely someone to hang onto in this world, a world which had suddenly become so empty.

And he knew at that moment that he had to regain something of himself in all this emptiness. And he had no one to turn to except Margaret, and at that moment he allowed himself to miss her, terribly, for the first time since they had parted.

And he knew then that he had been fooling himself. Fooling himself that he could simply start a new life without Margaret, put a lid on everything that had passed, proceed into newness, decorate a space for himself, without first determining what had gone wrong, and trying to fix it, or lay it to rest.

And as he was thinking these things he was crying, trying not to shake as he held the car for support, crying freely in the sunny car park at the Botanic Gardens, and fearing for himself, and fearing for everyone in the world, everyone who seemed so alone in this God-forsaken and God-forsaking world, and wishing that somehow, today, he could find his way home.

CHAPTER 27

In which Tony is removed.

The sun was setting, the winter sky deepening as the taxi approached the busy, five-way intersection at the centre of Dolphin's Barn. The old Toyota stopped in the midst of the fray, its right indicator ticking, waiting for the stream of on-coming traffic to ease.

'That's the church there, missus,' the driver said from beneath his cap. 'Our Lady of Dolour.'

'Thank you,' Margaret replied from the back seat. She stared out of the window at the imposing grey building, noted the fragmented groups milling around the entrance.

The taxi driver finally cut across an opening in the traffic. He slowed for two elderly women crossing the road, drove ahead for a bit, came to a space between the cars along the street and pulled in.

Margaret reached into her bag, scrounged for her wallet, and then realised that she had been clutching a five-pound note in her hand throughout the journey. She passed the crumpled note to the driver.

'Thanks,' she said, waving away the change.

'I'm very sorry for your troubles,' he responded, casting her a sympathetic look. 'My wife passed away just two years ago.'

'Yes. Sorry. I mean, I *am* sorry,' she replied, distracted.

She climbed out of the car, crossed the road and approached the bland, featureless church. Groups of mourners huddled together in the small courtyard: men in leather jackets and jeans; elderly women in wool coats and hats with veils; groups of young girls in short jackets and black trousers.

Margaret stood alone, shivered in the evening air. She told herself not to look around.

Irish funerals, she thought, scanning the crowd. Bloody awful things. Don't know where they got their reputation.

She could see the reddened eyes in the faces of those waiting outside the church. Young men stared nervously, their hands squeezed into their pockets to ward off the chilling air.

One well-groomed man, older than Margaret, paced nervously around the perimeter of the crowd. Tightly trimmed beard, silver-streaked hair, one blue sapphire earring. He appeared to be studying the scene: the church and its hard angles, the shadow of the sun setting behind the belltower, the cigarette smoke rising like mist from this crowd, enveloped by winter, by grief.

Damn, Margaret thought. Don't know if I can do this.

I should really leave, right now. Nobody here knows who I am. Nobody cares about UCD. None of these people care that Tony was studying at UCD, or that I was his tutor, or that I'm supposed to represent the College at this funeral.

She looked down at her shoes, scuffed from walking across the road. Should have worn my suit, she thought. She inhaled smoke from someone's cigarette, felt a rawness at the back of her throat, swallowed.

It was as if she had felt nothing, nothing at all, for over a day, for the however-many hours that had passed since she'd got the news. Yesterday afternoon a numbness had set in. A cloud of unfeeling had enveloped her as she left the office, walked home through the icy air without buttoning her coat, ignored the phone that was ringing so insistently when she arrived home.

She didn't sleep that night. She tried to read. She had wanted to phone Paul, over and over. But she didn't know what she would say. She had drunk all the wine in the house but still felt nothing but anxiety, raw nerves.

Now, standing beside the church where Tony's body lay, waiting, waiting with these strangers for Tony's relatives to arrive so they could finally enter, Margaret became aware of her feelings for the first time that day: the hollowness in her chest. The fear he had caused in her. And even, somewhere, deep down, the helplessness, the guilt that he had gone through this terrible death, and that maybe, somehow, she could have intervened.

A moment later two large black cars arrived. The crowd drew back to allow them to pull into the courtyard of the church.

From the first car emerged a couple whom Margaret assumed to be Tony's parents, and then an array of younger brothers and sisters. His father was a burly man, middle-aged, short-cropped hair, his dark coat creased from the car journey. He held the door for his wife, a small woman, clearly

distraught, shaking her head at those who circled around
the car, accepting their embraces, talking incessantly, *don't
know how I'll get through this day, oh Jesus how could they do this
to my Tony* . . .

The crowd followed the family into the hollow expanse
of the church. From the open door Margaret could hear a
lone soprano singing 'Ave Maria', accompanied by a wheezing organ.

Margaret waited for the rest of the mourners to file
in. She took her place at the rear of the church as the
priest appeared at the altar: a tall, grey man, tired-looking,
in soothing, cream-coloured vestments. The wooden coffin
rested on a cart before the altar, covered with a multifarious
bouquet of pinks, whites and lavenders.

Margaret couldn't focus on the ceremony. The prayers were
muttered with tired familiarity; the music was chanted with a
note of empty formality.

She noticed little of what was happening around her, her
thoughts wrapped coldly within herself. No one knows, she
thought, who I am. Why I'm here. What I know.

But then, when the congregation seated itself, Margaret
noticed a girl beside her at the far end of the pew. She was
in her late teens, with long, straight hair, and cheap make-up
smeared from her tears. She sat upright, with a fixed, hardened
expression on her face, her look piercing the coffin, that coffin
where Tony's body lay.

The priest approached the pulpit.

'Friends, relations of the departed,' the priest began.
'I know it is slightly unusual for me to speak during a

removal ceremony. But on this occasion, this especially difficult occasion of our bidding farewell to a young man from our community, I wanted to take this first opportunity to offer my deepest condolences to the family, and to so many friends gathered here, of Tony Dunne.

'I believe I knew Tony as well as any of you. I first came to this parish over twenty years ago now, and I met Tony Dunne when he was still a boy. And I've known the qualities in Tony that many of you also knew. As a younger man he was impulsive, perhaps a bit too prone to anger, a tendency that as he matured he struggled hard to control. He was a singularly *reserved* young man who rarely showed his true feelings. And most certainly, he was also a very clever young man. Yes, he had an agile brain, our Tony. A certain way of looking at things that will be sadly missed by us all. Indeed I, a priest in this parish, must admit to you that I will miss Tony's rare gift of insight.

'On occasions such as this we are all at a loss. We are at a loss for what to say, what to feel, how to explain how this appalling deed could take place in our midst.

'And we feel, all of us, at times like these, that we're grasping for something. Something solid. When so much is changing before our eyes – our jobs, our family lives, our values, our goals, our ways of dealing with one another – so much, my friends, is changing, slipping away from us as this century gets off to its uncertain beginning. Tony's so sudden, so *unnecessary* death to me seems such a symbol, my friends, such a symbol of what's happening in our society today. A symbol of just how deep the divides are setting in, just how much we're losing touch with each other.

'The last time I spoke with Tony, which was just four days ago, he phoned me out of the blue, late in the evening. I invited him over for a chat. And, my friends, I can admit to you all that we took a wee drop together that night. And how strange it seems to me now that, just four nights ago, we were discussing this very fact, this very *life*, and how the goodness of it all seemed to be slipping away from us as never before.

'And, my friends, I think Tony knew what God had in store for him. Because Tony told me some frightening things on that night, not four nights ago, some frightening things about what he had seen, what he had noticed in our community.

'My friends, Tony also told me about his beliefs, his deepest feelings. And to Tony, the very weakness of these vessels, our bodies, was a startling fact – a humbling fact, indeed. In the end, Tony said, all we have is our bodies. Nothing else. Only ourselves, and each other, to hang onto, in this fast-changing, ever so *temporary* world.'

He stopped, then, and stood back from the pulpit, visibly emotional.

'My friends,' he continued, 'today, and tomorrow, during this time that we will take to remember Tony, let us remember his words, Tony's wise words. Let us begin to love one another again, even as we struggle to get ahead, even as we strive to make the most of this new prosperity. Let us pause to remember ourselves, our frail bodies, our relationships with one another. Let us stop, let us please stop this murderous, deadly attitude of self that has taken such a hold of our society. Because it was this worship, this false ideal of self that killed Tony Dunne. Yes, my friends, it was not a bullet but an attitude, an attitude of greed and selfishness and evil that killed Tony Dunne.

'Let us leave this removal and the funeral tomorrow mindful of this attitude, my friends. And let us begin to live anew, and to love anew.

'And now, let us pray . . .'

And there was silence in the church as he prayed. Margaret could feel the influence of this priest amongst his people, working through them like a spirit. And Margaret turned to see the girl next to her crying, tears streaming down her cheeks, tears of anger and tears of love for what she believed she had lost.

After the removal ceremony, Margaret had no way to get home. It was dark now and she hadn't any cash, and her head was swimming with confused feelings. She felt as though her body had suddenly shrunk, contracted, become frail, cold and vulnerable.

So she began to walk through the grey streets, with their lurid streetlights, now heavy with Friday-night traffic. The temperature had dropped hard and before long she could feel the skin on her face drying in the bitter winter air.

It took her nearly an hour to walk home. When she reached the house she was weak from emotion, from hunger, from the long, cold walk.

But despite the cold and the exhaustion of what she had been through, she felt a certain wholeness. She felt truly better now, after having been there with Tony today, having said her goodbyes, there, with those people who would miss him most. And she actually apologised, out loud, for lacking the ability to come to his aid during these past weeks, and to give a disturbed young man the assistance that he truly needed.

And so, upon entering the house, even before she took off her coat, she went to the phone, and dialled the number of Paul's mobile, ready to make amends, to tell him everything, to beg him to see her, to do whatever was necessary to get him back, and to get their lives together once again.

But unfortunately, Paul had switched his phone off. For at that moment he was himself receiving instructions about life, and what mattered. And he would have to wait until tomorrow before Margaret's message would finally get through.

CHAPTER 28

In which Declan reveals all.

'Hello, Jack?'

'Who's this?'

'It's me, Paul. Back at the office.'

'Paul, me old flower! How the hell are you? And where are you at all?'

Paul could hear a crowd in the background.

'I'm back in the office, Jack. I need to talk to you.'

'Sure, you can talk away there, Paul, but it's all over, don't you see? By Jaysus, Paul, we're fucked, so we are. I'm telling you, boy, I've been fucked before. But this time we're fucked entirely, the whole fucking lot of us. Absolutely fucked, so we are!'

'Jack, listen to me. It's going to be okay.'

'*Okay?* How can you say it's going to be okay? We've no money, me old flower! We're swimming down the proverbial shit-hole. Those chaps at MountAgro are raging. They thought the whole thing was a cod. They think we're all a crowd of old chancers. Irish lefties. Fucking *Bolsheviks*, that's what they think. It's no good, I'm telling you. We're washed up.'

'Jack, please. Just try to listen for a moment. I think there's a way out of this . . .'

Then Paul explained. About meeting Elaine. About Northern Ireland and the advert in the *European Journal* and the requirement for the educational program. About rewriting the MountAgro proposal and getting it back to Elaine by Tuesday.

'Ah Paul, listen. Paul, me old flower. You're a life-saver entirely. Why don't you get over here, my friend, and we'll have a little celebratory drink. I'm at the Goat, you know. I've been here the entire afternoon. I'm a bit low, to tell you the God's honest truth. I've lost Spyral, I've lost the love of me life. A bit of company right now would be just the thing . . .'

'I know, Jack,' Paul replied. 'But we're going to be okay. And I think I'd better hang on here and get this proposal fixed.'

'Right. You're right there, Paulee boy. We're gonna pull through this thing. You know, you're a great lad, Paul. I'm damned lucky to have you. And you're a lucky fellow, so you are. You've a lovely wife at home, haven't you? Waiting for you to come home? Maybe a bit of dinner in the oven, eh? God, you're a lucky fellow . . .'

Paul had difficulty ending the conversation. Jack talked at such length that it was nearly 5:30 before he finally rang off.

Then Paul settled into revising the proposal. He typed for two hours, finishing a first draft. Then he wrote himself a schedule of items requiring attention on Monday and prepared to leave the office.

Business, he thought. So tidy. So responsive to good management. So much better than real life.

Before leaving the office he composed a crisp, clear e-mail for Elaine regarding their meeting that afternoon, confirming that the proposal would reach her within the agreed timescale, and saying that he looked forward to discussing 'this exciting opportunity' with her at greater length next week.

Then he clicked on 'Send', switched off his computer, turned off all the lights, and walked out of the door of the empty building.

'Paul!'

'Who's that? Declan?'

'How's the form, mate?'

'Don't ask. What's up?'

'I'll tell you what's up. Chris Potter. Dave Holland. Tonight. Stakis Hotel.'

'Potter? Here? Wow. But I tell you, Declan, I'm a bit wrecked . . .'

'Paul, look. He's only in Dublin for one night. I've got a ticket for you. And there's somebody I'd like you to meet. All you have to do is get here.'

'Right, okay. I need to eat something. Can I see you later – say nine?'

'We'll be here . . .'

Paul entered the Stakis Hotel at 9:15. An office crowd milled around the bar, hangers-on from their pint after work. White and chromium fixtures offset dark business suits. Strategic downlighting. Sophisticated shadows. The black water of the canal flowing outside the window.

Paul located Declan in a glassy corner at the far end of the lounge. Declan's image was reflected behind him in the glass.

As he approached, Paul saw Declan, and Declan's reflected self, wave in tandem.

'Paul! Good to see you, mate. Why the worried expression? A handsome divil like you! You'll have a pint, won't you?'

Declan hailed a waitress.

'Two more of these, when you're ready.'

Paul sat down, surveyed the crowd.

'I've never been here before,' he said.

'Really? European looks, what?'

'Yeah. But we're in Ireland,' Paul said.

'Oh no, you're not going to go all Irish on me, are you? Would you prefer a shamrock motif?'

'Maybe. I'm a bit culture-shocked. I was in the Botanic Gardens this afternoon.'

'The Botanic Gardens?' Declan said. 'What were you doing there?'

'Long story. It was supposed to be pleasure, but it turned out to be business. Where's Sally?'

'What?'

'Sally. You know, your wife. Isn't she coming tonight?'

'Ah, no. Not tonight.'

'So she's sitting home, and you're out here enjoying yourself?' Paul asked.

'Look, she's not into jazz, right, and I am,' Declan said, suddenly defensive. 'She's a grown woman and she can do what she likes.'

'Okay, hey, relax,' Paul said. 'I was only asking where she was.'

Silence. Two pints were delivered by a brusque Spanish waitress.

'Look, I'm sorry for snapping,' Declan said, reaching for his drink. 'I just get fed up sometimes.'

He stared out into the canal. He looked as though he were about to continue, but just then a voice intervened.

'Good evening, gentlemen!'

A tall man with wavy blond hair walked towards them from across the lounge. Australian accent. Black leather trousers. He smiled broadly, looking down at them with an air of easy confidence.

'Barry!' Declan said, suddenly brightening. 'Glad you could join us!'

Declan shook hands with the newcomer.

'Why so surprised, mate?' Barry asked. 'Think I wouldn't show?'

'I never know with the likes of you,' Declan said. 'This is Paul. Paul, Barry's an agent. For musicians. He got us the tickets for tonight.'

'Nice to meet you,' Paul said, extending his hand.

'Barry fixed the Rainey gig last week,' Declan explained.

'No kidding.'

'Yeah,' Declan said, turning towards Barry. 'How's Rainey doing in London anyway?'

'He's doing really well,' Barry replied. 'He's playing to great houses. And you know, English jazz fans are terrific.'

'Terrific at what?' Declan asked.

'Terrific at everything,' Barry said, with a wet smile.

'Ah Jesus, and you'd know, wouldn't you?' Declan said. 'Can I buy you a drink?'

'No, not just yet. I still have to talk to a guy about the

arrangements for tonight. But I'll be back to you shortly. And then I want to learn more about your friend here. Don't go away, right fellas?'

He waved with his fingers, and then walked back towards the bar. Brief silence as both men watched him walk away.

'So,' Declan said. 'What do you think?'

'Hmm? About what?'

'About Barry,' Declan replied.

'What do I think? Nice guy. Where'd you meet him?'

'In New York. Two years ago.'

'I see.'

Silence. Both drank deeply from their pints.

'So,' Declan continued, with forced cheerfulness. 'Have you spoken to Margaret?'

'No, not yet. I will, though. I'm going to call her. Soon. When the time is right.'

'That's what you want, then?' Declan asked.

'Yeah,' Paul replied. 'It's gone on too long. I really miss her.'

'Funny,' Declan said. 'I wondered which way you'd go.'

'Which *way*?'

'Yeah. Look, Paul, maybe you've got it better than you think.'

'How so?'

'On your own. A single man again.'

'Don't think so, Declan. I'm a bit out in the cold.'

'Yeah, but no ties. You're in control. Your money is your own. You've got free time. Jesus, Paul, I'm in up to my tits. Fucking obligations, you know?'

Declan lifted his glass, finished off his pint.

'It's not all it's cracked up to be,' Declan continued. 'This breadwinner crack. It's pressure, you know? I can't seem to relax. I'm losing weight. I'm not sleeping nights, Paul. And then I look at you, and I think maybe you've finally got the right sit.'

'But you get disconnected,' Paul said. 'You lose touch with things when you lose your wife. A wife reminds you who you are. Gives you a sense of proportion.'

'But the problem is you don't have any bloody choice in the matter,' Declan said. 'Once you're married, she calls the shots. And I've got other interests, you know what I mean? I'm just not interested any more.'

Paul looked at his friend. Declan seemed to be working something out in his mind.

'Declan, are you okay? Look, is it another woman?'

'No! For fuck's sake, what would I want with another woman?'

'So what are these "other interests" you're talking about?'

Now Declan looked directly at Paul.

'Paul, I don't think you'd get it.'

'Try me.'

'Paul, this is big stuff, you know? I'm looking into the abyss here.'

'What are you talking about?'

Declan paused for a moment, and seemed just about to speak. At that moment, Barry appeared, as if out of nowhere.

'Now, gentlemen!' he said in his Australian accent. 'Let's staht the pah-ty!'

*　　*　　*

The more Paul drank that night, the more it sank in. So simple. So obvious.

Declan. Barry. Together.

Paul had had inklings, perhaps, in the past. Nothing direct. No sexual overtures, nothing like that. Rather it was the way Declan spoke of women. The way he never seemed interested when they approached him – and they did, they always had, especially before he married, in Illinois. Strings of women. They seemed to follow him, pursue him, mesmerised by his good looks, his easy Irish charm.

But Declan had never seemed to notice them, these women. Even when he became engaged to Sally, he never seemed to want to spend time with her. Jazz, or work, or even Paul, had always come first.

And so tonight, watching Barry and Declan together, Paul felt he was watching something that made sense, that should have been happening long ago.

Oh, they were discreet, certainly. They practised the social restraint that gay couples in straight environments become so used to practising. They included Paul in their conversation, and there was nothing in their body language that would suggest more than fraternal camaraderie. The talk was of standard stuff: music, work, travel, money, even women.

Even as the night progressed, and the music deepened, there was no bodily contact, no clues to outsiders as to the nature of their now mature relationship.

But Paul could sense it, all the same: tangible, strong, their attraction hung in the air like a sweet odour. Half-formed gestures of attentiveness; tiny, suppressed smiles of reassurance.

And as the night wore on, a feeling of comfort in their simply being together.

The jazz that night was good, very good: smart, high-energy jazz, with driving rhythms, free-ranging melodies. And looking at the two men, Paul felt saddened – saddened that he seemed to be losing a friend, saddened that Declan's personal life was now divided, with no easy outcome for him, for Sally, for the twins.

Paul decided to escape before the final set. He felt increasingly uncomfortable, an extra in this new drama. A sensation of relief overtook him when he stood to go. And then, a heavy loneliness, as he made his way out of the hotel.

When he entered the fresh air for the short walk home, the night was crystal-clear, and very cold, and eerily silent.

'Sally?'

'Yes, who's that?'

'It's me, Margaret.'

'Ah Margaret, how are you?'

'Sally, I'm just great. And what are you two lovebirds doing tonight?'

'I tell you, Margaret, this lovebird is having a rather boring Friday night in. The other lovebird is out at some jazz do. I think he's with Paul.'

'Oh dear. Why don't men ever grow up?'

'I don't know, Margaret. But maybe it's for the best. Little boys are so much easier to manage . . .'

They laughed.

'Listen, Sally, I'm sorry to bother you so late, but I wonder if you could do me just a little favour?'

'Anything at all.'

'I'm trying to ring Paul.'

'Oh Margaret. I'm so happy for you.'

'But I can't seem to get through on his mobile. And I don't have another number.'

'I'm afraid I don't either, Margaret. But I tell you what, I've the next best thing.'

'What's that?'

'I can tell you where he's staying.'

'Oh God – it's been so long. Do you think I should just arrive?'

'Sure why not? Time's a-wasting!'

'I know, I know. But I think, if I'm going to drop in on him, I'd better leave it until tomorrow.'

'But Margaret, why? Why don't you just sneak over there in something slinky and have a cosy little reunion?'

'Because if I go over tonight and catch him in bed with some little tart, I'm likely to kill both of them.'

'Wise move, Margaret. Wise move. He's at 29 Sandford Road, just around the corner from you.'

'Really? Imagine! Thanks, Sally. I think I'll pay him a little visit. Tomorrow. During the day.'

'Oh, it's so exciting! And Margaret?'

'Yes?'

'Make sure you get a good night's sleep!' Sally said, laughing.

'Oh God, you're dreadful, Sally, you know that? Really and truly dreadful!'

CHAPTER 29

In which our hero is ill but soon recovers. And Margaret finally meets Mamie.

Throbbing, Paul thought. Everything throbbing.

Head. Everything.

Guinness, he thought. Amazing stuff. Leaves you throbbing all over. Must be the iron.

He sat up in bed, felt the icy air against his skin. Sleety rain pelted the window with an irritating, insistent rhythm. A backdrop of bright sunshine beyond the clouds. Brilliant light filled the room.

He stood, lurching out of the bedroom to the small kitchen, careful not to bang his aching head against the slanted ceiling. He bent down to peer into the fridge.

No eggs. No orange juice. Bread too old to think about.

Shit. Freezing. I'm falling apart here. Going to freeze to death, right here. They'll find my body in a month, frozen solid. What a way to go.

He returned to the bedroom, climbed into his jeans, pulled a sweater over his head, threw on his winter coat, and descended the stairs.

Outside the rain cut his face as he ran across the road to the newsagent's. Head pounding, he gathered essentials for breakfast and a large packet of painkillers. A can of soup for lunch.

Worry about dinner later.

He paid the boy behind the counter, a lad with thick, dark-rimmed glasses. By the time he returned to the house his jeans were wet through to his skin and his winter coat was darkened, heavy with the icy rain.

And he had no keys.

Eventually Mamie responded to the raucous doorbell.

'Ah Paul, good morning to you, and what a dirty morning it is – come in, come in! Aren't you great to be up and about on such a morning!'

'Terribly sorry to bother you, Mamie,' Paul replied, noting her colourless dressing gown, her grey slippers.

'Not at all, I'm so glad I caught you, I wanted to ask you all about the preparations for today.'

'Preparations?' Paul asked. Beads of sweat were forming on his brow.

'Yes, weren't you talking to Martin? He was here. Yesterday. He brought fifteen litres of paint and rollers and brushes and what-d'you-call-them covers for the floors. He's got two men coming over to clean the chimney and set the fireplace right. He says he hopes you'll have a chance to finish the painting today so it's all dry by Monday when the floorboards are going to be sanded and polished.'

'He wants me to finish the painting *today*?'

'Yes, that's what he said. I thought he'd spoken to you.'

'It'll need two coats.'

'Yes, he said that. But that's why he brought you such a load of paint.'

Mamie smiled up at him with just a hint of mischief in her expression.

'He's delighted with the room, Paul. He's delighted with everything. Delighted to see me, so he was. Hugged me when he arrived. Hugged me again when he was leaving. He's in great form altogether.'

'Okay,' Paul said. 'I'll get started right away. I'm just going to have some breakfast.'

'Righty-o, Paul. But first, get out of those dreadful wet clothes!'

Bread, she thought. Paul always liked the bread I used to bake when we lived in Illinois.

Margaret sat at her kitchen table in her dressing gown, watching the rain beat against the window, streaming down in eager little rivulets. She was writing items on a sheet of notepaper, sipping abstractedly from a mug of milky coffee.

So I'll need yeast. Some heavier flour. I'll have to go to Donnybrook. Not Ranelagh – too near Paul's house.

Okay, what else? Oysters, she thought, smiling. Can I get oysters at McCormack's? Might ring them. And lemons. And maybe a bit of salad. With artichokes. And I'll get a good bottle of white Bordeaux. Put everything in that basket Declan and Sally gave us. Of course I'll look a right fool walking in the rain with a picnic basket!

And then she shivered. God, I don't even know if he'll be in. And if he is there, I don't know if he'll want to see me. And he might not want to eat.

She put her pencil down, rubbed her face in her hands.

Look, Magsie. If you don't go over there, this is just
going to go on, and on, and on, and the whole thing will
fall apart. Your whole life will fall apart if you don't do
this. Today.

Gosh, she thought. There's a lot riding on this loaf of
bread.

When Paul entered the room, a mug of black coffee in his
hand, it was just as Mamie had reported.

Heavy canvas cloths were folded and stacked in the corner.
Beside them were three tall cans of paint. Serious, businesslike paint, with straightforward labels. *Colortrend*, with the
American spelling. No fanciful names – 'Robin's Egg' for
light blue or 'Chelsea Morning' for yellow – just an austere
sticker reading 'Emulsion 7103'.

Beside the paint were brand-new accoutrements: a new,
large brush. A roller, a roller pad, a roller pan. White plastic
stirring sticks, 'MRCB Paints' in red letters. Even a white
painting cap, adjustable for head size.

The last throb of Paul's headache tensed his skull, rolled
down through his neck as he surveyed the walls, the walls
that had received so much of his attention during these weeks
without Margaret.

He mused for a moment, sipping his coffee.

These walls, he thought, will never be seen again. From
today, they will be backdrop only, a blank surface, an expanse
behind a painting or a matching suite. They might get marked,
and then washed or repainted, but they will be ignored, with
no meaning of their own. After today, no one will ever again

see this pink surface, these smooth white repairs, the quiet domestic history recorded in this plaster.

He paused to touch the walls again, to run his hand along the pale surface, to feel its coolness, sense with his fingertips the tiny, invisible imperfections which the creamy paint would now fill in, cover over, and complete.

'Ah Paul, there you are,' said Mamie, entering the room behind him. 'That was Martin on the phone just there. The chimney men will be here this afternoon. They can only do the work if the rain stops, but it's supposed to clear later today.'

'Okay,' Paul replied. 'I'll be here.'

'Goodness, Paul,' she said, looking around the room, 'won't these walls be lovely when they're finally covered?'

Margaret lowered lumps of moist brown yeast into a bowl of warm water. She spooned honey into the mixture, and then stirred it slowly for a moment, watching for signs of activity. A few minutes later, creamy foam began to cloud the water, indicating that the yeast was alive and well.

Why do I feel like my mother, she thought as she sifted flour and salt into a large bowl. My mother never made bread, not that I can remember. The seventies, she thought. I was brought up in the sophisticated seventies, when we were escaping all this. Instant packets of dessert and cheap, store-bought, sliced white bread.

This is what we need, she thought, pouring the yeasty water into the bowl of flour. This is what Ireland needs – a touch of the fifties again. And two tablespoons of olive oil – one, two – for the new millennium.

She stirred the mixture. Then, sprinkling flour onto the table, she kneaded the dough, pulling, lifting, and pushing away with a steady rhythm. She could feel the muscles in her arms as she worked the soft, receptive ball, feeling a strength there of which she had been unaware for some time. A physical strength, which she had missed for these weeks, for so long.

Yes, she thought, let's just feel good today. If he rejects you, well, *you* rejected *him* two weeks ago. But he'll eat the bread anyway. And he loves oysters. And the wine was expensive – he'll like the wine, I hope.

It'll be a start, she said, putting the kneaded dough into a clean, ceramic bowl. Then she rubbed more olive oil over the dough, and covered the bowl with a warm, damp tea towel.

At least we can make a start.

Ready to roll, he thought.

Lifting a heavy can of paint, he poured it into the black rolling pan. Heavy, creamy liquid, with a hint of gold, a suggestion of rich, coppery gold, he thought. The paint smelled clean and new and homely.

He picked up the roller, onto which he had slipped a bright new roller pad. Just touching the paint at first, he rolled back and forth in the pan to get an even covering on the roller. Then he worked the roller into the paint more deeply, until he had achieved a heavy, even soak.

Then he climbed the ladder, stretched up into the corner, and pressed the wet roller onto the wall.

Thus the recovering began.

The work went quickly. One square patch at a time he worked his way across one wall, then the next. He worked the roller as deep as he could into the corners, carefully, leaving just a thin line to be filled in, later, with the brush.

The walls seemed eager for the paint, he thought. Like a balm on dried, gently ageing skin. As he rolled the paint over the dry plaster, he felt as though he were rubbing oil into a cool naked body. Soothing and welcomed and intimate.

Christ, he thought. I've been alone too long.

The coverage was good for a first coat, and even in the cold air the paint dried well. A second coat would be needed, though, to cover the shadows that seemed now to lurk on the dull golden walls.

He'd use a brush for the final coat, he thought. He always preferred the texture left by a brush. More appropriate, he thought, for an old house. These old walls deserve the soft attention of the brush.

At around two o'clock he stopped for lunch. The rain had eased off, though it was still cold. He figured he'd need another two hours for the second coat. Just as he was leaving the room to go upstairs, the doorbell rang.

Two men in clean, blue coveralls stood at the door.

'Are you Martin Walsh?'

'No, but this is his place,' Paul replied.

'Is there a fireplace here needs cleaning?'

'Yeah, come on in.'

Paul led the two men into the freshly painted room.

'Chipper Chimneys' was written in white lettering across their backs.

'Here it is,' Paul said. 'Do you guys need a hand?'

'No, just leave it to us. We'll give this fireplace the once-over to make sure it's all hunky-dory, right? Then we'll clean the chimney and be on our way.'

One of the men bent down for a closer look at the ironwork of the fireplace. 'Ah Jaysus, Danny, isn't she lovely?'

'Gorgeous, Bobby. Worth a few bob, I'd say,' Danny replied.

'But look,' Paul said. 'I'm supposed to have this room painted today. The dust. It'll ruin the paint.'

'Ah now, you work away there, and leave the dust to us. The fact is, if we do our job properly, there won't be any dust. Right, Danny?'

'You're right there, boss.' Danny nodded his assent. 'We'll look after the dust all right.'

Paul went upstairs for lunch. He could hear the clanging of tools down below. Then he could hear the sound of heavy machinery outside. Looking out of the front window, he encountered Danny's face rising before him, lifted on an industrial crane, on his way up to the roof.

Returning downstairs, he found Mamie and Bobby standing in the centre of the room, both wrapped in animated conversation about Dublin's house prices. A black plastic container filled the fireplace. The whole house reverberated with the sound of brushing, up and down the chimney.

The floor was spotless.

'Ah here's Paul,' Mamie said. 'He's come all the way from

America. And isn't he doing great work for us here?'

'God knows enough of us Irish went the other way,' Bobby replied.

'And worked hard as well.'

'Worked themselves sick,' Bobby said. 'Sure, half of America was built on the backs of Irish labourers.'

'It was indeed,' Mamie agreed. 'Surely it was. But look at us now. Aren't the times changing in our favour at long last?'

Paul smiled a weak smile and reopened the paint.

Paul worked steadily all afternoon. The rich paint covered quickly and well, and the interstices in the corners, missed by the roller this morning, required only one coat. By half past three, half the room had been painted; by five o'clock, the job was nearly finished, and the walls were bright with fresh, true colour.

Bobby and Danny were true to their word. No soot entered the room. Nothing. Bobby replaced bags in the fireplace as the afternoon wore on, and eventually used a dustpan and brush to pick up the tiny residue in the grate. Paul was able to complete his edging around the fireplace as the men packed their equipment into their truck.

Night had fallen and the temperature had dropped considerably by the time the men were about to leave.

'Now, Paul, my good man,' Bobby said. 'That fireplace is as good as new, safe and sound. You'll want to have it cleaned every year, though, to keep it in top condition. I leave you my card for your future reference.'

'Super. Thanks for your help. You guys sure know your business.'

'Service, Paul. I'm telling you, it's all about service. We'll leave you with our complimentary bale of turf briquettes. Would you like us to light the fire? It's a cold night, and the fire would help your paint to dry.'

'Yes, please, go ahead, light the fire.'

As Paul refolded the drop cloths, Danny placed the briquettes in the grate and set them alight. The flames soon cast a warm glow across the freshly painted room. As they were leaving Paul shook both men's hands, which, he noted, were remarkably clean.

He could hear the men chatting at the front door before they left, and then he heard the door close, and he was alone.

Now the fire blazed and began to emit real heat. Paul was tired. He pulled a drop cloth over to the fireplace, switched off the bare bulb overhead, and sat on the floor before the leaping flames.

The light from the fire played on the freshly painted walls. As Paul watched, figures seemed to dance around him. They seemed to move in circles around the warm, amber room – women in dresses, and children jumping and dancing, and men holding up their arms – figures from the past, now returned, to visit the room once again, to enjoy this home space, to feel the warmth that had been absent for so long.

And then Paul heard the door open behind him. He expected Mamie, and he didn't turn, but waited for her reaction, to the room, to the fire, to him sitting in the dark.

But instead someone sat down beside him, placing a wicker basket on the floor. And he turned, and it was Margaret.

Margaret, sitting beside Paul on the floor before the fireplace, wore a nervous, enigmatic smile. Her smile slowly faded as she looked into the flames, which leapt and brightened in the dark room.

She looked older, he thought, even though it had only been two weeks. Her face was thinner; she had lost weight. Her hair was different, shorter but softer than the style he remembered, and she wore a soft grey sweater, which gave her a new appearance of gentleness.

Approachability.

She breathed audibly, as though she was catching her breath. Perhaps, he thought, she had run in from the rain.

Paul didn't smile. He couldn't bring himself to speak, so many feelings rushed in upon him.

'So,' Margaret said, breaking the silence. 'How have you been?'

'Fine, thanks. And you?'

'Grand,' she said. 'I've been grand.'

She paused for a moment.

'Is this where you've been staying?' she asked.

'Yes. Upstairs. There's a flat upstairs.'

'This room is lovely.'

'I've just finished painting it,' Paul replied. And then, with an unbidden note of resentment in his voice, 'I painted the room rather than pay the full rent.'

'I see.'

She looked around the room. 'The colour is very nice,' she said.

'The painting is only the final step,' he replied. 'The walls, the plaster underneath had to be prepared first. The paint is only the covering.'

'It must have been a lot of work.'

'Why did you ask me to leave you?'

She looked down at the floor. The fire crackled in the grate before them.

'I don't know,' she began. 'Things weren't going well, Paul. I was so ashamed. I've been in hospital – I was worn out. I needed time.'

She looked at him.

'I'm sorry,' she said.

Silence.

'So you're here now,' he said.

'Yes, I am,' she said, nervously. 'I've brought some things, in the basket.'

She opened the basket, and pulled out the wine, and a loaf of bread, and the other things she had prepared, setting the meal before them on the drop cloth.

'Margaret, look,' Paul interrupted. 'I'm trying to get a handle on this. Two weeks ago you decide you want some space, so you kick me out of the house. Then tonight you show up with a picnic as though this little peace offering is going to sort everything out between us. I'm sorry, Margaret, but I'm going to need a bit more, I don't know, *preparation*.'

Margaret stopped unpacking, lowered the lid of the basket, looked up at him as he spoke.

'I know,' she said. 'This is the whole problem. I don't know why you'd want to come back.'

He didn't reply.

'Paul, I asked you to leave because I felt I had nothing to offer you any more.'

He turned towards her.

'Couldn't I be the judge of that?'

'I kept feeling, Paul, that I'd dragged you away. From something. And I didn't know what I'd brought you *to*.'

'I wasn't complaining.'

'But you *should* have been complaining,' Margaret said. 'Maybe I *wanted* you to complain. I wanted to hear that you were frustrated that my career wasn't going anywhere. I wanted to hear how frustrated you were that we can't afford our own house. I wanted to hear all these things, because then at least I could fight back.'

'But look, Margaret, can't I make up my own mind?'

'Yeah, sure, but the burden is still on me, isn't it? It's still my responsibility that you're here. And I just couldn't take it any more. I wanted to be on my own, to be free of the worry, the weight of knowing that, just maybe, I had ruined your life.'

For a moment, the only sound in the room was the soft flicker of flames.

'Margaret, have I really been that much of a burden?'

'No, of course not. Paul, you've been a saint. But that's the problem. I can't go on living with you unless I know that you're happy. Here. In Ireland. With me.'

Tears glistened in her eyes as she searched his face for an answer.

'Margaret,' he said, 'I don't know what to say. To convince you. Look, these walls. The walls in this room, they have memories, hidden memories. I've spent the last two weeks encountering the hidden memories of this house – the families, the parties. The decorating, the tearing down. The artistry and the tawdriness of a hundred years of everyday Irish life. Ireland is in this room, Margaret. It's under my fingernails. I don't know how to say this, but I want to stay here, Margaret. With you. Here.'

She looked at him with a sceptical expression, as though listening to good news that she was reluctant to believe.

'But Paul, what will we do?' Margaret broke in. 'I'm working so bloody hard, and I don't seem to be getting anywhere, and you're putting so much into your job, and I don't know if you're happy there – sometimes I feel like it's never going to be right.'

'Yeah, but it doesn't matter, does it?' Paul said. 'That's how life works. The bits don't fit together. There are cracks and gaps and fissures. It's texture, Margaret. Life isn't surface, it's *texture*. It's all in the imperfection. And you have to go with it. Experience the bumps, the tangles, and the smooth patches. Because that's it, *that's* the beauty.'

Margaret looked into the flames.

'Right,' she said. 'So here we are. Imperfection, through and through. But we need to decide. Now. Are we going to give this a go? Can we try, again? Can you forgive me, Paul, for this mess?'

He smiled gently.

'Sure. Give it a go, as they say.'

'And Paul, you'll tell me, won't you, if you're getting miserable?'

'Yes. You'll be the first to know.'

'And Elaine?' she said, watching his face closely. 'You'll get rid of her, whoever she is?'

Paul didn't flinch.

'She's a business associate, Margaret,' he said. 'Strictly business. Word of honour.'

'Good,' Margaret said. 'Better keep it that way.'

She smiled. And they both felt their breathing relax. And then there passed between them, for the first time since she had entered the room, that palpable, tangible current that passes between two people who love one another, soul, and mind, and body.

And they bent towards one another, and they kissed, for the first time in many, many days.

'But Margaret,' Paul said. 'Just one more thing, before we go upstairs.'

'Yes, Paul,' she said, looking deep into his eyes.

'Could we possibly explore that basket a bit further? I'm really starving.'

The next morning Mamie McDevitt walked slowly from her flat, down the corridor, and into the newly refurbished room.

The sun streamed into the back garden, glistened off the deep green foliage, flooding the room with light. She looked around at the fresh, clean walls, felt the warmth still glowing from the fire from the night before. And she smiled.

Feeling suddenly energised, she began to climb the stairs. First one flight, then the next, as her breath continued to come easily. She turned up the third flight, then paused for a moment, and climbed the fourth flight, suddenly feeling her age, in her legs, in her lungs.

By the time she made it up to Paul's flat she was quite out of breath.

'Helloooo, Paul!' she called in through the closed door, panting. 'Do you mind if I come in? I'm collapsing out here.'

'Hrmph, sure, yeah, wait, Mamie, I'll be out in just a moment!'

But she didn't hear his response, and she opened the door to find not one, but two figures in the narrow bed by the wall.

'Ah, good morning! You must be Margaret. Mamie McDevitt. *So* pleased to meet you!'

Margaret pulled the sheets up over her chest with one arm, and reached to clasp Mamie's trembling hand.

'You've got a lovely fellow there, Margaret. And he's told me all about you. I look forward to getting to know you better. Now look, you two, how would you like a nice breakfast downstairs with me? I could do something appropriate, one of my old American specialities – do you like pancakes, or, better still, eggs Benedict?'

'Mamie, really, there's no need to go to such trouble . . .' Paul interjected.

'No trouble at all. Now you two lovebirds take your time, and come down to me in half an hour, and we'll get to know one another a bit better over breakfast before I head off to Mass. Is that all right?'

'Yes,' Margaret piped up. 'We'd like that very much.'

'Righty-o,' Mamie replied. 'See you soon!' And she waddled out of the door and back down the stairs.

And they began to laugh.

'Might as well,' Margaret said. 'Where else would we get a decent breakfast at this hour?'

'Yeah. Might as well.'

Then, a moment later.

'Margaret?'

'Yes, Paul.'

'It's been a very long time.'

'For what, Paul?'

'You know.'

'Yes, Paul. Nearly eight hours.'

'You know what I mean. Did you miss it?'

'Miss it?'

'As much as I did?'

'Paul?'

'Yes, Margaret?'

'I missed you terribly, Paul.'

'Mmmm,' Paul replied. 'Me too.'

EPILOGUE

*In which a day passes, making a significant difference
to all concerned, and leading us to our conclusion.*

Years later, Paul and Margaret would remember the perfect
start to that day. The morning's conversation. The warm
lovemaking. And then the journey downstairs to Mamie
McDevitt, eating breakfast together at the table in Mamie's
snug sitting room.

Mamie admitted to them that she heard Margaret arrive
last night. She had heard the voices through the walls of that
big, silent house – heard the low tones, then the raised tones,
then the soft laughter as the conversation wore on, as comfort
reestablished itself between them.

So Mamie had risen early that morning, and she had taken
out her old cookery books and looked up her favourite old
American recipes, for 'English muffins' (nothing English
about them, she thought), and hollandaise sauce (sure they
never had this in Holland when I was there, she thought)
and eggs Benedict (who was Benedict, anyway?) made with
Irish rashers (something familiar, finally, she thought).

And she knew they would join her for this special breakfast. Indeed, even before meeting Margaret, Mamie had a
little plan that, just maybe, the couple might come round

every Sunday, just like this, for a lazy breakfast together in her flat.

The rest of the day, too, went by so easy, so relaxed, spent where else but in the room itself, where another fire was set, and the walls were touched up and finished, and the new skirting boards coated a creamy, glossy white, and Mamie got to thinking about her sofa, and her comfy chair, and her hearthrug, and how those lovely old boards were crying out to be polished, walked on, and lived on again.

The late winter sun did its best to shine that day, and then day eased towards night, and Paul went upstairs to gather his things, and there was that long, awkward moment standing before Mamie's door, hesitating before knocking, to say goodbye.

At that same moment, though, towards evening, as the sun was setting, another entrance was taking place, in Sandymount, at the home of Declan and Sally Sheehan. Declan came home at that hour to greet his bouncing twins ('Daddy, Daddy!') and to face his wife ('So, where on *earth* have you been?'). There were strange, difficult, adult silences in between the children's excited shrieks, and the tense distance between husband and wife grew, and then came the curt announcement ('I'm not staying') and the angry tears, and the raw confusion as their lives were turned upside down, never again to return to where they had been, because Declan was declaring his freedom, in the first act of a long, slow, painful dissolution of his and Sally's marriage.

A few hours later, around eight o'clock, just as Declan was performing that act of separation, a man was dialling the telephone from his local pub in Glasnevin. This man entered our story only briefly, on the fringes, back in the Department of the Environment in the magnificent eighteenth-century Customs House on the quays. Tonight he is placing a phone call to a number in Northern Ireland, a number he had never dialled before, but which he knew well, which he had rehearsed so many times before. He had had one or two pints of ale to fortify himself, and he knew he had to return home soon, but he walked calmly over to the public telephone during this quiet time in the pub, and he dialled that number to speak to Elaine, just to let her know that, in his capacity as Principal Officer in the Department of the Environment, he would be visiting her offices in Belfast in the morning, and he was wondering especially, if it wasn't too short notice, whether Elaine might possibly be free to join him, at Malone's restaurant, beside the Wellington Park Hotel, where he would be staying, for dinner, tomorrow evening.

To which request Elaine, hardly surprised by the call, returned a non-committal yes, and rang off, and tried to recall, during the many times she had met him, had he ever mentioned any details about his wife, apart from the fact that she did, indeed, exist.

Elaine was not the only one to experience the stirrings of a new romance on that February night. Shortly after eight o'clock Felicity heard the doorbell ring, and wrapping her dressing gown about her, went out to discover not a visitor, but a box left on her doorstep. She brought the parcel indoors, and was surprised to find, upon untying the string – a puppy! A live, healthy, whining puppy, golden, with oversized ears and a pair of sad, imploring eyes, and a note, from Jack at the office, *hope you like him, KNOW he'll love you*, written in a nervous scrawl. Ten minutes later, the puppy was happily lapping up its mushy puppy food on her kitchen floor, and Felicity was crying, heavily, sweetly, as the hungry puppy splashed, and spilled, and slurped.

But alas, there were darker events taking place on that fateful Sunday in Dublin. In Dundrum, in the comfortable modern-day suburban surroundings of the Walsh household, there was pain, heavy physical pain racking Martin Walsh, and his wife Deirdre, and his mother-in-law Joan. Somehow, after that grand Sunday dinner, at which Martin, and his wife, and their daughter, and his wife's mother, had enjoyed such a lovely roast, with potatoes and cabbage and carrots, and even if Martin's wife smoked through the meal everything was grand, and sure the wine was flowing and it was so relaxing to sit there in the new kitchen, and even the little tiff that Martin had with his daughter hardly spoiled the day, and so what if she left to see her new boyfriend before the dessert, to leave the three adults to their awfully boring old chat.

But not long afterwards didn't it hit them, all three, a fierce tightening in their nether regions, and didn't his wife turn sick altogether while the mother-in-law was retching and couldn't seem to bring anything up, and by the time the ambulance arrived wasn't the mother-in-law in an awful state entirely, and how much worse can it get only didn't she die, that night, from food poisoning, that must have been in the pâté, as his daughter, who had refused to touch the stuff, was grand, and what a dreadful way to end one's life, and after such a lovely meal, and herself supposed to be flying out that evening on her way to the sun for a short holiday?

And the next day, and the next, wasn't Martin away from the office out of respect for the old woman, and yet while he was recovering, and while the funeral arrangements were being made, didn't he find time to phone his bank manager and explain the situation, to point out that a significant legacy would be forthcoming from his mother-in-law's estate, and that an advance of fifty thousand pounds to enable him to buy into the Stoneybatter Property Consortium – why, it was a no-brainer, of course he'd be in a position to repay the loan!

During that week, while Martin Walsh was regaining his health and making phone calls and ensuring that he could capitalise on his investment opportunities, Paul was back at work, and working very hard to complete Spyral Multimedia's proposal to develop online training materials on the subject of genetics for the Irish Department of the Environment, addressed to the very man we met earlier in this chapter, who in turn was on such wonderful form that, on Elaine's recommendation, he reviewed the proposal very quickly, confirmed that it stood head and shoulders above the other entries, and proceeded to offer the two-hundred-and-thirty-thousand-pound contract (for Phase 1) to Spyral Multimedia (subject to satisfactory passing of the Department's financial controls) thereby saving the company, and the employment of all within.

But to return to the Sunday afternoon at hand: when Paul and Margaret finally plucked up their courage to say goodbye to Mamie, she was of course ready for them. She had prepared her arguments very carefully to recommend that they consider moving out of their current rental accommodation and into her house, where the flats upstairs could be very nicely renovated to their satisfaction by who else but Paul himself, in consideration of greatly reduced rent.

An offer which they considered carefully that evening, when they weren't busy considering one another.

And so, the next day, Margaret began packing her things, and preparing for the move, when the post arrived, with a letter from the *Literature and Psychology Review*, indicating their extreme pleasure with her article on 'Woolf, Dalloway and Culture Shock', and their intention to include the article for publication in their summer issue.

As for the future, we can only speculate based on the brief contact we have had with the surfaces of these characters' lives. We can of course predict with confidence that there will be ials ahead for this couple as they recover from their exte ed, and profound, separation. But interspersed with th effort to build a solid foundation for their relationship, e may also sense the presence of sunshine, patches of warm sunshine, in the back garden of Mamie McDevitt's house, where, too infrequently, but so beautifully, tea will be served to Paul and Margaret, on Mamie's white china tea service, on fresh, sunny, summer afternoons.